A Biographical novel

Begum Samru

A Reign of Romance, Royalty and Restrain

Raj Gopal Singh Verma

Vitasta

Published by
Renu Kaul Verma
Vitasta Publishing Pvt Ltd
2/15, Ansari Road, Daryaganj
New Delhi - 110 002
info@vitastapublishing.com

ISBN: 978-81-963329-2-1

First Edition 2023
MRP ₹495

This novel is entirely a work of fiction. Names, characters, events and incidents are entirely imaginary. Reference to real places, actual regions, institutions or community practices has been made in a fictitious manner. Any resemblance to actual persons, living or dead or actual events is purely coincidental.

Edited by Soumitro Das
Cover Artwork by Vandana Joshi
Typeset & Cover Design by Somesh Kumar Mishra
Printed by Vikas Computer and Printers, New Delhi

Contents

Preface

For some people, history is a dull and monotonous subject, one that numbs their minds and lulls them to sleep. For them, reading about historical events *per se* is as tedious as sneezing while keeping one's eyes open. Writing about it is well… an entirely different story. According to such people, history simply weaves some disputes, conspiratorial behaviour, wars and archaic customs that have no substantial significance in the modern era. There are so many preconceptions regarding historical events, that somewhere along the line, facts are left behind.

The trouble is that we view this subject solely from our prejudiced perspective. More than often, we fail to maintain a neutral standing. In many cases, unjustified beliefs and prejudices are passed down from one generation to the next. These are transmitted through the food we eat, the water we drink and the air we breathe.

The experience of writing this biographical novel has been an exhilarating one. After years of planning, dedication, extensive research, countless interviews and immense effort, I have been able to give final shape to this book. While penning this story, I experienced a plethora of emotions- some happy and some sad. After all, the sun shines only after rain. Thankfully, my willpower has remained strong. This was possible only because of the immense support I received.

Since my formative years, beginning from childhood, I got plenty of opportunities to discuss the exploits and triumphs of Sardhana's matriarch and to marvel at the great palaces with wide eyes. Yet, it was important to analyse and interpret it. As I began to view the palaces and her life from an unbiased standpoint, the layers and chapters in the history of human civilization began uncovering themselves.

Historians from alien lands cannot be expected to write a credible and sincere account of our nation's past. Naturally, the events in their version will be distorted and prejudiced. It is, however, deeply saddening when even Indian historians present an unreliable account. Historical character-oriented novels are sometimes placed under the genre of fantasy and the facts presented in the story often mislead the readers. Such novels should be considered nothing more than fiction. Though if the subject specifically concerns a female, the author should be doubly careful about sticking to the facts. The writing should not become a smear campaign against any woman's character or reputation.

Farzana, also known as Begum Samru, is an indispensable component in the history of India during the latter part of the eighteenth century and the initial half of the nineteenth. As a fifteen-year-old nautch girl, Farzana earned a livelihood by dancing in the courts of the emperors in old Delhi. Not many people had apprehended that this seemingly ordinary dancer would one day become the ruler of Sardhana.

Naturally, people tend to find discrepancies in the events of the past. However, without any factual information, one shouldn't arrive at unjustified conclusions and malign another individual's character or reputation. People often lack understanding and empathy when they evaluate female rulers. However, history is perpetual and facts cannot be disputed.

The legend of Begum Samru is truly riveting. Her journey from a destitute dancer to an able ruler is nothing short of inspiring. She led her people to such a victory, that even great rulers were brought to their knees. The begum upheld the dignity of women in her kingdom, perfected war strategies, worked immensely to ensure the wellbeing of her people and kept an eye on the proceedings in her territory. Despite being an Indian, she married a German and later a French warrior and even converted from Islam to the Roman Catholic faith.

In childhood, she was surrounded by extreme poverty. However, during the time of her death, her net worth was estimated to be billions of dollars. She had indisputable morals and was extremely magnanimous. Her heart was pure and she did not harbour greed or hostility. Yet, when the time came, she assumed the role of an objective and skilled ruler without hesitation.

The begum devised innovative strategies to ensure the independence, sovereignty and autonomy of her kingdom. She relentlessly cultivated discipline in her ranks. She was also a builder of the largest Cathedral in India. She singlehandedly rescued the Mughal emperor Shah Alam, without paying heed to the danger she was putting herself in. She could have easily taken advantage of the situation then to usurp the power but she did not do so. In the aftermath of her death, she was remembered for her adeptness, generosity, administrative capability and religious tolerance.

The resourceful matriarch managed the administrative affairs of her province so proficiently, that there was always prosperity, security and communal harmony. Most importantly, she did all this when northern India was transitioning from a Mughal empire to a colonial state. It certainly wasn't easy to do so during this era of wars, complicated situations and conspiracies. Begum Samru was extremely practical that way. She was aware of the fact that there was only a certain extent to which an invader could be stopped. Moreover, if the opposing party was a major stakeholder in the country's administration, then fighting a battle was equivalent to suicide. The Begum wisely decided to dedicate her resources to ensure the welfare of her people, rather than crossing swords with a powerful enemy.

The inspiration for this book struck me first in a meeting with Anil Maheshwari ji, a former staffer of The Hindustan Times, who gave me valuable material on her.

Professor late Dr Mahendra Narain Sharma, the principal of M.M. Degree College in Khekra, district Baghpat assisted me in my writing venture. He shared with me a copy of his research work titled 'The Life and Times of Begum Samru of Sardhana.' If our paths hadn't crossed, I would have perhaps not been able to write this book well. After almost four and a half long decades of hard work, he was able to conclude his detailed, authentic and meticulous research work. The information presented by him is considered a much relevant and credible source of knowledge even today.

The credit for analysing Begum Samru's life in a transparent manner goes primarily to three people- Brajendranath Banerjee, Professor Dr Mahendra Narain Sharma and Nicholas Shreeve. In his historical novel 'The Dark Legacy,' which chronicles the life of Begum Samru, Nicholas Shreeve has given research credits to Professor Dr Mahendra Narain Sharma.

Professor Dr Mahendra Narain Sharma's research work, 'The Life and Times of Begum Samru,' is devoid of any romantic imagination or assumptions because he mainly focused on proven facts. The amount of research and hard work undertaken by Professor Dr Mahendra Narain Sharma cannot be matched by any other writer. Unfortunately, this book published by the Indian Historical Research Council is no longer available in the market. Professor Dr Mahendra Narain Sharma's son, Rakesh Sharma, a professor in Ancient history, helped me bring this issue to light. He also provided me with several other books. I would like to extend my heartfelt gratitude to him.

Brajendranath Banerjee published an English novel titled 'Begum Samru' in 1925. His book was a much authentic source for his research. He also derived information for his book from the English, Marathi and Persian records that were available then. His novel does not display facts collected from any vague source of information or word of mouth. This was the speciality and defining characteristic of his account which chronicles Begum Samru.

It is said that a society without the knowledge of its history, origin and culture is like a tree without roots. Such a society, which lacks enlightenment, becomes aimless. If man treads on the winding alley of history, he can gain knowledge about his physical, cultural and societal past. Society requires history, not historians. Some historians employ their imagination to study and explain the past to society as per their whims. However, history inspired solely from imagination and distorted facts is misleading. Historians need to connect unrelated events and build a concrete explanation for the actions of antecedents. Historians must have benign motives for doing this. They must never use their abilities and knowledge to garner publicity.

Quoting the renowned historian and author Edward Hallett Carr:

'If we do a detailed and thorough analysis of the past, history will be able to provide us with the assurance that dark times can be overcome. It can light a spark of hope in our hearts for the future. We should await such a time when humanity will enthusiastically take a step to establish a social order wherein non-Europeans and Europeans join hands to facilitate the development of their culture and origin. Humanity has been deprived of such a harmonious alliance for centuries and aeons."

People who are interested in gaining knowledge about the post-Mughal and colonial period of India must study Begum Samru's life in detail. Though there are many misconceptions about her I strongly feel these are due to several novelists, and biographers not having done justice to her character. As a student of history, I consider this book very close to an accurate historical account chronicling Begum Samru's life. Factual information is of the utmost importance to me. This book is based on credible sources only. The purpose of my writing isn't to determine the Begum virtues and morals. Through this historical work, I have tried to present to the readers a glimpse of the woman whose existence left deep dents in the pages of Indian history. Readers can arrive at conclusions and form opinions after studying the available sources of information and understanding the circumstances of that time. The begum's role in the history of India, a role she built and preserved diligently, isn't particularly old. But, because she was a woman, she has been shown in a bad light. That's my take.

For this book, I have studied Hindi as well as English versions of various history books, novels, newspapers, journals, research papers and translated accounts chronicling aspects of Begum Samru's life and times. Additionally, I have examined records maintained by the government, letters and gazettes related to the subject at hand. Meetings with the priests in the church built by Begum Samru and interactions with some officials from the Training Council have also been tried which could contribute to this book.

Amongst the people who have supported me in my venture, I would like to extend my gratitude, first and foremost, to senior journalist, Mr Anil Maheshwari, who is a sort of mentor to me. His words motivated me to write and filled me with self-confidence. I owe a heartfelt thanks to him.

I would also like to thank Mr Raj Kishore Sharma 'Raje', the author of several popular historical books, A special thanks to him, who, as a seasoned expert in Indian history, contributed immensely to make my book a worthwhile read.

—Raj Gopal Singh Verma

CHAPTER 1

The first sight

THE colossal doors were encrusted with numerous multi-coloured shards of glass. As they swung open in their majestic grandeur, a pair of round doe-shaped eyes coyly peered inside. She hesitated only briefly, before slowly walking in. With each step, a gentle tinkling rose from her ankle bells. The melodious music seemed to bounce across the hall. The colourful chandeliers that were dangling from the roof of the palatial room reflected the flickering lights of the candles. However, their magnificence seemed to fade beside her dazzling beauty, which was dripping from her petal-like eyes to her luscious red lips.

A diaphanous veil covered the damsel's face. From behind the sheer material, her eyes locked into a pair of unfamiliar pupils. She curtseyed gracefully.

'I pay my obeisance to His Majesty…'

She looked like a heavenly nymph in the intricately

embroidered and sequined white and gold costume. She had draped a dupatta in the Mughal style over her jacket and churidar outfit. Her beautiful features shone with youthful radiance. The gaze lingered on her bewitching face whenever she turned. The ensemble covered her slender frame completely, leaving a great deal to the imagination. Owing to the veil that was draped over her head, the onlooker was able to see only glimpses of her face. Despite that, he was mesmerized.

Just a few moments ago, the maid had brought in glasses, beautifully carved in silver, and had poured liquor in them from a jewel-encrusted pitcher. Only a pint of alcohol had been slurped till now. The celebrity guest was tottering on the brink of intoxication. He hadn't crossed the line yet.

The damsel was still standing with her head bowed in obeisance. The glow of the candles that illuminated the resplendent hall had dimmed in her presence. Her feet moved gracefully to the melodious music in the background. The tinkling of her ankle bells pleasantly complemented her dance.

His majesty tried to rise by taking the support of the throne. Seeing this, the damsel said, 'No...no! Please don't bother, your majesty. I will come to you.' She glided forward so that there was a distance of only four steps between them.

However, his majesty had already stood up. Pleased, he smiled and said, 'I haven't lost my taste for such extraordinary beauty and charm.'

When the damsel smiled gently, it felt as though the twinkle of the most beautiful stars in the universe had shone in that hall. His majesty chuckled and bowed to her.

'It's my honour,' she said. Both faces were radiant with joy. It was as though they had known each other forever. His Majesty noted that the damsel's features emitted profound warmth. Her innocent doe-shaped eyes, luscious enticing lips, rosy cheeks, long artistic fingers and slender body bewitched him. The word '*Mashallah!*' was straining to escape his lips. She was petite- a little above four and a half feet. But, one doesn't fall in love based on height. Love, at first sight, is simply influenced by beauty, grace and charm.

One glance at her had caused him to fall head over heels in love with her. After all, she was no ordinary girl. She was an accomplished artist. Every cell in Farzana's body swayed with the music. When she sang, he felt as though he could listen to her melodious voice for the rest of eternity. It was very easy to fall in love with her. He felt certain that Goddess Saraswati herself lived in Farzana's heart.

'I wish to get acquainted with you. Perhaps you could slip the veil off,' suggested his majesty. She obeyed. He was dumbstruck by her flawless beauty. It was as though someone had suddenly lit a thousand candles in that room. His majesty was unable to tear his eyes away.

From then on began the string of chatter. Farzana wasn't just some doll to love and adorn. That was evident from what she said.

'What would you like to listen to, your majesty? If you are an admirer of beauty and art, you must be fond of Kathak.'

He was pleased by Farzana's words. He smiled and said, 'Are you asking or testing me? I must admit that I am a stranger to this art. So, educate me...what is this Kathak?'

'Alas, I am wretched, your majesty. How can I teach you? However, since you have ordered me to do so, I can't refuse. Kathak is a form of storytelling. One can perform this art to narrate a tale, without speaking a word. Kathak originated during the era of the Mahabharata, it later became a form of Krishna devotion and is now used to adorn Mughal courts. I am certain that you will enjoy watching it,' said Farzana and she met his majesty's eyes.

He was entranced by her intelligence. 'How are you so knowledgeable... that too at such a young age?'

'No, your majesty. I know nothing. I am just a means of entertainment. Had I received an education, I would have certainly become someone like you,' Farzana said with childish charm. The lady's maid arrived with a tray, which displayed a collection of sweet *paan* wrapped in silver, tobacco glazed *paan*, cardamom, peppermint, fennel... and whatnot.

His majesty politely declined the tray. 'But your knowledge at such a tender age is truly astonishing, Farzana.'

Before he could speak again, she placed a finger on his lips. 'No, don't say that. Please don't use your sacred voice to speak my name. I am not worthy of even your words.'

He wasn't able to believe that Farzana was standing so close to him. He felt as though he was in a fairyland. He had been deprived of his wife's touch for a long time too. 'You are stunningly beautiful Farzana… and worthy also.'

'No, your majesty. I am worthless and this beauty will last only so long. Anyway, the Lord has bestowed this to us women. It has nothing to do with me.'

Farzana was like the intoxication of liquor. His majesty felt as though he could drink in her beauty and charm forever. There was something oh-so irresistible about her. He couldn't find the right words to say to her. He felt exuberant after meeting her. Such beautiful moments come only once in a lifetime, after all. Anyway, his majesty was almost three decades older than Farzana. He had been bound by the sacramental vows of marriage even before she had taken birth. However, those blissful moments with Farzana seemed to carry a promise, that one day, they would alter the course of history.

She was well-acquainted with the intricacies of Kathak. People who are fond of this art can spend hours bathing in its charm. Farzana could dance for nights on end without getting tired.

The fifteen-year-old damsel sought his majesty's permission to begin her performance of Kathak. The artists had taken their seats with percussion instruments, the pakhawaj, the tabla and the sarangi. Farzana sang two lines which marked the commencement of her performance. Those lines had once been sung by Gulbadan.

The flames of love were strong earlier,
Now they have burned me to ashes.

His majesty couldn't help but exclaim,

'Wow!'

Farzana bowed in humility. She sang another verse at his majesty's request. The devotional song composed by Meera Bai was-

I may not relive this birth,
To be born human, I must have merited
Life expands every moment, yet it is over in no time
Like the leaf that withers, and never returns
The deep ocean of identity can swallow one
The name of the Almighty shall sweep you to the shore
Life is like a game of chess. When the die is thrown,
One will either win or lose.
Wise men say that life is momentary,
Meera wishes to spend her brief time with her beloved Krishna.

The amused special visitor rose to his feet in respect for the marvellous dancer. He paid his obeisance to her beauty and talent. Since he had travelled to almost every nook and cranny of India, he was well-acquainted with pure Hindi, Urdu and Persian. Yes, there were a few words that were out of his reach. However, Farzana explained their meanings articulately.

He couldn't help but say, 'Today, you have presented before me, the one of the most sublime aspects of the culture of northern India. Your songs carry the beauty and colour of the Ganga and Yamuna rivers.'

Farzana peered into the eyes of the ivory-skinned man. She felt as though he, an artistic philanderer, was hiding behind the mask of a stern-faced warrior. 'Your honour, if it were up to me, I would have swept the culture and stories from the Seine river that flows through your country.'

The visitor playfully cocked an eyebrow and smiled. 'You are slightly off the mark, Madam', said he. 'I hail from Germany, where Marshal Reese was born. It's just that I worked in France for many years.'

Farzana was not accustomed to giving up easily. She smiled endearingly and said,'Certainly, your majesty. But, rivers and oceans aren't ensnared by the boundaries created by men. We are obsessed with the idea of restricting love and culture. Besides, the Rhine river flows in Germany as well as in France. It is not restrained by the wall that exists between the two nations.'

His majesty was stumped by the ethereal damsel's words. He kept gazing at her, presumably rendered speechless. He had no choice but to accept defeat. He smiled and nodded.

Farzana tightened the bells that were wound around her ankles and said,

'Allow me to dance for you, your majesty. These worldly conversations can wait.'

'No, I wish to get to know you better. You should get acquainted with me. Your dance has already lured me,'

The visitor, Sombre murmured dazedly.

'Please go ahead, your majesty. Ordinary people like me have little to share. Exemplary men like you, on the other hand, are angels in disguise, who spread love and joy wherever they go. You might have a lot to tell me.'

The ball was in Farzana's court. Her words had, yet again, rendered him speechless. She commenced her performance then. She said, 'Hold your breath, mister'. An embezzled Sombre watched as began Farzana's dance of love on the song,

'It feels as though the moonlight is melting,
The moon hid when you came.
Neither is the night moonless nor are there any clouds.
Where is the beautiful moon today?
I wonder how long it will hide.
How will the moon return if you stay?

These were the wordings of Hindi and Urdu couplets on which she danced. The performance was truly a treat for the eyes. His Majesty had heard the song before. However, he had never gotten the opportunity to watch Kathak. Both the art and the dancer had enchanted him.

At that time, he was oblivious to the fact that his infatuation with Farzana would irrevocably change the course of history. With every step, verse, and tinkling of the bells, the damsel was gradually sneaking into his heart. All this was happening almost effortlessly. At that point, neither the damsel nor his majesty was aware that they were together writing a new chapter in history. Yet, there is nothing extraordinary about that. History is like a piece of fabric threaded out with such miraculous incidents.

His majesty had no idea how much time had passed. Time, like everything else, seemed to flow effortlessly in Farzana's company. He had arrived in Delhi to fight alongside the Jat ruler of Bharatpur, Jawahar Singh. They had lost the fight, which had considerably weakened his morale. But now, it felt as though one defeat had led to another victory. The magic that flared from Farzana's fingertips had already dug up a spot in his heart. He found her to be even more charming and beautiful in real life than in the stories he had heard.

They had touched upon almost every subject in their conversations. Music, dance, history, politics, diplomacy…you name it and they had discussed it. The first encounter… or rather the first glance had enraptured the so called German warrior. Both of them fostered a flame of hope in their hearts that somehow time would slow down. However, the hours slipped through their fingers like grains of sand.

This scenario belonged to a place of dance and music, near the stronghold of Mughal power, Red Fort in old Delhi. This particular place had become very popular over time. Powerful and wealthy men, along with indulgent courtiers regularly used to pay visits. Farzana's presence had further contributed to its charm. Khanam Jaan was aware of the fact that Farzana was the key to their enterprise's prosperity and wealth. Special care was taken of her because of that reason.

On that day, Farzana bade goodbye to his majesty at the crack of dawn. She climbed down the three-storeyed building and reached the threshold. His Majesty was still in a trance. The desire to drown himself in Farzana's charm and beauty was overwhelming. Khanam was also awake in her room. Her loud yawns were audible even from outside. The gentle footsteps on the staircase informed her that Farzana had returned.

'Congratulations', murmured Khanam groggily, but Farzana wasn't in a mood to talk. Her disinclination to the conversation was not just because of the strain of the night. There was also the fact that she felt dazed after meeting his majesty. She glanced at her once, and smiled briefly, before flouncing out of the room.

'Aha...look at that! She is nothing but behaves like a queen. The pompous girl didn't even reply,' fumed Khanam. But, she bit her lip to keep herself from saying more. She knew that Farzana could get offended by her words, which could potentially stir up a storm. Khanam was dying every day. She had her hopes pinned on the damsel.

Farzana's beauty was truly exemplary. Her style, charm and grace had broken many hearts in the past. She had diligently learnt Urdu and Persian. She was also able to recite verses written by acclaimed poets with beauty and clarity. Farzana's name was taken with respect owing to her grace and chastity. She wasn't just an ordinary member of the brothel. She didn't indulge in prostitution, nor was she simply a beautiful doll to toy around with. She only danced and conversed. Yet, she was enchanting.

Rays of light streamed in to announce the crack of dawn. The sun was peeping from behind the clouds. In those days, the Chawri Bazar in Delhi was relatively tranquil. It was largely devoid of the usual hustle and bustle. One could easily watch the sun rising and setting from the roof of the tallest building. Farzana was awake at such a time after many days. As she admired the orange streaked sky, the word, 'Wow' escaped her lips.

She held her hands before her and bowed to the Sun God. She marvelled at the view for a while, before returning to her room and letting out a yawn.

Farzana began undressing. She first removed the headgear, necklace, the four gold bangles that adorned her slender wrists, colourful bangles separately, flowers, armlet and other gold jewellery. She placed them all in a special box padded with cotton.

This was a glimpse of a bright morning that fell on the wealthy mansion in Chawri Bazar, Delhi in 1767.

CHAPTER 2

Era, Time and Evolution

THE time we are talking about was an important historical transitory phase. After the demise of Aurangzeb in the year 1707, the pace of the collapse of the Mughal empire in India was accelerated. In the latter half of the 18th century, history began to draw a new map, which depicted the scattered and fragile state of the Mughals. Rulers were busy resolving internal disputes and fighting battles during this period of increasing foreign intervention. India had, at that time, become a festering ground for mismanagement and conflict.

The Marathas had conquered Delhi, but they were unable to shoulder the responsibilities of the massive empire. Emperor Mohammad Shah, who ruled from 1719 to 1748, had neither authority nor intelligence to govern the kingdom. He had little interest in fulfilling administrative duties. He was the last Mughal emperor to sit on Shah Jahan's peacock throne.

Afghanistan's Abdali clan's ruler, Ahmad Shah's repeated attacks ripped the Mughal empire to shreds. The next emperor to sit on Delhi's throne was merely a puppet. He danced at the orders of Afghan rulers. For the thirty-two years that followed, the throne of Delhi was hegemonized by Afghan and Maratha power brokers. In reality, the throne belonged to them, not to the emperors who occupied it. Nadir Shah had changed the dynamics of Delhi's power battle in 1739. Emperor Mohammad Shah and chancellor Asaf Shah died in 1748. The fragmented empire finally collapsed then.

Mohammad Shah's death in 1748 marked the commencement of the era of conspiracies, betrayals, complicated inheritance laws, assassinations and rebellions all in the name of the throne. The Mughal empire was on the brink of destruction. The old empire was breaking up piece by piece.

Owing to Mohammad Shah's absence, conspiracies began festering within the kingdom. It was impossible to manage the affairs of the empire efficiently. His son, Ahmad Shah was illiterate. Due to this reason, he was unable to understand administration and was not capable enough to control the vast empire.

Ahmad Shah loved to indulge himself in sensual pleasures. Moreover, there was no elderly person to supervise him. This further contributed to his apathy and lethargy. He spent too much time enjoying life. It is rumoured that his harem was one mile long. In such a situation, important administrative duties were neglected.

In 1752, when the Mughals were trying to attack the Rohilla clan with the help of the Marathas, Ahmad Shah Durrani conquered Punjab. Next year, the Mughal empire handed over the remaining areas of Punjab along with Kashmir to him, apprehending a possible ambush. The Maratha leader of that time challenged Durrani's authority in Punjab with the help of his brother, Raghuba. His army compelled Durrani's forces to flee from Punjab. He also captured Lahore and drove Durrani out. The entire area was under the control of a Maratha governor.

Later, Jahandar Shah's son, Muhammad Azeem-Ud-Daulah was proclaimed emperor of Delhi. He was bestowed with the title of 'Alamgir II.' Delhi's political condition worsened under his rule. Ahmad Shah Abdali planned repeated attacks and captured Punjab. Delhi was becoming fragile, but the Marathas were slowly gaining power. One day, a minister murdered the king to crown another Mughal prince. In this situation, prince Ali Gauhar, the true heir to the throne, sought asylum with a minister of Oudh to keep himself safe.

Ahmad Shah Abdali was angered by the minister's betrayal and the Maratha empire's intervention. He arranged a large army and marched to war. In the battle of Panipat in 1761, Ahmad Shah Abdali crushed the minister's army. The Marathas also met a gruelling end which took them almost one and a half decades to recover from. Ali Gauhar was proclaimed king. He was honoured with the title of 'Shah Alam II.' On Abdali's orders, Shuja-Ud-Daulah was made a minister and Rohilla Najeeb-

Ud-Daulah the commander-in-chief. Matters were in control for a few days. In 1764, Shah Alam, as a prince, fought against the British, alongside his allies- the Nawab of Oudh and the Nawab of Bengal. He met a crushing defeat, which considerably weakened his strength.

In the aftermath of his defeat, emperor Abdullah Jalaluddin Abdul Muzaffar Hamuddin Muhammad Ali Gauhar titled 'Shah-e-Alam II' Sahib-e-Quran Padhshah Gazi had to hand over Bengal, Bihar and Orissa to the British. In return, he was given Allahabad and other small provinces along with twenty-six lakh rupees on an annual basis. Until 1772, this emperor was under the control of the British. He was just a king for name's sake as he exercised little control over the affairs of the kingdom. His empire was limited to Delhi and Agra.

The kingdom authorities were caught up in a string of conspiracies and were dragging the kingdom to doom. Shuja-Ud-Daulah's death in 1775 and Nawaz Khan's death in 1782 had further weakened the emperor. He struck an alliance with Mahadji Shinde. The emperor wanted Shinde to take over the empire completely. However, his decision was met with great opposition within his kingdom. Several advisors and ministers of his joined hands with the Rohilla clan.

This was the situation in a majority of provinces in northern India. Several princely states start clamouring for independence. This was the time when any gutsy person with 100 horses, 100 rifles, 100 soldiers and a little bit of cleverness could declare independence. People weren't motivated by patriotic emotions, and nor were they restrained by a guilty conscience. Even people with alien origins who had settled here, did not hesitate to make use of their army against their armies, providedthey were given a fair remuneration.

The British, Portuguese and French, disguised as either traders or warriors, had already started establishing authority in this fragmented land. Members of the East India Company had planted the sapling of their dominion and had also begun to intervene in war strategies and regimentation. They started providing mercenary services to the local land-owners and rulers of princely states. Such small rulers desired only one thing-to enjoy life in the lap of luxury. They were oblivious to the fact that their carelessness could cost them their position as rulers and could potentially reduce them to the status of grantees.

The year 1773 marked the emergence of the British and French in India. At that time, the French had reached the pinnacle of their power. The areas under French control danced at the fingertips of governor Dupleix. French power was at its peak owing to his influence, enthusiasm and energy.

However, just a short while after Reinhardt Sombre arrived in India, the French suffered heavy losses. They lost several trade battles and the ownership of princely states. Secessionist groups started raising their voices too. The prescient French government withdrew Dupleix from India, thereby accepting its incompetency.

This was the golden era of British domination under king Mohammad Shah and British war strategist, Richard Wellesley. Yet, their actions did not seem to be motivated by their political interests at that time. The emperor and the small rulers considered the Britishers as only soldiers.

The wheels of time spun rapidly and the string of conspiracies, betrayals and malevolent intentions stretched onto half a century. The rulers neglected patriotic emotions and acted in their interest. The royal army of Mughals had irrevocably dropped its morals and principles somewhere along the way. The presiding British government began eyeing the national treasury and started exploiting the natural resources of the country.

The man, who irretrievably drowned himself in Farzana's charm, was still as much of a mystery as he had been when he had first crossed the borders of the country. People knew him as the foreigner from Strasbourg or Treves. But, no one knew for sure whether he was from Australia, France or Germany. According to some, he was born in Luxembourg or Switzerland. However, the documents accounting for his existence recorded his birthplace to be a small village in Isenberg, Germany. The register kept in the protestant church in this town bore a description of his birth. He arrived in India in 1750 and became proficient in Hindi, Urdu and Persian in less than a year. It was evident that he was not an ordinary man. Besides getting a grasp on the languages, he had carefully analysed and understood the politics and people of this nation.

Historians have nicknamed him 'Dyed Fox.' He joined the French army at a very young age under the alias of 'Samar' and thus began a fresh chapter in life. During that time, he managed to join the ranks of the Swiss army in West Bengal. However, the army drove him to boredom in only fifteen days. Samar then used his luck to get into the combat wing of the Safdar'[1] forces. He drifted away from there too and later became the trusted advisor and commander of Bengal's Nawab Mir Qasim.

He was nicknamed 'Samru' by his fellow commanders, who considered him a pensive, despondent and brooding person. When he noticed that the French were grasping at straws, he approached Mir Qasim and offered his services. He was also a commander in the army of Jawahar Singh of Deeg and he fought from various sides in different battles. Yet, he was solely motivated by the promise of fair monetary remuneration.

As the sun rose on the morning of 1757, baby Farzana wailed helplessly beside her unconscious mother at the footsteps of Jama Masjid. She was pleading with the almighty to spare her mother. The mysterious man who was to come to her life years later had fled from Chandernagore, the French enclave on the Hooghly and was now wandering in search of a new purpose to his solitary existence. He had managed to escape by disguising himself as an Indian man. He offered his help

1 He was a royal person from Bengal.

to the nawab of the nawab of Bengal. He was known as Sombre, the French youth who was always willing to help for money. He became an ally and advisor of several Indian rulers and was popular as Samru in the bureaucratic circles. He was able to switch sides easily since he did not conform to any particular ideology.

Instead of marvelling at the wonders in the beautiful city of Paris in France, Samru was wandering amidst the old mansions and brothels in the Chawri Bazar in Delhi. There was a reason behind this. He had arrived in Delhi to support king Jawahar Singh's 'Head to Delhi!' mission. The Mughal emperor wasn't so fragile that he would allow the ruler of a small province to shake the throne of Delhi. Thus, Sombre's mission was rendered unsuccessful and was flushed down the bin of historical failures. He had wandered off to a brothel to seek out new pleasures. Little did he know that something unexpected was going to happen.

Initially, foreign soldiers had seemed to have the sole intention of training Indian soldiers in the art of war. As the wheels of time spun away, the masks had slipped off their faces to reveal their nefarious intentions of occupying the nation.

Akbar the Great had sowed the seeds of the vast empire with unmatched proficiency and Aurangzeb had ruled with an iron hand. However, their successors were so incompetent that the Marathas were easily able to snatch Bengal, Madras and the remote areas of southern India from them. The Battle of Panipat in 1761 had proved to be fatal for the Marathas. Although the Marathas had sprung back to power two decades later in central India, the cup of victory had been snatched by the princely states. They were able to hold on to the throne of Delhi only for a short while. After the demise of Mahadji Shinde, even that victory wasn't sustained.

History witnessed the emergence of several small provinces that eventually vanished without contributing anything. Their obsession with warfare and military led to instability, which ultimately became the root cause of their downfall.

In this era, people were apathetic to patriotic emotions and national welfare. Anyone could take the help of foreign mercenaries to usurp and rule a small province. Such small rulers had begun to dream of occupying the throne of Delhi and getting hold of the treasury. In such expansionist projects, the European commanders were awarded gold and silver souvenirs, diamonds, priceless jewellery and artefacts. Many Europeans were fixated upon draining the treasure chest that belonged to such small princely states.

CHAPTER 3

Physical Conditions of Pre-existing Colonies

THE culture, geographical conditions, lifestyle, dialects and cuisine tend to change after every few miles in northern India. This pristine civilization, demarcated by religion, caste and sub-caste, must have had something special. For, the lascivious gaze of the modern, progressive and influential world was fixed on it. It is important to understand the people of this land, who have shed blood, sweat and tears to plant the roots. The soil of this civilization has been watered with unbridled love, dedication and hospitality. These virtues run deep in the country's value system and spread the message of peace and harmony, just as veins are embedded in the human body to carry blood to different organs.

In understanding Begum Samru and her land, it is helpful to know that besides the Marathas, several other clans and tribes were equally aggressive and dominating. These included the Jats, Sikhs, Rohilla Afghans and a few foreign powers.

No other people was as religious as the Sikhs at that time. They were prominent in Punjab and the surrounding regions. Guru Gobind Singh taught this pious community to sacrifice their lives to ensure religious autonomy. He came up with innovative solutions to make his people militarily independent. After Guru Gobind's death, Guru Banda became the leader. He raised his voice against the growing strength and influence of the Mughals in Saharanpur. In 1767, Ahmad Shah Durrani sent his soldiers to disband the Sikhs, but he was unsuccessful in burying their patriotic feelings. The Sikh population grew day by day. Finally, they were successful in driving the Afghan forces out of their territory. The Sikhs established themselves in Punjab. They granted administrative powers to Ranjeet Singh.

Meanwhile, the Rohillas had occupied the north-western region of Oudh along with the mountain ranges in Kumaon and terrain in the fertile middle Gangetic plain. At that time, a majority of the population was composed of Hindus. However, the changes that were implemented in 1740 resulted in an alarming spike in the Muslim population. The numbers had touched such unprecedented limits, that a migrant warrior was made the ruler of this region. An Afghan Pashtun, who hailed from the Rohilla clan, became the ruler. These Afghans had fled from their land before the commencement of Nadir Shah's tyrannical rule. The Rohillas were said to be perspicacious. People also believed that they were crafty, deceitful, immoral, and aggressive. It was common for such people to commit cruel and violent crimes. Hafiz Ahmad Ali, the ruler at that time, was apprehensive of the Mughals. Despite the aggression and violence of the Rohilla clan, he took several steps to increase the fertility of the soil. He also attempted to dispel the rumours and stereotypes concerning them. He was known as the old ruler with a white beard, who was capable of bringing the enemy to his knees.

The Rajputs faced a lot of hardships during the eighteenth century. They were unable to live up to the legacy left behind by their ancestors due to their laziness and disinterest in warfare. They had entangled themselves in the messy web of internal conflicts and property disputes. They were tormented by the fear of being attacked by the Marathas and Afghans. Anarchy, violence and financial instability further contributed to their worsening condition. This community was slowly drowning in the ocean of doom and despair. Unfortunately, there was no way to rescue them. Owing to their lack of unity, Maratha warriors looted the Rajputs as and when they wanted. They behaved cruelly, but the Rajputs were too fragile to raise their voice. They had stopped paying obeisance to the Mughals, just like the others. They did not hesitate to hoist the flag of rebellion.

The only clan that was ruling with an iron hand was the Jat community, in the princely state of Bharatpur. They had established themselves in the region near Agra. They were known for their proficiency in laying a bed of nails for their enemies. On 7 June 1756, the Jat king, Badan Singh passed away. During the rule of the Mughal king, Ahmad Shah, Badan Singh's son and heir, Surajmal became the ruler. Surajmal was effectively considered the most powerful ruler of northern India. He was a legendary strategist and warrior who was loved by the populace. The gallant and capable Surajmal expanded his kingdom, crossing boundaries. There was a time when Agra, Mathura, Dholpur, Hathras, Mainpuri, Aligarh, Etawa, Rohtak, Mewat, and Rewari all came under his sovereignty.

On 5th December 1763, a deceitful Mughal commander and member of the Rohilla clan, Najib-Ad-Daulah surrounded and killed Surajmal in the Hindon area in Ghaziabad. Surajmal's son, Jawahar Singh was declared ruler of the Bharatpur province in haste. He altered his strategy slightly and brokered an alliance with the Marathas. He actively participated in several campaigns against the Mughals and the East-India Company along with Tukoji Holkar. This was the time when Walter Reinhardt Sombre offered his services to the Jat state. King Jawahar Singh set aside his contempt for foreigners and gratefully made use of his skills to fulfil his purpose.

It is important to understand the world of foreign mercenaries who participated in the invasions of that time without any restraint. These soldiers of fortune greatly influenced the regional rulers. The transitory years were economically propitious for these mercenaries. This was the era of rebellion and instability, which was detrimental for the disciplined European armies. The British, French,

Dutch and Portuguese soldiers were willing to stake their lives to get their hands on the tremendous wealth that was stored in the treasury of these areas. The collapse of the Mughal empire and the complexities arising from the independence of small provinces invited the foreign mercenaries to jump into the field. A time came when British or French commanders were recruited to manage the provincial armies efficiently.

Ren Maddock, Thomas Legge, Ramond, Walter Reinhardt Sombre, George Thomas, Benoit de Boigne, and General Perron were some mercenaries who managed to scale great heights in their occupation. Owing to this, they were each given a few pages in the book of Indian history. English educated soldiers, athletes, henchmen, cooks, merchants, unsuccessful traders-- all attempted to become a part of the siege laid by the mercenaries. Some reached heights they had never dreamt of. Others earned so much that they could live the rest of their life in the lap of luxury. However, most of them were unable to return to their country and died without seeing the faces of loved ones. They were all buried in unmarked graves like the majority of soldiers in these pointless wars. The rest of the survivors became prey to poverty and disease.

French warrior Ren Maddock's life was synchronous with that of General Samru. He was also rash and daring like Samru. They were companions but they split up after the incident of Buxar where the rash Samru brutally murdered several French officers, Maddock kept his distance and ran away to Delhi. He became a favourite of

Najaf Khan. Later, he fought in the battle of Barsana. He spent some time in the service of the Jat king of Gohad. In 1782, he exchanged his army in return for being permitted to board the ship that was sailing to France. He was attacked and killed by a rival there.

George Thomas, an inhabitant of Ireland, was one of the most popular and powerful mercenaries of his time. Despite being illiterate, he was remarkably daring, hard-working and diligent in plotting out war strategies. Initially, he deflected the responsibilities that came with his sailing job and wandered all across the country. He learned the art of war during his stay in the princely state of Hyderabad. He was also a part of a band of robbers which he deserted it as he wanted to focus on his future.

George's initiation in the mercenary business began when he joined Begum Samru's army. He proved his worth in several famous wars. Owing to some conspiracies, he was compelled to leave Sardhana. He joined the Marathas and turned over a fresh leaf. He is considered the founder of the Hansi Estate, which is situated between Rohtak and Hissar in Haryana. George Thomas didn't live long. He passed away within fourteen years.

Mercenary De Boigne also played a major role in the war dynamics. He was a meticulous warrior and strategist. The credit for single-handedly bringing in the use of scientific European technology and imposing a ban on illegal weaponry goes to De Boigne. He was blessed with exceptional talents and skills.

This was the time when the socio-political conditions

of north-western India had become truly deplorable. At that time, Sardhana wasn't a known principality. According to the accounts penned during Akbar the Great's time, Sardhana was a part of a small district. The Sardhana of that time also included a significant portion of the Muzaffarnagar district. During Mohammad Shah's reign, the jagir of Sardhana was handed over to Wazir Kamruddin Khan. Later, this area went to Alamgir II's advisor, Yaqub Ali Khan.

In retrospect, Sardhana became an essential component of history only after Begum Samru's coronation. The legendary queen watered the soil of Sardhana with unconditional love and care.

CHAPTER 4

Farzana's Journey

THE tales and whispers about a nautch girl in the fleabag markets of old Delhi have grabbed as many eyeballs as the endless string of political, social and cultural scandals from the bygone ages. Due to the lack of an efficient transportation-communication system at that time, one couldn't travel from the Bharatpur province in Rajasthan to Khanam's brothel in Chawri Bazar, Delhi and return the next morning.

Although Bharatpur came under the jurisdiction of Rajasthan, it shared its borders with Mathura, which was governed by the Jats. With time, many elements of cultural practices of the Jat community became intertwined with the rituals followed in Bharatpur. This was perhaps the only province which was cognizant of the malevolent intentions of foreign mercenarics. Jawhar Singh was wary of them, so he made use of their services only to advance his army. That was the reason why Bharatpur remained autonomous for a long time.

Farzana was a Kashmiri. That is a proven fact. In the past, there was a certain amount of speculation regarding her nationality. Some people believed that she was from Afghanistan, whereas others suspected that she hailed from the ethnic group of Arabs. Historians have scrutinised credible records that account for this fact. A letter was found in the possession of a French curator in Pondicherry to support this. She was known as Zeb-Un-Nissa and Johanna Nobilis. It is also proven that Farzana was born in a village named Kotana, in Meerut, a part of western Uttar Pradesh. On the surface, she seemed like any ordinary child. However, the maturity she possessed was remarkable for such a precocious age.

The region within the borders of Meerut, Baghpat, and Muzaffarnagar was prosperous. The fertile land yielded sugarcane, mustard, and wheat of superior quality. It is said that water in the streams that ran through the town was sweeter than sugar. However, the people residing there did not withhold the sweetness of their land. Their harsh words concealed the beauty of their culture. If you happen to stay there, you will notice that their so-called 'crude' language is punctuated with love.

Lutafat (Lutf) Syed Ali Khan was a Muslim. It is said that he was ethnically an Arab. Although history is tight-lipped about him, there are certain accounts which claim that he was a courtier of a Mughal emperor and he later settled in the Kotana village in Meerut. The taciturn Khan Sahib married twice. Farzana was born to his second wife, Jahan, who was Kashmiri, in 1751. Syed

Ali Khan passed away when she was just six. After his demise, Farzana's step-brother started misbehaving with them. The distraught mother and daughter left home in search of shelter. They collapsed with exhaustion after wandering through Meerut, Agra, Rohillakhand, Bharatpur, and Deeg. The mother-daughter duo finally reached Delhi in 1760.

The Mughal emperor Shah Jahan had abandoned Agra to make this city his capital. Delhi was the first mapped and planned city in India. The eight-mile-long area was covered with broad roads, galleries, lush green trees, and scenic gardens. This beautiful city could attract anyone.

Opulent mosques and a few temples were built here. The markets were generously stocked with all kinds of goods. Luxurious residential wings were constructed for courtiers and officials within the fort itself.

When little Farzana arrived in Delhi, her mother, Jahan had no choice, but to hand her over to the infamous brothel in Chawri Bazar. In this way, the strings of Farzana's destiny were pulled by the brothel. However, this brothel did not engage in prostitution. It was a congregation ground for aesthetes.

This was the time when a wave of anarchy was sweeping throughout the country. There was no law and no law-abiding citizen. On the contrary, the seemingly responsible soldiers and officers spent nights relishing the pleasures of brothels. In such a lawless society, the business of sexual trafficking of nubile girls was flourishing. Mothers voluntarily sacrificed their gullible daughters' chastity. As soon as they reached puberty, their destiny was determined by their buyers.

Some girls were auctioned like cattle and were sold to nefarious strangers. Others were taught the intricacies of dance. Farzana belonged to the second category. Her journey is intriguing.

Farzana had arrived in Delhi with her mother. They were seeking shelter in the vast city. They wandered to a residential colony in search of a distant relative. However, no one came to help them. This relative, who supposedly lived in a small hut in Chandni Chowk, had passed away three months ago. For the eleven days that followed, an anguished Jahan and a weary Farzana wandered from one place to the other, in vain. They hoped against hope that the passing shoppers, soldiers, merchants, traders and devotees in mosques-churches-temples would come to their aid. This memory haunted Farzana for years. Passers-by gave them odd stares wherever they went. They survived on pieces of bread and drops of water. They thanked the kind, old lady who had permitted them to stay in her small hut for just a few paise. With time, even that meagre money got exhausted, and so did the lady's generosity. She closed her doors to the mother-daughter duo.

The two of them began appealing to the passers-by in the name of the Lord. They sought relief from the scorching sun under green trees or oxcarts, where they shared a place with squirrels, rats and dogs. They spent endless nights in strange places. Jahan would cradle innocent Farzana to her chest and grovel at the feet of passers-by. Initially, they hovered around others in an attempt to gather alms. After a while, they started begging while sitting in one place. Jahan's fragile body could not bear the strain of the day. Later on, she begged while lying on the pavements. But, this was the vibrant city of Delhi- the land of vivacious people, who carried a flame of *joie de vivre* in their hearts. No one had the time or patience to empathize with the mother-daughter duo. Occasionally, some passer-by, who might be feeling generous that day, would toss a coin or two and saunter away. That was enough for them. Matters worsened once Farzana's mother's health began deteriorating.

It was particularly cold and rainy that day. Enormous grey clouds were rumbling menacingly. Streaks of lightning split the overcast sky into two fragments. Braving the unpleasant weather, Gulbadan Jan gingerly stepped out of her cosy carriage. A veil covered her face, so it was difficult to recognize her. She was frightened by the weather and wished to return to the safety and warmth of her mansion. Her carriage was moving past the Jama Masjid when the heart-wrenching cries of a child reached her ears. Disregarding the cold winds, she ordered the henchmen to halt.

Through the diaphanous veil, Gulbadan's gaze fell on a child who was pitifully wailing beside her exhausted mother.

'Someone help! My mother is dying. Her life is in

danger. O' children of God, help me! What do I do?'

Gulbadan approached them with the caution that one reserves for ferocious animals. The child must have been around seven or eight. Her clothes were dirty and scruffy, her hair unkempt and she looked as though she hadn't eaten for days. But, her beautiful entrancing eyes, which seemed enormous for her malnourished face, were shining with extraordinary self-confidence. Gulbadan's gaze fell on the mother too. Her mind procured a hazy old memory. When she learned the woman's name, the clouds of doubt faded away. Yet, Gulbadan maintained a poker face, which didn't betray her astonishment.

'Who are you and what do you want?' she asked.

This eminent lady was the owner of the infamous brothel in Chawri Bazar, where Lutf Khan had fallen in love with Jahan. Gulbadan's sharp eyes discerned Jahan's identity. Yet, she maintained her composure and remained tight-lipped.

'We wish to reach Gulbadan Jan's mansion. Exhaustion and disease restrain us from reaching our destination. We are relatively new in this big city and do not know anyone here,' Jahan whimpered weakly.

It was Gulbadan's turn to be caught off-guard. She wished to get acquainted with the daughter, not the mother. Just as how a connoisseur can discern the feeble spark of a diamond buried underneath the ground, Gulbadan recognized Farzana's extraordinary beauty through the veil of torn clothes and matted hair. She was never wrong about such matters.

Hiding her astonishment, Gulbadan briefly introduced herself.

'Come with me. I will take you there.'

She beckoned towards a carriage. Gulbadan's carriage rode upfront and the second carriage, seating the mother-daughter duo, followed her. Finally, the two carriages halted outside an opulent, but weathered mansion. The henchman who was waiting at the gate bowed before Gulbadan. She ordered him to take the mother-daughter duo to the guest wing. Jahan realized that Gulbadan was not an ordinary woman. Utterly exhausted and worn out, she was unable to recognize the kind, eminent lady who had taken her under her wing.

Gulbadan's brothel had lost its glamour and charm. Call it the antics of time or simply bad luck- the bygone era was history now. The threshold of the mansion was battered and worn out now. Gulbadan's influence ensured that the mansion and brothel remained intact at least.

Ironically, that particular brothel, which Jahan had once abandoned, became a silver lining for the mother-daughter. The demise of her father, cruelty at the hands of her step-brother, financial problems, and a life of poverty had irrevocably muddled Farzana's childhood. But, every night is followed by a beautiful morning.

As Farzana matured into a beautiful teenager, happiness somehow seemed to find its way to her. She was so stunning, that it was difficult to not be dazzled by her. Khanam, who would provide sensual pleasure to men, was also struck by Farzana's beauty. The Shahjahanabad of that time is known as old Delhi today.

Jahan realized that every nook and cranny of the lavish room, from whose ceiling hung an opulent chandelier, hid delectable memories. This room had been the life of the mansion twenty years ago. The paint was peeling off the battered walls and the curtains were torn and dirty now. The teak furniture, had, however, survived the passage of time and shone resplendently.

The past came knocking back on Jahan's doors. She felt honoured to have been invited to stay in that magnificent room. Countless army generals, merchants, traders, and intellectuals had spent nights there. A wave of panic suddenly knocked her off her feet. The thought that this was temporary and she would have to return to her pitiful life again terrified her.

In the afternoon, a lady's maid came to take Farzana away. She was bathed in rose water. Her hair was disentangled and she was asked to wear new clothes. She was also made to wear anklets and small bangles. The lady's maid then took her to meet Gulbadan.

Gulbadan was mesmerized by Farzana's newfound beauty and charm.

'Come, my child,' she said endearingly and embraced her. Farzana hugged her back. She felt as though she had found her lost mother.

'You are my lovely doll,' whispered Gulbadan and lovingly stroked her hair. She brought in a doctor to treat Jahan. A sumptuous dinner was prepared for them that night. Jahan's condition had begun to show signs of improvement. She was grateful to Gulbadan. Her old memories were gradually surfacing again. She began to remember Gulbadan's youthful days.

'Your dance used to be captivating, sister!'

she said respectfully.

Gulbadan smiled and said, 'Those days have passed. Now all that remains are these battered walls. People have forgotten us.'

'Why, sister? I remember that every night, dancers would entertain men in these rooms. Shining tiles, cushions and settees, fragrances wafting in the air, bewitching atmosphere, and a large group of percussionists. Aesthetes were always swarming around this mansion. But, things have changed now. Why is that so?' Jahan asked curiously.

'You know that it is difficult to sustain our business. Delhi's ruler funded and supported us then. Now that the Mughal empire is on the brink of extinction, it has become impossible for us to survive,' Gulbadan said, passing the platter of mince pies, goat meat, pleated bread, kabab and biryani to the mother-daughter duo.

The little girl was unable to follow the esoteric conversation. Yet, her beautiful eyes remained glued to Gulbadan's face in amazement.

'Have this, child,' Gulabadan said and dropped two pieces of meat and curry onto her plate.

Farzana smiled gleefully and began to eat.

'On the night of Eid, Nadir Shah laid siege to Delhi. That prowler was furious because someone had attacked him here. He ordered his army to destroy Chandni Chowk and Chawri Bazar. His soldiers robbed jewellery as well as eatery shops. They even raped innocent women. No one was spared. Thousands of men, women and children died that night,' Gulbadan said.

'People loathe Nadir Shah. His arrival in Delhi has been the cause of our downfall.'

Gulbadan chuckled as she spoke. But, her eyes betrayed the sadness and pain that was simmering in her heart.

CHAPTER 5

Who was Reinhardt Sombre?

ALTHOUGH this tale is about Begum Samru's legendary life, it is imperative to analyse Reinhardt Sombre's birth and childhood. He was said to have been born in the year 1725.

Historians must have been impressed by his background. It is claimed that he was born in Germany. However, there is little evidence to support that claim. The name 'Reinhardt' has its roots in Germany. People hailing from this family are primarily located in Austria and Switzerland, and in the southern part of Germany. Despite this conflicting piece of information, it is said to be a proven fact that Reinhardt was born in Germany. The descendants of his father, Leonhart Reinhardt still live in Baden-Württemberg.

Reinhardt was also rumoured to be an illegitimate child. His mother worked for Leonhart Reinhardt, who was a butcher. Reinhardt Sombre was a product of their liaison. As soon as the news about the ill-fated pregnancy reached Leonhart's ears, Reinhardt's mother was removed from the small farm where she worked. A gipsy family in Eisenburg came to her aid then. Reinhardt was born in the midst of one of their wanderings and he grew up as a nomad. Although his mother was a Catholic, he adopted Protestant Christianity as his religion owing to the influence of the gypsies.

As a typical German, he was a man of faith. He believed in the innate goodness and kindness of humanity. His friends fondly recall that he truly believed the myth of a silver mine beside the fort in their area. He narrated the tale of the mine earnestly and even expressed his concern about people misusing the knowledge.

When Reinhardt was just fourteen, his mother sent him to Wurzburg to learn the butcher's trade. She returned to her former profession of providing domestic help. When she told the teen about his father's whereabouts, he turned red with rage. He gathered all his resources and burned his father's farm. To save himself from his father and the local authorities' wrath, he fled to Strasbourg and enrolled himself in the ranks of the French army. He was made the keeper of the treasury and thus became a trooper. He proved his worth by playing a key role in the Battle of Beltzan. After that, he bid farewell to the army, sold his horse and set off on a naval expedition to Holland. He wished to reach Spain, where he wanted a job in the Spanish Guardia. He desired to work specifically in the freelance wing. Upon reaching

Middelburg, he encountered a ship which was about to sail to India. Without giving it much thought, Reinhardt climbed aboard and reached Pondicherry. This happened in 1750.

At that time the East India Company was struggling to establish itself in India. The local rulers were being educated about their financial condition, landowners were facing exploitation and harassment, and British factories were expanding throughout the country. Sombre was an ordinary soldier then. He was clever enough to understand that the French were tottering on the brink of collapse. He realized that if the tables didn't turn, the British would flourish in India and French power would meet a miserable end. He began opposing the French and started devising infiltration tactics for the British.

This was the time when there wasn't any significant difference between the military tactics devised by India or European nations. Due to this reason, foreign soldiers were considered inferior to Indian soldiers during Akbar and even Aurangzeb's reign. They worked under the supervision of Indian authorities. Indians had developed only one kind of defence mechanism. There was little innovation in military technology in India in the decades that followed. However, a wave of technological advancement swept throughout Europe, which led to several changes in the social hierarchy. The European commanders earned some respect in the Indian army ranks and they swelled with pride.

The situation altered so dramatically that the

Europeans who used to address the rulers as 'Your Majesty' began demanding superior positions in the courts in the seventeenth century. They became successful in climbing a rung on the ladder of power. After a point, the local rulers became puppets in the hands of European courtiers. The Indian soldiers, commanders and even the emperor himself started believing that the proficiency of European commanders couldn't be contested. They considered Europeans to be superior to the native Indians and began entrusting political and military decisions to them. This was the time when Sombre rose from dust and became a key player in power dynamics.

In 1757, Sombre reached Chandernagore or Chandan Nagar in Bengal. This was his second stint with the French army. This area, which is located beside the serene Hugli river in what is now West Bengal was under French control. It is rumoured that along with some small districts, this area was established by the French. It was later discovered that this region had already been accounted for in 1696. Within years, the French managed to turn the city into a haven of prosperity and wealth. Almost a century later, in 1756, Chandernagore became a battleground for the British and the French. The British army began shelling and managed to overthrow the French on 23rd March 1757. Sombre was in league with the French. When he noticed that his army had become flimsy, he cut off all ties and fled the battle, in line with his fugitive tendencies. Sombre, the sergeant of the French army, disguised himself as a native and slyly slipped out of Chandernagore.

He wandered in different districts of Bengal, where he stumbled across Mir Qasim's Armenian General, Gurgin Khan. He demonstrated extraordinary skill and valour under him. Later, he organized and led Nawab Mir Qasim's army in a European fashion. Sombre had a morose and sullen personality and he developed a monomaniacal obsession with warfare. He had a wheatish skin tone, which prompted his friends to nickname him 'Sombre.' In French, Sombre refers to dark skin colour. Later on, the name was altered slightly and thus became 'Samru'.

As and when Sombre came in contact with Indians, his holistic persona showed significant signs of improvement. This remarkable transformation was reflected in his opinions and body language. He professed a keen interest in Indian festivals and carnivals, the Mughal regalia was his favourite attire, and Indian culture left a lasting impression on him. He became proficient in Persian and Urdu. He could fluently converse in those.

The scales of fortune were leaning in Samru's favour. Despite his contempt for foreigners, Mir Qasim had developed a soft spot for him. Although he was a good-natured man, he harboured an implacable hatred for the British soldiers and the officials of the East India Company, who had attempted to rob him of his kingdom.

Young Sombre had considered Bengal only because it promised a propitious future. He enrolled himself in the ranks of a Swiss battalion of the East India Company. It is rumoured that he had registered himself as Sumer, or

Samar or Samru to conceal his true identity. It appeared as though the name, 'Samru' was a distorted version of Sombre.

Bengal's Nawab, Siraj-Ud-Doulah was exasperated with British interference in the affairs of his kingdom and their expansionist policies. Factories were being set up illegally and the Nawab's opponents were being indulged.

The Nawab was a shrewd man. He never decided in haste and intelligently planned a siege to overthrow the British. The East India Company officials were so jubilant of their success that they did not pay heed to the Nawab's wrath. On the contrary, they openly humiliated and ridiculed his messengers.

When there was no scope left for an amicable compromise, the outraged Nawab had no choice but to order the destruction of British factories and buildings. In retaliation to an obstinate ruler who was in league with the British, the Qasim Bazar Factory was conquered. In 1756, several British factories were made defunct. A proportion of the opponents surrendered to the Nawab. Those who fought were butchered. Sombre fled from the pitiful scene once again, and chose not to fight along with the East India Company, alongside several other company officials and authorities. He was successful in keeping himself safe. Sombre worked for the British Crown for just eighteen days. When his seniors fled the battlefield with their tails tucked between their legs, how could Sombre be expected to demonstrate valour? The logistics department of the British hadn't even arranged boats for the army's retreat. They were only concerned about saving themselves. In 1756, Sombre journeyed to the French colony of Chandernagore, where he was appointed sergeant.

Although the Nawab had managed to defeat the East India Company officials and establish himself in that region, the sovereignty of his state didn't last long. Clive and Watson succeeded in ousting him from Kolkata. The debilitated and helpless Siraj-Ud-Doulah was forced to bow before the British and accept the unjust conditions they had put forth. Somewhat consoled by the fact that the region remained prosperous and happy, the Nawab had to extend the benefits of those unreasonable terms to the French in Chandernagore. The Nawab was going through a tough time. He felt threatened by the knowledge that the notorious Afghan rebel, Ahmad Shah Durrani, was advancing towards this region. In this situation, the Nawab decided to take the help of the British army and grind Ahmad Shah Durrani to dust in Patna. However, the East India company had other plans. They agreed to help the Nawab if he offered his resources to them to overthrow the French in Chandernagore. The British wanted to break the ties of friendship between the Nawab and the French and thereby conquer this area.

By taking the assistance of the Nawab to defeat their rival, and simultaneously getting an estimation of the Nawab's prowess, the British killed two birds with one stone. The Nawab did not have the luxury of time to make a decision. He wanted peace and harmony in his province. He agreed to this condition also. On 13th March, Reno and Clive sent a formal notice to the French in Chandernagore, asking them to surrender the province. When they received no reply, they attacked the French colony on the morning of 14th March. After examining the unnerving situation, Sombre was convinced that the French were going to lose. So, he fled the scene. He was successful in escaping even before the actual battle had begun by donning Indian clothes. Subsequently, he became an officer in Siraj-Ud-Doulah's army.

On 23rd March, the East India Company won the pre-decided battle. They implemented stringent policies to tighten their hold on this province. As per the new measures, they decided to get rid of the uncertain Nawab, who was torn between his allegiance to the French and his desire for peace in his kingdom. A web of conspiracy and betrayal was laid out for the Nawab. Fake news was circulated throughout the province by the British for this reason.

This brought in a new set of challenges for the Nawab. Clive and Watson removed him from the position of commander of the army. On 1st May 1757, the Executive Committee of Fort William decided to crown Mir Jafar, a relative of the Nawab, instead of the Nawab himself. After deceitfully winning the Battle of Plassey, Clive placed Nawab in captivity. In such a situation, Reinhardt Sombre decided to betray his master and flee. He abandoned the Nawab and left for another destination.

He spent the next few years travelling to different

places. In 1760, the coveted title of Commander of the Purnia army was bestowed upon him. This designation meant that in effect he became the Governor of this district. Sombre was made commander of a battalion and he organized the army in a European fashion. This army did not achieve anything remarkable in the first battle, but it filled Sombre with ambitions to control larger armies and provinces. His foresight and experience had taught him that such opportunities could be explored by wandering in Bengal. The British did not frighten him anymore. He would have never returned to Bengal if that had been the case. He blended himself in by donning Mughal regalia and adopting the native traditions.

At that time, the political landscape of Bengal had altered dramatically. The East India Company had crowned Mir Qasim, instead of Siraj-Ud-Doulah. But, his condition had deteriorated too. The British authorities did not pay heed to his desires. On the contrary, they regularly humiliated and insulted him. Mir Qasim now began dreaming of freedom. He started employing capable European mercenaries in his army. This responsibility was shouldered by Gurgin Khan, a skilled warrior, who had close relations with influential families in India. Along with becoming Mir Qasim's advisor, he was also the commander of the army. He entrusted Sombre with two battalions. This was the time and place where Sombre struck gold.

Mir Qasim had decided to expand his kingdom now. He acted on commander Gurgin Khan and Sombre's advice and attacked Nepal. However, he lost miserably. Despite that, he did not give up and continued to devise strategies to overthrow the Britishers. The populace was encouraged to harbour patriotic emotions and was told to boycott the East India Company. Anyone caught aiding the Company would be severely punished.

In an attempt to crush the rebellion against Nawab Mir Qasim in Patna, in 1763, British rebels from Munger were executed under Sombre's watch. This was a black mark on his conscience. Sombre had come to India as a nomadic soldier and he had risen to great heights owing to Gurgin Khan. Khan was beheaded because he declined to execute the Nawab's order. In 1763, Sombre mercilessly executed more than a hundred Englishmen on the Nawab's orders. He knew that if he hesitated to obey the Nawab, he would be killed like Gurgin Khan. Sombre entrusted this gory work to his Hindu soldiers, but he assisted them as and when required. He eased his conscience with the knowledge that this was a minor incident in the era of war.

Sombre's brutality resulted in British fury towards him. He was threatened by them, but he received protection from the Nawab. On 6th November 1763, a cannon was fired, but Mir Qasim, Sombre and several other people fled before the attackers swarmed in. They reached Awadh on 19th November 1763 and approached Nawab Shuja-Ud-Doulah.

At the beginning of February 1764, Mir Qasim hounded the Hindu kingdoms that had challenged Shuja-

Ud-Doulah's authority twice. Sombre efficiently managed the army there. The opposing army could not stand too long before his skilled and disciplined soldiers. Najaf Khan was in the service of a Hindu king at that time. He advised the latter to employ Sombre to train his army in a European manner and equip it with advanced military technology. This battle has been viewed as Sombre's big break. Shuja was impressed by Sombre's prowess. Taking into consideration Mir Qasim's repeated requests and emotional appeals, he accepted his friendship and agreed to help topple the British empire in India.

Naturally, the British authorities were displeased by this turn of events. They threatened to go to war if Mir Qasim, Sombre and other fugitives weren't handed over to them. There would be no dialogue if this demand wasn't fulfilled. Shuja-Ud-Doulah was a stubborn man. He threatened the Britishers by saying that,

> *'If those who disrupt peace remain entangled in the web of insubordination and pride, the sword of justice will slice them into pieces.'*

Upon realizing that Shuja was adamant and war was inevitable, a formal declaration was sent out to commence the battle. Men of different religions and castes composed Shuja's army. Only the wing managed by Sombre was disciplined and skilled. He was commanding three brigades but even his war strategies were ultimately rendered unsuccessful. This worsened Mir Qasim and Shuja's ties. It is rumoured that Mir Qasim ordered Sombre to shoot Shuja, who was retreating from the battleground. This war, which left its mark in the pages of history in August 1764, proved to be indecisive for both parties. This was because Shuja wanted the province of Bihar before any dialogue took place. On the other hand, the East India company had put forth the condition that they wouldn't engage in any peace talks until Mir Qasim, Sombre and other French fugitives were handed over to them. However, none of the conditions was accepted.

The senior authorities of the company altered their game. They tried to influence the Muslims from the opposition. They were asked to help capture and arrange for the surrender of Mir Qasim and Sombre. That approach did not work, but differences and conflicts kept intensifying between Mir Qasim and Shuja. Shuja shrewdly convinced Sombre to side with him. Sombre, along with his soldiers, captured Mir Qasim and demanded that he be paid for his services. Mir Qasim did not hesitate to compensate him. He advised him to keep the two battalions that he had been entrusted with. He also told him to keep the weapons that belonged to the soldiers. However, Sombre did not pay heed to Mir Qasim and said that the true owner of the artillery was the one who had rightfully won it.

Sombre severed all ties with Mir Qasim. His tent was installed beside Shuja-Ud-Daulah's tent. Later on, Awadhi soldiers surrounded Mir Qasim's camp. He was released from captivity after a short while. Shuja, who wanted to befriend the British, told them that Mir Qasim had been punished appropriately. However, the British governor and his council insisted on fulfilling the conditions that had been put forth. They threatened to crush the Nawab if Mir Qasim and Sombre weren't surrendered. Major Munro of the East India company was ordered to head to the battleground to teach them a lesson. The Company wanted to create a situation wherein Shuja would be compelled to hand over Mir Qasim, Sombre and other fugitives.

Major Munro reached Buxar on the morning of 22nd October 1764. The next day, Shuja arrived on the battleground for this pre-decided war. Sombre was on the ground too along with his English companions, Gentil and Maddock, and eight skilled and disciplined battalions. The British were strongly contested in this war. At one point, the Indian soldiers felt as though they had managed to defeat the British. However, because of the widespread confusion, the army was unable to stand before the British forces. Sombre's battalion did manage to weaken the enemy to a great extent. Only his battalion did some justice to the war. However, Shuja was greatly angered by this defeat. He insulted Mir Qasim, Sombre and others and accused them of betrayal. He initiated a dialogue with the British to reconcile with them. This discussion was carried out with the guidance of the charter of rights. He advised the governor to give up the condition to surrender Sombre with Mir Qasim because he had no control over the soldiers and weapons owned by Sombre.

It was decided that as soon as Shuja allied with the

British, he would have to dismiss Mir Qasim, Sombre and other French mercenaries and he would also have to withdraw the funds that were allocated to them. Later on, two senior British officials declared that an alliance between Shuja and the Company couldn't be brokered without Mir Qasim, Sombre and other mercenaries. Both parties remained engaged in war preparations. He departed from there to launch a campaign against Benares. The British dominated this battle too. However, Sombre's pragmatic tactics kept Shuja out of the way. Shuja invited several provinces of Northern India to contribute to the ferocious battle against the unjust British forces. He placed his family and valuables under the watch of Sombre's skilled and disciplined army and immersed himself in the task at hand.

The Battle of Kora, which was fought on 3rd May 1765, led to the defeat of an ally province. Shuja was now heavily depended on the mercy of the British. The East India Company told Shuja to hand over Mir Qasim, Sombre and other fugitives or execute them publicly and prove their death.

Sombre knew that the British were tough opponents. His army was small and he had pledged his allegiance to an indecisive Nawab, who was reluctant to ask the Marathas for help.

Shuja ultimately joined hands with the British. Because of the constant presence of skilled soldiers and officers around Sombre, Shuja couldn't lay a finger on him. Sombre wanted a new job. He found this opportunity with Maharaja Madho Singh. This ruler of Jaipur founded the city of Sawai Madhopur and was thus known as Sawai Madho Singh. Sombre couldn't stay there for a long time. Later on, the Jat ruler of Bharatpur, Jawahar Singh employed him to reorganize his army.

When the East India Company heard about this, they started hunting Sombre. The ruler of Bharatpur State Jawahar Singh offered state protection to him and his companions. On 7th June 1765, the Bengal Governor, Robert Clive wrote the following letter to the Jawahar Singh on 19th August 1765,

> *'You have provided shelter to the man who brutally murdered hundreds of innocent Englishmen. If you surrender Samru to us, we will befriend you. We are gracious friends and will help you as and when required.'*

Through this letter, the company tried to pressurize Jawahar Singh into surrendering Sombre. Jawahar Singh knew that presently, there was not a strong province, not only in the peripheral region but miles away also that could even look Bharatpur in the eye. Provinces governed by the East India company were too far to even pose a threat. Jawahar Singh decided to reply to this letter in the following words,

> *'The intention behind helping Samru is not to worsen relations with the British. The ruler wishes to strengthen his army by incorporating European war tactics and modern technology alongside advancing the organization of his*

infantry and artillery wing. For this purpose, solely, he has employed a European commander.'

Jawahar Singh wormed his way out of this situation by brokering a seemingly friendly and protective alliance with Clive, by proclaiming Sombre's surrender unnecessary. In this way, he managed to keep his Jat province out of the vicious clutches of the East India Company.

Sombre trained the Jat army and marched to Pushkar for a battle. He halted in the Marwari area of Jaipur and invited Vijay Singh to unite the Rajputs against the Marathas. Rajputs were terrified by the idea of opposing the Marathas. The battle was ultimately fought near Manda. As the Rajput army marched through the valley, they split apart owing to the fear of being robbed. On the other hand, the Bharatpur army, which had been trained by Sombre in a European fashion, advanced steadily and was successful in protecting their king.

Jawahar Singh was destined to die young. An agitated soldier murdered him due to a slight provocation. This incident marked the commencement of a new chapter of conspiracies and family disputes. Naval Singh succeeded Jawahar Singh to the throne of Bharatpur. A significant portion of the military force was said to be in his favour.

The Marathas and the Rajputs clashed in a terrible battle on 6th April 1770. In the war council, Sombre and Maddock urged the king to halt the battle after sunset. Their plea fell on deaf ears and the battle continued. Two hours of brutal bloodshed convinced Naval Singh to retrace his steps and pay heed to what Sombre and Maddock had said. He was forced to escape so hastily, that he had to leave behind all weapons and valuables. If Sombre hadn't used his intelligence and demonstrated extraordinary courage, even the two cannons wouldn't have been salvaged. Perhaps even the army would have been completely slaughtered by the skilled soldiers of the opposition.

Sombre played a major role in the battle fought between Najaf Khan[2] and Naval Singh. He slew two commanders in Najaf Khan's advancing army. However, Najaf Khan acted boldly. His morale was boosted by his determined General. Sombre fought bravely, but Bharatpur lost the battle because of Najaf Khan's absence and also because they were greatly outnumbered by the opposing army. Owing to Sombre's foresight and disciplined soldiers, they were able to save a major portion of the forces.

This battle proved to be fatal for the Jats. Sombre's decision to abandon this province worsened the situation. As a gesture of gratitude for having stayed in Deeg and Bharatpur and as a symbol of reverence, Sombre was given a small village that was situated a mile away from Deeg. This place is known as 'Samru-ka-Nagla" even today. A few acquaintances of Sombre were even buried there. The residential wing of the Bharatpur Palace, where Sombre

---

2 A powerful courtier of Mughal darbar.

had lived with his wife, is still in existence there.

When Sombre left Bharatpur, he was accompanied by his trained and armoured army. After collecting a princely sum of two lakh rupees as his fee from the king, Sombre was en route to the Marathas territory. Impressed by his efficiency in handling his army, Najaf Khan was eager to employ him. In the royal court, Najaf Khan's rival group wanted to bag all the credit, despite being on emperor's side. The leader of the group, Abdul Ahad Khan approached the emperor Shah Alam II and tried to convince him to give up Sombre. He told the Nawab that the rebellious Sikhs posed a serious threat to the throne of Delhi. If Sombre joined hands with them, it would worsen the situation. He offered Sombre thirty thousand rupees per month. After a string of conspiracies, Sombre finally joined the Mughal emperor. He explained to the emperor that his ties with the British had been severed beyond repair. He wanted to keep his distance from any kind of dialogue between Shuja or the Mughal emperor and the British.

The emperor reassured Sombre that the Mughal empire wouldn't broker any kind of alliance with the British and Sombre himself would be protected around the clock. It is rumoured that the emperor had even promised to make Sombre the ruler of the Bengal province. Sombre became the official ruler of the Sonipat and Panipat provinces. It was also decided that Sombre would immediately become the owner of the province he usurped from the Sikh leader, Kuchet Singh.

At that time, Sombre possessed a huge number of weapons, ammunition, five canons, six elephants, two-hundred horses, and an army of 1900 soldiers, a few of whom were Europeans. This army wasn't big enough to win a battle, but it was quite disciplined and skilled. British spies had alerted the quick-witted Governor-General, Warren Hasting about the alliance between Sombre and the Mughal emperor Shah Alam II.

As per the agreement with the Mughals, Sombre's army defeated the Sikhs in Samalkha on 25 June 1774 and occupied the *pargana*. Sombre started heading towards the Sonipat-Panipat province. However, the British were extremely displeased by Sombre and the Mughal emperor's alliance. Shah Alam II was even sent a letter expressing the company's displeasure. The emperor immediately sent a diplomatic reply to the British stating that he had employed Sombre to fulfil his immediate needs. However, Sombre would be dismissed immediately.

The Mughal emperor later declined to fund all raids carried out by Sombre. The sly Minister Ahmad Khan did not even acknowledge Sombre's complaints. However, Najaf Khan was a clever man, who had realized that Sombre could be a valuable ally. He wanted to use him to topple the Jats of Bharatpur. He knew that Sombre was well acquainted with that province's strengths and weaknesses. He warmly welcomed Sombre even after he had been dismissed. He gave Sombre an increment to hold him in place. Under the influence of Ahmad Khan, the Mughal emperor locked horns with Najaf Khan for having employed Sombre. Najaf Khan cleverly obviated the emperor's anger and concern.

Concerning Sombre's war tactics, Major Lewis Fernandez, an expert in the field of warfare and military said,

> *'The Battalion led by Samru wasn't known for any particular victory in war. Their intent wasn't to gain or lose something. Yet they were notorious for strategically retreating from the battlefield. Samru routinely assembles his army in a straight row and then begins shelling. He would manoeuvre his soldiers in a wheel formation and would then retreat.'*

Sombre was able to create troubles for Naval Singh from the Mughals' side as he had worked for him and he knew his weaknesses. He proved to be a thorn in Naval Singh's side where the province of Bharatpur was concerned.

CHAPTER 6

Reinhardt Sombre Fervent Love

THE political atmosphere of India was dichotomous at that time. While one half of the society was preoccupied with conspiracies, military insurgency, instability and the fear of the British, the other half, which was constituted by soldiers of fortune like Reinhardt Sombre, viewed the power dynamics differently. By the time Samru's gaze fell on this distressed damsel in Khanam's brothel, she was already known by the name of Farzana. The irresistible charm that emanated from her had lured many to this brothel. Rumours about her bewitching beauty had travelled to almost every nook and cranny of Delhi. When Sombre saw her for the first time, he couldn't take his eyes off her. She was even more beautiful than he had imagined.

As they frequently rendezvoused, they grew closer to each other. Farzana's knowledge at such a precocious age was enough to unsettle anyone. Her inquisitive nature and eagerness to learn, especially about stereotypically patriarchal fields such as warfare and the military, were astonishing. She professed a keen interest in discussing Sombre's military exploits.

This stiff-backed soldier had understood that their acquaintance was not a monetary affair, but a romantic one. Sombre's thawed stone heart had melted in the flames of love. His wife had been ailing for quite some time. Also known as *badi bee,* she had little interest in Sombre's military exploits, diplomacy and politics. The middle-aged Sombre had found love in young Farzana. He had fallen prey to her beauty and intelligence. She was exactly the type of companion his heart had been yearning for. Farzana's attraction towards Sombre was evident too. These encounters continued on a routine basis. Soon, both hearts were enraptured with love.

'For how long will we continue meeting in this dark, dingy attic and for how long will you keep waiting for me?' Sombre asked Farzana one day, as she lay on his lap.

'That is for his majesty to decide. I am his slave, am I not? I cannot make decisions,' she murmured gazing into her lover's eyes.

Sombre planted a kiss on her palm. 'You have stolen my heart with this charm of yours. I do not have words to tell you what you mean to me.'

'Oh, you! Reveal the feelings that simmer in your heart to me. We are not strangers anymore. I have never dreamt of spending so much time with another person before, as I have spent with his majesty. You are all I have.' She turned away to hide the tears that had welled up in her eyes.

'May I say something…if you permit?' Sombre murmured.

Farzana dried her tears and brightened up. 'Permission? From me? Don't pull my leg, Mister! My soul and heart belong to you. Ask away, your honour.'

'Listen carefully. What I am about to say next will irrevocably change the course of history. I want you to marry me. Unless you wish otherwise, you will be christened Begum Sombre.'

A dumbstruck Farzana gaped at Sombre. She felt as though her troubled and lonely world had been flipped upside down for good. She had always thought that her love for this army man was unrequited… simply a means of pleasure. He was like a king and she was an ordinary nautch girl in a nondescript brothel. The Almighty had perhaps entwined their souls in heaven. She had never dreamt that the love of her existence would one day show up at her threshold with the proposal of marriage. The mere thought was enough to sweep her off her feet. Farzana reminded herself that this was reality, not a dreamy musing. She wanted to pinch herself just to make sure anyway.

'Your honour…,' she whispered as a pearly tear swam down her delicate cheeks.

Without wasting time, Sombre hastily tucked Farzana away in the saccharine heart that hid behind his strong, muscular chest. He smothered her face with kisses, as though signifying the commencement of their relationship. Farzana was on cloud nine in his honour's arms. Those moments were desperate to be etched in the chapter of everlasting love in the tome of history.

Both of them had decided to become one. There was no one to stop them. It is rumoured that Sombre gave the owner of the brothel a hefty compensation in exchange for Farzana. Owing to this reason, her relations with Sombre and Farzana remained amicable for a long time. The wedding ceremony meant, in effect, that Farzana had a legal right to love Sombre.

Age factors weren't able to sneak in between the nubile Farzana and the forty-two-year-old Sombre. The love, respect and status Sombre had extended to her were enough to compensate for the ill-treatment she had suffered at the hands of her family. He was less of a husband and more of an uxorious and besotted lover.

Sombre did not want to waste any time in making Farzana his. He had spoken to Gulbadan, the owner of the brothel. Farzana wasn't aware of the terms of their agreement, but she had heard that Gulbadan (Khanam) had no problem with their relationship. Gulbadan had grown increasingly fond of Farzana as she had watched her flowered into a young woman. A mother-daughter relationship had grown between them over the years, which had, in time, blossomed into a friendship. Gulbadan often poured her heart out to Farzana.

On the other hand, It was rumoured too that Gulbadan had struck a deal in exchange for Farzana.

The terms of the deal were never revealed. The bargain must have been a profitable one, for Farzana, Sombre and Gulbadan remained on good terms till death.

There is one incident that took place even before Farzana entered Sombre's life. Sombre and Mir Qasim had become friends. The two of them would pour their heart out to each other whenever they met. Instances of Sombre's cruelty were revealed in those days.

This happened in 1763-

Sombre was waiting impatiently in Mir Qasim's guest wing. He was finally allowed to enter.

He curtseyed in the Mughal style. 'I extend my greetings to his majesty.'

Bengal's governor, Mir Qasim shifted restlessly. 'You took your time, friend. I have been waiting for forever.'

'I am at your service, your majesty. Command me.'

Sombre was a shrewd diplomat. He was a glib talker who could capture hearts with his sweet words. Additionally, he had made Islamic culture a part of his lifestyle. This quality of his contributed to the fact that he was often preferred over other European mercenaries.

'I am worried... because of some treacherous rascals. You know how I hate such men, Reinhardt...'

'What is the matter, your majesty? Please elaborate. We will always stand by you,' Sombre interrupted.

'These alien people have revealed their true colours. They were always a treacherous lot. I curse myself for strengthening my ties with them,' Mir Qasim exploded angrily.

He then composed himself and said, 'Alice, the Britisher is the most treacherous person I have ever met. He used to grovel before me. This is how he pays me back for sheltering him and his men. I can forget and forgive other mistakes. After all, there is no harm in dreaming big. However, he dared to commit atrocities on my populace. He even tried to usurp Patna. There is no way I can pardon him.'

'Certainly, …he is a pathetic man. I have heard that he even imposes taxes on your kingdom. If the populace is made to pay taxes to two different rulers, there will be instability and rebellion,' Reinhardt said, adding fuel to the fire.

'You are right. I must ask my people to not pay taxes to them. The fact that he dared to tax my province angers me. Alice must be punished in a manner that even his descendants remember what the repercussion of messing up with me is.'

'Your honour, I heard that you have taken him hostage,' Sombre said knowingly.

Mir Qasim puffed up with pride. 'You heard correctly. We have captured Alice along with 150 of his mercenary friends. The Indian army has also been taken captive.'

'Bravo, your majesty! I pray for the success of your forces. Rest assured every drop of my blood in my body is and will remain loyal to you,' Reinhardt said.

'That is the sole reason why you occupy a special place in my heart. I will drop dead otherwise,' the Nawab fumed passionately.

'This life is insignificant, your majesty. I am forever indebted to you.' Reinhardt saluted the earth to show his reverence for the Nawab.

The Nawab's iridescent eyes shone with hope. The spark was replaced by sternness and anger in a matter of seconds.

'Listen, Reinhardt. I have something in mind for that bastard and his operatives.'

'Command me, your honour,' Reinhardt said punctiliously. He was always the first one to voluntarily commit himself to the Nawab. He was standing beside him even today.

Distorted versions of other mercenaries and Sombre's life portray them as cruel and heartless men. These anecdotes live on as stubborn stains in the pages of history. The Nawab's merchants promised to give them the princely sum of four crores to set themselves free. Their pleas fell to deaf ears. Sombre and his mercenary comrades paraded them in shackles and then shot them dead.

Sombre was a shrewd warrior. He knew that disobeying the Nawab would have dire repercussions. He would be beheaded just like Gurgin Khan. He had no desire to suffer a similar fate.

During this time, Sombre re-organized his battalion. However, he did not find any satisfactory employment. He wandered throughout the country and ended up in King Jawahar Singh's province of Bharatpur. In April 1765, he offered his services to the Jat king.

This was the time when the stiff-backed soldier struck gold and Farzana entered his life.

CHAPTER 7

A New Dawn

MATTERS had taken a definite turn. The time was an auspicious one.

Sombre rented a carriage one evening. The royal carriage was designed to not only cater to Farzana's dreamy desires but also to reinstate the luxurious life that was befitting her elevated status. The cosy carriage was adorned by rich velvet curtains and intricately embroidered carpets. Armed security was arranged to parade the carriage. Two coachmen were also hired for Farzana's convenience. The opulent carriage seated the young, flowering bride whose thoughts were shrouded by a veil of desires and uncertainties.

She alone could comprehend the potency of her troubles. For the first time in her life, she had the luxury of time to muse and reflect. The decision to marry Sombre was hers alone. Although Sombre was a stranger to her, she felt a distinct sense of familiarity and security in his arms.

The exhausted and overwhelmed Farzana effortlessly slipped in the warm embrace of sleep. The future was an abyss of uncertainties. However, Farzana had found solace in the arms of the stranger. The glimmer of hope in his eyes had entranced her.

In the early hours of the morning, when the new Begum was still asleep, Reinhardt Sombre decided to halt the caravan and check on her. The rays of the sun that streamed in through the uncovered windows illuminated her lovely face. Till then, Sombre was accustomed to seeing her only in the dark of the night, with dim lanterns or flickering candles. This was the first time that he was seeing her face in daylight. She was undoubtedly the most beautiful creature on earth. She looked like a heavenly nymph who had just descended from the heavens.

The sunlight roused Farzana awake. As her eyes slowly fluttered open, her gaze fell on her lord... her first love. The sight filled her heart with joy.

'How is my Begum today?' Sombre asked reverently.

She sat up and bowed respectfully.

'We are near the *Braj* area. We will spend the day and evening with a friend of mine. I have dined with him earlier also, but he longs to meet you. This occasion of happiness will be marked by a feast. My companions will also get rest and food. We will start again in the day and eventually reach our city. Any concerns, Begum?' Sombre continued.

Begum smiled gently.

'No, Mister. I have no problem-now that you are

here. I can see you, touch you and feel you. That's the very reason why I slept so soundly tonight… as though even sleep was waiting for these moments. How are you feeling? You spent the whole night on the tough back of a horse. You must be tired,' Farzana said with some love, grace and some concern.

Her tantalizing words were like an arrow. The prey was already injured.

'No, Begum… I am fine. And you can take my name. Walter… Reinhardt, Sombre or even Samru…anything is fine. I am used to this tough, nomadic life. The rough horseback is my companion for the night. My worry, however, is justified…!'

Begum could do nothing but smile. That was enough to charm the brooding lover.

They reached the Agra Fort the next morning. Farzana had spent her childhood and youth near the Red Fort of Delhi, which was the stronghold of Mughal power at that time. Farzana had walked past those intriguing red bricks countless times. She had always wanted to touch those bricks. How she wished to see beyond those familiar bricks and stroll amidst the beautiful buildings to inhale the intoxicating scent of the flowers that bloomed inside.

That dream was before her eyes today. The Agra Fort was as magnificent as Delhi's Red Fort. Farzana knew that although these were happy times, there would be plenty of hardships too. She had been fortunate enough to be with the man of her dreams. This was something others could only dream of. Her chest puffed up with pride at the thought. The future excited her.

She had entered Delhi's Red Fort only once. She performed there in a dance show. The smooth red sandstone and the magnificence of the royal court had stunned her.

The Agra Fort seemed even more opulent to her than the Delhi Fort now. Farzana had only seen the part of the fort that had been reserved for them. She made a mental note to check out the entire fort in time.

Reinhardt Sombre had acquainted himself with the symphonies of her heart. For, as soon as he entered their bedroom, he said, 'Come, Begum. Unless you are feeling tired, let me show you every nook and cranny of this fort. These walls yearn to befriend you, just as you long to know them.'

Farzana had finished dressing up. She had had some snacks and was in an adventurous mood. She did not hesitate even once. The words seemed to topple down her lips by themselves. 'Yes, your honour.'

Sombre had invited Amelia, the wife of one of his colleagues to befriend Farzana. Amelia was a garrulous person, a lively lady. She had porcelain skin and a willowy figure. Twin dimples appeared on her cheeks whenever she smiled.

Having lived there for a long time, she was comfortable in Urdu and Hindi. She had even taken additional tutoring in these languages. She understood them almost as well as Farzana.

Amelia's bubbly personality drove her to the meeting

spot even before Farzana had arrived. Both women were pleased with the other's company, for they promised to meet again. Both had meandered in the memory lane of nostalgia as they recounted their life stories. Sombre smiled and walked away when he was told that the fort could wait.

Farzana was mesmerized that she was there, before the smooth red sandstone walls, the intricate carvings, the public courts and the royal courts that she had fantasized about in the past. Her dreams came true today.

Meanwhile, Sombre had become an indispensable part of Jawahar Singh's politics. His chemistry with Farzana was also synchronising beautifully. Though Jawahar Singh's expedition to Delhi was a failure, despite that, Sombre remained loyal to him. As it was, Farzana preferred the scenic beauty of Deeg over the noisy Delhi, which was booming with drums in anticipation of the relentless war. There was a high probability of encountering dangerous situations in Delhi. On the other hand, the Jat rulers of Bharatpur had turned Deeg into a haven of prosperity and happiness. Just as how an oasis in a barren desert quenches the thirst of tired travellers, Deeg proved to be a silver lining in the scorching, blood-lusting India. Even an alien bird would think twice before flapping its wings in this province, which consisted of strong walls, forts bounded by cliffs and drawbridges, castles and other monuments. All this comforted Farzana. Later on, they went to live in Bharatpur also.

The gardens and fountains in the palaces in Bharatpur were adequate for a pleasant evening. They not only provided relief in the summer season but also helped calm her mind and provide succour. The lake carved out by Jawahar Singh's father, the legendary Surajmal had become a haven for native as well as migrant birds. The stay in Bharatpur was truly priceless for the girl who had spent her childhood amidst the hullabaloo of Delhi's Chawri Bazar. Even a concerned Sombre had found happiness and solace here. It was an open secret that the British were thirsting for his blood after the gory massacre of Buxar. Samru could live in Bharatpur without any concerns about his safety. He was respected and feared here because of his status as the commander of the Jat king's infantry and artillery. The political situation was tense though but Jawahar Singh was grateful to Sombre.

Sombre and his wife remained loyal to the royal family till the demise of the incumbent in 1772. Sombre, naturally offered his services to Jawahar Singh's successor, Naval Singh. The new bride had irrevocably stolen this stoic warrior's heart and now she was toying with it. As a result, Sombre had temporarily halted his military expeditions. All he desired was the company of Farzana. He would spend hours with her. Even this Begum wanted her husband to forget everything else and spend time with her.

When a province requested for Sombre's services, she said, 'For how long will you keep running away from yourself? If there's a will, there's life. These worldly affairs will always knock on your door. You should take some time out to rest and relax.'

The history knows Zulfikar-Ud-Doulah by the name of Najaf Khan. He was the most trusted courtier of Shah Alam II, the Mughal emperor. He decided to take undue advantage of the property disputes that were sweeping Bharatpur. Upon learning this, Naval Singh discussed it with Sombre and decided to go to war with his disciplined European army and a few French authorities.

The two armies clashed fiercely in October 1773 in Barsana. Although the army of Deeg had to accept defeat owing to a weak armoury and a lack of funds, they did not back down without leaving a lasting impression on the enemy.

Najaf Khan was now determined to catch General Sombre. He believed that with Sombre by his side, he could effortlessly recapture Agra from the Jats and rule wisely. After weighing the pros and cons, he offered a hefty sum of Rupees 30 thousand per month as remuneration to Sombre.

Although Najaf Khan's offer was tempting, Sombre's life changed dramatically. He did not want to betray the Jat king. He took his time to arrive at a decision. Later, he handed over the letters of offer to his lord and sought permission to quit.

CHAPTER 8

Welcomed by the Mughals

'HIGHNESS!' The cry came from an attendant who appeared at the doorway with her head bowed.

'What is it? Don't you know that Shah Alam is relaxing in his harem? How dare you disturb him, insolent wretch?' exploded the emperor of the Delhi darbar.

'Your majesty, I tried to make the Nayab understand, but he just wouldn't leave. Please forgive me for my insolence,' the girl continued with her head bowed.

The emperor composed himself and said, 'What does he speak?'

'He wishes to meet you, your majesty.'

'Hmm… Alright. Make him sit in the guest room. I'll be there,' said Shah Alam as he sobered and retrieved himself from the embrace of his pretty queen.

Abdul Ahmad Khan, the nayab was sitting in the guest room. His wrists and ankles were shackled and his head was bowed. He curtseyed before the emperor, who sank down on the plush cushions of the *diwan*, initially without uttering a word. The emperor then glanced around and said, 'Speak, What do you want to say Nayab.'

'Your honour, the Sikhs have crossed all the limits. They are spreading anarchy without any restraint. They do not fear your rule…'

The Nayab lowered his voice conspiratorially and began to fill the emperor's ears.

'Is that so?,' the emperor queried, his tone a mix of anger and astonishment.

The Nayab gathered his wits and began to speak again.

'They have looted and burnt down Shahdara, which is not far from Delhi. If not stopped, those scoundrels might turn to Delhi too.'

The Nayab paused for a few seconds to see if his words were having the desired impact on the emperor.

'Then?' the emperor said worriedly.

'I think that we should get General Sombre on our side and convince him to help us stop the rebellious Sikhs. We don't have time, so we have to decide quickly.' The Nayab gazed into the eyes of the emperor, who had never refused to heed his counsel.

'You have a better understanding of these matters. Your wishes will be honoured. Send an invitation to Sombre tomorrow afternoon. I will personally welcome him. I also realize that Sombre can be a valuable ally.'

The Nayab bowed low. The emperor stood up and dismissed him.

This was the time when the emperor's kingdom was in a fragile condition. He was considered a weak and ignorant ruler, who was simply a puppet in the hands of his shrewd minister. Envious of the increasing popularity and strength of Najaf Khan, Ahmad Khan decided to fill the emperor's ears against him. He later realized that recruiting Samru would allow him to kill two birds with one stone. He would succeed in snatching this opportunity from right under Najaf Khan's nose. Sombre would also be indebted to him and he would remain loyal to him in the Mughal empire.

The next day, at a predetermined time, Sombre entered the historic fort of Delhi. A few senior officers of the army mounted on horses and elephants, along with a battalion of foot soldiers, were waiting to receive him. The entire corridor to the royal court was marked by white chalk and millet grains. The floors were sparkling. Pitchers had been used to sprinkle water everywhere. Artists even painted murals in some places overnight. Smartly uniformed soldiers were standing guard at the corners.

An amused General Samru was brought in from the main door in a carriage pulled by two horses. The carriage halted at the doorway of the Diwan-e-Khaas, where a delegation of courtiers stepped forward to receive him. A round of customary gunshots was fired in his honour. Thc pompous procession, marked by *Ransinghas* (brass instrument) and trumpets, welcomed Sombre to the court.

General Sombre was overwhelmed by the emperor's warmth. He paid his respects to the emperor by reassuring him of his loyalty.

Once the terms of the deal were brokered, the emperor ordered Samru to undertake a military campaign against commander Kuchet Singh. He was notorious for having captured Karnal, Sonipat and Panipat and declaring himself the ruler of those provinces. The Delhi ruler was facing an all-encompassing financial crisis due to his interference.

The emperor promised to hand over those provinces to Sombre in the event that he succeeded in usurping them.

Sombre agreed, and marched to the battleground with five new cannons, a number of tanks, about 1900 soldiers, a few European soldiers and six elephants from his stockpile. However, Najaf Khan had his eyes elsewhere. He was desperate to get Sombre to initiate a war against the Jats of Bharatpur. He was aware of the fact that Sombre's knowledge of the Jat courts, military force and their war strategies was unparalleled. To convince Sombre to side with him, he sent an alluring offer to him through a secret messenger.

Sombre had already agreed to start the campaign against Kuchet Singh. He had even set out to do so. However, the lack of an inflow of funds effectively meant that he didn't have the resources required to proceed. Contrary to what he had hoped, he was denied assistance on his journey to Bharatpur. He sent a message to Abdul

Ahmed Khan saying that the lack of funds for his army and allowance for himself was serving as a hindrance to his initiative. Sombre had even invested his savings in this campaign. Even after capturing several provinces, he was struggling to meet ends. To add to the insult, there was an eerie-like silence at Ahmed Khan's end.

General Sombre must have sent a number of reminders to Ahmed Khan but it was all in vain. This sorrowful situation had the potential to depress any respectable man. Sombre even suggested to Ahmed Khan to permit him to seize a few more provinces to gather all the funds he would be needing. Upon receiving no response, Sombre began re-evaluating his alternatives.

Najaf Khan had struck gold by winning rapidly in the Jat province of Bharatpur. This helped reinstate the Delhi darbar's authority and influence in him. Jabita Khan was the son of Najeeb-Ud-Daulah, the ex-army chief of the Mughal army. The area of Nazeebabad in Bijnor was named after him. Meanwhile, the British East India Company was expanding and gaining influence. After the debacle of Buxar, the British were intent on hunting down Samru. They wished to stir conflict between him and Delhi. Alienating Samru from the Mughals would allow them to capture and punish him. However, emperor Shah Alam II was so pleased with Samru's loyalty, proficiency in warfare and diplomacy, that he was willing to lock horns with the British on this issue. Shah Alam II did not allow Samru's foe to cloud his judgement.

The emperor had handed over the province to Najaf Khan. Najab Khan was ethnically Persian and used to regularly accompany the emperor on his expeditions. Jabita Khan was enraged to see this and ultimately rebelled against the emperor. Najaf Khan was well-acquainted with Samru's qualities. He had heard enough stories to know about Samru's unwavering loyalty towards Mir Qasim and his deftness in administering punishment to rebels.

Trusting Samru's valour, the emperor ordered him to punish the rebellious Jabita Khan, who had gone into hiding. As soon as Samru began hunting for him, he fled to the mountains. He went into hiding in the remote areas of Oudh, but Samru got hold of Jabita Khan's ancestral and stolen wealth which were left behind by him in haste.

However, Samru was tired of these military initiatives. He yearned for a peaceful life. Najaf Khan convinced emperor Shah Alam to bestow upon him the province of Sardhana. Once Samru usurped Saharanpur from Jabita Khan, the pleased emperor handed over this province to him. Samru was awarded a particular region, out of which he chose Sardhana as his capital. The area of this region extends from Budhana in Muzaffarnagar to Tappal of Aligarh. In this way, Samru's province of Sardhana was carved on the map in the year 1773. He henceforth wished to ease this burden of maintaining and leading a mercenary army. Samru now longed for a place he could call home! Sardhana now promised this and much more to him.

Sardhana used to be a historically prosperous province.

In the era of the Mahabharata, it was said to be a part of the Pandavas' Hastinapur. The famous Mahadev Temple which was built here during the Mahabharat era is still intact. The Pandavas had prayed in this temple situated at the confluence of the Kali and Hindon rivers before falling right into Duryodhana's trap of the inflammable palace of lacquer.

The province of Sardhana, which yielded the princely sum of six lakh rupees along with the resources from the Doab of the Ganges and Yamuna rivers, proved to be a priceless gift for him. Situated on the banks of the Ganges, this province was considered a strategic location. The British empire had divided the Doab, which stemmed from the Shivalik mountain ranges and flowed to Allahabad into three parts- Upper Doab, Middle Doab and Lower Doab. A significant chunk of present-day Uttar Pradesh was included in the upper Doab. Along with Sardhana, some areas of district Muzaffarnagar like Budhana were also a part of this. Important provinces or areas of that era, such as Karnal, Barnawa, Baraut, Kotana, Tappal and Jewar came under the jurisdiction of this *jagir*. Baraut, Binauli, Barnawa and Sardhana used to be prosperous areas. Meerut wasn't a part of this region. However, the area had gained importance for trade and commerce. Baghpat was a supposedly lucrative region as it helped meet the revenue demands of the territory.

Begum Samru was increasingly fond of this region, owing to its proximity to her birthplace. This hamlet hosted an old, tapering palace from the Mughal era, which Samru had transformed into his temporary royal abode. Samru longed to slip into the warmth of his Begum's arms. The Begum continued to support him unconditionally in helping him fulfil his dreams.

In the bygone years, Samru had also served as the Chief Security Officer of the Agra Fort. He had built a residence for himself, away from the Red Fort. This palatial mansion was located in the Shahganj area of the city, on the road which led to the historical town of Fatehpur Sikri from Agra. The exterior of his mansion was an octagonal structure. Samru's dynastical emblem with the year 1763 was also engraved on the entrance door. Remnants of only two storeys of this palatial building have survived the test of the time. Most parts of the mansion have been vandalized and encroached upon. Only two pillars that encircle the mansion remain.

Samru possessed a strong mind and heart. The scorching heat of tropical India, which was usually unbearable for the Europeans, didn't seem to bother him. He wasn't addicted to alcohol. However, he occasionally had a sip or two. His diet was restricted to *dal-chapati* and *milk-jalebi*. He loathed tobacco as he believed that it was a sin to consume it. To maintain his fitness and health, he used to prefer having almonds on a routine basis and adopted a simple, yet balanced diet. Despite that, his health had begun to deteriorate with advancing age.

CHAPTER 9

Agra's Alliance...or Invitation to Death

SAMRU was felicitated with the coveted position of Agra's civil and military governor along with Sardhana's *jagir*. This was a supreme honour for him. He had spent his days ensuring the welfare of Sardhana, but now he had to be relocated to Akbarabad with his Begum. Samru extensively worked on the scheme for the restoration of an ancient church here. The emperor Akbar the Great, had provided the land to build this church during his reign. However, some internal disputes had gotten in the way. Since the establishment of the church, Samru was talked about with great respect and pride in the local Christian communities.

However, destiny had a different plan. Agra was known for its scorching heat. Conflicts of the heart, battles with conspiracies, and the fatigue of old age were ill-suited to Samru's job as the military and civil governor of Agra.

It was the fourth day. Samru was ailing with a high fever. Hakim Sarfaraz Hussain was routinely paying visits to the palace in Akbarabad. However, his medicines had no effect whatsoever. High fever, infected lungs, bodily discomfort, uneven breathing, fluctuating pulse and bouts of coughing- these symptoms were truly worrisome.

The Begum gazed into her lord's eyes. She wordlessly told him to stay put. She clasped his hand and began stroking his forehead lovingly. Samru could only smile then. Words failed his fragile body.

The royal Hakim arrived by then.

He measured the patient's pulse, felt up his stomach, examined his pupils, touched his forehead and said, 'Your highness, although this is malaria, the unpleasant weather has worsened matters. It has led to the onset of pneumonia. I have brewed a decoction and have prepared some medicinal herbs. I will send them soon,' Hakim reassured him worriedly.

'Hakim Sahib, how could I not worry? It's been four days and his fever hasn't improved. Look how pale he has become," the Begum said, expressing her concern.

Her words referred to the corpse-like stillness of Samru's face. His face was drained of colour, almost as though he had been ailing for months.

'Don't worry too much. God-willing, we will get some good news tomorrow night… this fever is stubborn. It comes of its own will and leaves on its own terms. Trust me, his honour will recover soon,' Hakim said respectfully as he stood up.

Although the Begum permitted him to depart as she sat by Samru's bedside, her heart was slowly shattering into a thousand tiny pieces. It was the summer season. Samru's forehead was drenched in sweat. The Begum lovingly stroked his forehead. Two female servants were deputed for rapidly flapping hand fans. Finally, at peace, Samru closed his eyes. It seemed as though Samru wished to express his gratitude to his Begum for staying by his side till the very end. However, his fragile body restrained him from doing so. He managed to clasp Begum's hand and place it on his chest.

She ran her hand over his chest with the unbridled affection that one reserved for a child. His heart was pounding erratically. She was alarmed to see that his pulse was accelerating unusually.

She began to panic. The servant who had gone to fetch the medicine had returned by that time. Upon the cook's insistence, she agreed to drink a glass of milk. However, she was unable to sip even a drop.

'Let me bring some decoction for his honour,' Hakim said. "It will improve his condition in just half an hour.'

The Begum simply lifted her head and beckoned him to bring the decoction.

In about ten to twelve minutes, Hakim reappeared with a glass of the decoction and a dose of medicine. Begum helped Sarmu drink that decoction. He was so weak that Hakim had to support him by wrapping his arm around his waist. He had reached the stage where he could not peacefully sip even the decoction.

Darkness began to creep up. A servant brought four candles and one lantern into the room. Samru's face looked forlorn and slightly yellowish in the light of the lamps. The Begum's heart was melting as she beheld his doleful expression.

The ill-fated day was the 4 May in the summer season. A wave of despondency wreaked havoc on the Begum's life as Walter Reinhardt Sombre breathed his last. He hiccupped once and then passed away.

Samru was rumoured to have died because of his deteriorating health and Hakim's carelessness. He could not comprehend the seriousness of his condition. This was an unexpected shock for Farzana. The Begum's life was uprooted as she watched helplessly. She was unable to understand why the almighty, who had disentangled the strings of her heart, had left her at a fork in the road. Moreover, Sombre was not old enough to perish. Deep in her heart, she harboured dreams of relishing the warmth of her married life till old age. The outpouring of sadness had numbed her senses.

A mourning period of forty days was announced in the Sardhana *jagir.* There was no official decision made in this regard, however, the Begum's chief advisors had taken this decision. Begum descended into a state of depression and did not utter a word. During this mourning period, the Begum neither wore fineries nor adorned herself with jewels. She even refused to sleep on the bed and gave up non-vegetarian food.

As per the Christian traditions followed by the

Europeans, Sombre was buried in his mansion in Akbarabad. Later on, he was given a respectful homage in Agra's Roman Catholic cemetery. A mausoleum was built in his honour, which is present there even today as a mark of respect to the departed soul.

Farzana battled loneliness again. She had spent thirteen years unconditionally supporting Samru. She had never left his side. She accompanied him everywhere, irrespective of whether the place was the battleground or the occasion was the assessment of the army. She used to talk to him about politics, tough decision-making, and various other subjects. She was twenty-seven years old when Samru died. She was as youthful and beautiful as a fresh flower. She seemed even more enticing and beautiful now. However, she was completely alone. She plunged into a severe depression.

Farzana spent her days cherishing and recalling the soul-stirring memories of her love. However, she was aware that the affairs of the province couldn't be dealt with by drowning in the sea of cherished memories succumbing to waves of despondency. She also knew that the province of Sardhana and the army were willing to support her.

CHAPTER 10

Farzana to Begum Samru: A New Charade

AN eerie emptiness nestled in Begum Samru's womb. She could not become a mother. However, Sombre's first wife was a mother to a son. His name was Lord Balthazar Reinhardt. Upon the Begum's insistence, Shah Alam II had bestowed the title of Zafaryab on him. Unfortunately, the son couldn't follow in his gallant father's footsteps or live up to the legacy of his stepmother. He was known for being a man of weak character. He was so young, owing to which, Sombre hadn't burdened him with expectations. Neither the emperor nor his ministers had any reason to believe that he was capable of managing the administration of the province.

Zafaryab was not an intelligent man. His mother was rumoured to have descended into a state of depression after his birth. She was never cured. *Badi bee*, as she was referred to, spent her days within the four walls of her abode. Just like Farzana, she was a Muslim woman.

However, she hailed from a relatively respectable family. She also spent a significant chunk of her life in the part of the palace in Bharatpur which had been gifted to Samru by the Jat king. Because she never stepped on to the battlefield and was terminally ill, she posed no threat to the second wife of her husband Farzana.

Finally, eighty-two European officers and four-thousand soldiers of Sardhana's army insisted that the Begum alone could manage the affairs of the army and protect Sardhana from hostile invasions. The authorities wanted the Begum to step forward and fulfil her obligations in this crisis. Some officials even convinced a few Mughal emperors to allow the Begum to take charge. The Begum had already made a lasting impression on them by accompanying Samru to the battlefield.

Even the Begum understood that it was imperative to command the army with prowess to keep the province and the soldiers in check. She requested a deferment as she needed some time to make a wise decision. She did not want to rush into anything. This woman, who had morphed from Farzana to Begum Samru, was clever enough to evaluate and weigh all possible repercussions of her decision on the province of Sardhana. But, there was another reason underlying her actions. Losing this province would effectively mean that she would have to return to her old troubled life. How could she tolerate such a possibility; at the hands of her marital rival that too?

Although the Begum was in mourning for forty days, she wasn't oblivious to the flurry of activities surrounding her. She was so involved in the royal obligations and duties that sometimes even the secret messengers weren't permitted to present their findings to the chief of the division, Nawazuddin, before getting the Begum's approval.

Finally, at the insistence of the populace, the battalions and counsels, the Begum realized that Commander Samru's ambitions couldn't be fulfilled without her direct intervention in in affairs of state. As soon as Begum said 'Yes', Shah Alam authorized a directive which proclaimed Begum Samru, owner and commander of the province of Sardhana and its army.

Farzana set up her court for the first time. She addressed the courtiers from the royal throne, which Samru had occupied once-

> *"I am forever indebted to all of you for supporting me in this time of need, just as how you once supported the late Samru Sahib. As you all know, this is a period of mourning. No one can anticipate when death is going to snatch one. Sooner or later, all of us will be summoned to the Almighty's abode. What is truly important is how much time and energy we devote to the service of the populace and the Almighty!"*

As the Begum finished her speech, her voice cracked and her eyes welled up with tears. She composed herself and said-

> *"All of you constitute my family. The doors of my palaces and homes are permanently open. I*

place my faith in you and I hope that you will also be able to trust me. That's all I have to say. Our mutual trust should remain intact."

Saying so, she slowly stood up. This was the first time that the public was able to see the Begum completely unadorned. Her lithe frame was devoid of the royal clothing and pearl and gold jewellery. Despite that, her simplicity and natural beauty exemplified her persona.

A courtier stood up in the back of the hall and shouted enthusiastically, 'Begum Samru…!'

'Long live… long live," chorused the entire hall in unison, almost as though they had been waiting for this moment forever.

Begum remained standing for a few moments. As though she had suddenly remembered something, she closed her eyes and turned her head and hands towards the emptiness of the sky.

The assembly was adjourned.

The next day, the Begum stood before those trusted and loyal officers and soldiers of different battalions, who had given her the strength to take charge of the troops. Her four-feet six inch tall physique was frail with grief. Yet, she stood unwavering, perhaps reasserting her strength and inner will. She said-

"My gallant warriors....! This jagir belongs to you. If you hadn't supported us, or if you weren't this strong, Sardhana wouldn't have existed today. After the Almighty, I am indebted to you people only. Please keep in mind that I am not

saying this just to establish myself as the head of this province. I simply wish to ensure the wellbeing of the common people. I have been entrusted with the task of carrying forward the late king, Samru's work…, uplift Sardhana's status, and enable the province and all of you to flourish. You have to work side by side to protect our land. I am ready to be tested and questioned at any point in time."

As soon as the Begum ended this heartfelt and passionate speech and stepped down from the royal podium, the sounds of trumpets and *Ransinghas* blared in the background.

This was the beginning of a new dawn in Sardhana's history.

The Begum simultaneously managed the activities of the mourning period with the administration of the kingdom. She had engrossed herself in the affairs of the state. She would frequently discuss ways to add value to her *jagi*r with her courtiers.

On the fortieth day, the Begum had a *Fatiha* for a peaceful afterlife for her late husband. After that, she distributed grains and clothes amongst the poor and the needy. She ensured that no one should leave the palace empty-handed.

The forty-first day saw the conclusion of another task. On that day, Begum took hold of the reins of her kingdom. She dressed in the royal robes and began wearing dresses and ornaments suitable for the commander of the army. A gold chain adorned her neck, pearl earrings dangled from her ear lobes, an embroidered belt, a nose ring, a fat gold ring embedded with a mirror, attractive flower jewellery, feet encased in shoes warped in gold wire embroidery. The Begum was earlier known for her beauty and charm. The shining embodiment and allure that she possessed had resurfaced again.

CHAPTER 11

Farzana Christened Johanna Nobilis

THE Begum had drowned herself in the administration of the kingdom and the expeditions of the troops. She reminisced about Samru's memories ever so often. She regularly paid her respects to her late husband's grave in Agra. Exactly three years three days after his demise, the Begum took a historic decision which had far-reaching consequences.

It was on the 7th of May in 1781.

The Roman Catholic church in Agra had been decorated beautifully. Something unusual was destined to happen.

Begum Samru was the chief guest of the church that day. She bowed her head before the priest, Father Gregory, when he said,

> *"I, Gregory, proclaim that Sardhana's Begum Farzana Samru and her son Zafaryab now belong to the religion of Roman Catholicism.*

> *Henceforth, they will be known as Begum Samru Johanna Nobilis Sombre and Lord Balthazar Reinhardt. I hope that Christianity is fortuitous for them and guides them on the path of truth."*

In honour of the Begum, the priest even hosted a special program. Noblemen as well as commoners had been invited from distant areas. Several other priests also participated in the program and prayers.

Farzana turned into Johanna Nobilis and returned to her province. She not only performed numerous charitable acts for her people but also built several churches in due course.

People had divided opinions on the Begum's decision to convert to Christianity. While some interpreted this as an act of boundless love and devotion towards her late Christian husband, others believed that she had taken this decision from a political perspective. This was the period when Muslim rule in India was collapsing. Begum had perhaps realized that adopting European cultures and traditions was in the best interest of her kingdom. In retrospect, this shrewd political decision proved to be favourable for her. Despite all this, not many people know about this figurehead named Johanna. She was neither known as Zeb-Un-Nisa not Farzana and not even Johanna. History only remembers and recognizes her by the name Begum Samru.

Every evening, she lit candles beside her late husband's painting in her residence in Sardhana and prayed for him.

She would often spend hours gazing at his pictures. Her moist eyes revealed the soft heart that hid underneath the strong, commanding exterior. When the time came, she entered the battlefield and commanded her troops with the utmost efficiency. The string of events that followed proved that the emperor Shah Alam II trusted the Begum only because of the abilities which had become a part of her identity. She was a courageous woman; fearless on the battlefield. She had accompanied Samru in some of these battles earlier and had thus acquainted herself with the intricacies of warfare. Begum had become consummate in not just military tactics, but also politics and diplomacy.

In those days, General Paulie was the commander-in-chief of Begum's army. He remained the German commander of Samru's army, till his death, when they all lived in the province of Akbarabad. He was often involved in conspiracies and was not trustworthy. Owing to this reason perhaps, his head was found severed one day. Although the crime was a gruesome one, no one was particularly saddened by his death. Everyone was well-acquainted with his treacherous nature.

It is said that a woman has to protect herself from countless malevolent gazes, which search for something or the other… a conversation, company, sexual pleasure or marriage… it can be anything. However, Begum Samru was different. General Paulie's brutal death had stunned her officers also. The other authoritative figure in the army, Em Montenegre also had lewd thoughts about the Begum. It was rumoured that he wanted to woo and marry her to get his hands on her massive wealth. When he came to know that General Paulie's sudden death was a consequence of his desire to usurp Begum's property, he abandoned his malevolent ambitions.

Although Farzana had aged, she remained graceful. She managed to retain the charm and beauty of her early days when she had wormed her way into Samru's heart. Her beauty, charm, grace and clothing were always a subject of discussion and admiration. She wore a veil most of the time. However, those who had seen her claimed that the Almighty had blessed her with extraordinary beauty and grace.

Five years passed thus. She continued journeying to Agra to pray for her late husband's departed soul every year. On those days, she would distribute gifts amongst her people and would pray for the well-being of her province.

CHAPTER 12

George Thomas and the Begum

'YOUR honour! An army officer of some alien land has come to meet you. His name is George Thomas,' a servant informed.

'An alien? We've had enough! They seem to have no work in their countries, for they are constantly trickling into our land. Tell him I have no desire to see him.'

Begum said this without lifting her head. She took a sip of her tea and dismissed the servant.

'As you wish, your highness!"

The servant was retreating from the room when the Begum thought for a moment and said, 'Listen, tell him to wait for a while. I will be in the guest room shortly.'

'As you wish, your highness!'

The Begum allowed herself to take the taste of tea. Although alcohol was not barred to her, she preferred to keep a distance from it. Kashmiri tea warmed her body in the cold winter and thus she was fond of it. It kept her mentally and physically strong. She could never keep count of the number of cups she had in a day.

Begum placed her cup down and had a look at her dress. She placed a red turban on her head and draped a yellow Pashmina shawl around her shoulders. She then pulled on a floor-length gown which was covered in barbed Iranian embroidery, something she wore quite often.

The Begum descended two dozen steps and reached the guest wing. Her staff dutifully accompanied her. She beckoned her servants to bring the guest to her favourite room in the guest wing.

'I pay my respects to her majesty!' said the foreigner, bowing before the queen. His gaze trailed across Begum's physique and came to rest on her face. It felt as though time had frozen. His eyes were brimming with strength and self-confidence, an unusual rarity. He, a strapping young man with a fair, unmarked complexion truly possessed a magnetic persona. A twinge of self-doubt began kindling in the Begum's heart after casting a glance on him.

The Begum did not allow the unsettling feelings to betray her. She nonchalantly said, 'Please sit…so you are Thomas?'

He smiled slightly and bowed again. 'Yes, your highness…George Thomas!'

'Frankly, my experience with *firangis* hasn't been all that great. Anyway, I don't have a requirement or a vacancy for a new officer.'

'Forgive my insolence, your highness. Firstly, I don't consider myself a *firangi*. My complexion is not fair. I believe that the land I inhabit is my country. And if my skin colour doesn't blend with this land's coffee colour, then you have every right to question and accuse me, your highness…'

Thomas's words held such tantalizing charm, that the Begum could do nothing but stare unabashedly.

'Alright. Tell me then what can you do to improve my province, my army, my people's lives?'

The Begum could sense a unique personality behind his words. Somehow, his magnetic persona had convinced her to listen to him, even disinterestedly.

'Your highness, just give me one chance. One week is sufficient. It took just three months to learn this language. I won't take more than a week to understand your governance…'

The Begum couldn't hold back her laughter. She composed herself immediately and said sombrely,

'Isn't that a little too hasty… one week? I have spent half my life learning this language, learning new dialects, slangs and customs have worn me out now. Anyway, it's not so important to understand my governance. What is truly imperative is that you prove to be valuable for the army. Talk to Salauddin tomorrow morning. He will have a message for you.'

Thomas bowed again and said, 'I assure you that my service will be liked by you.'

An unusual smile flickered across Begum's lips. She

began heading towards her bedroom. Perhaps after decades, she had smiled twice in a day. Something about that soldier had touched her heart. There was a child-like innocence in his round eyes, which were twinkling with a thousand dreams. Her intuition told her that he was a skilled soldier. She didn't know if she was right or wrong in believing this. The strings of her heart, which had become stiff after Samru's demise, were trying to tell her something important. The Begum brushed those thoughts away and replaced the amusement on her face with sternness and rigidity.

In this way, George Thomas, a reputed soldier and nomad, made his place in the army. He was a native of Tipperary, a village in Ireland. In 1781, he travelled to Madras through the sea route, in the guise of an ordinary sailor. He left the seaport there and began his career in a small province in southern India and then joined some gangs which were engaged in unlawful activities. In search of a better life, he reached Delhi, from where he managed to worm his way into Begum Samru's army. The Begum had perhaps identified his potential and determination in their first encounter itself, for he started working in the army as a lieutenant. It didn't take long for him to be promoted to be the commander of a battalion.

Thomas's capabilities were revealed during several battles against the rebellious Punjabis from the Sikh provinces and other expeditions led by infantry. The strategies he had devised always succeeded in toppling the enemy. Sardhana's army owed its new-found popularity and pride in General Thomas's military efficiency and strength. The Begum's prestige was growing rapidly in the neighbouring provinces also. Needless to say, she was pleased with these changes. She became entranced by Thomas's skills and personality.

The Begum's heart was still young. There remained enough soil to sow the seeds of love. The period after Samru's demise had been a living hell for her. Her heart was plagued by loneliness and despair. Even after decades, the flames of love were burning in Samru's name. She knew that she owed her status and power entirely to him. If he hadn't entered her life, she would have still been an ordinary, nameless dancer in a nondescript brothel in Delhi's Chawri Bazar. With age, her popularity would have diminished.

The interplay between Samru's love and Farzana's fate had flipped her fortune, leading to the transformation of a small, insignificant village to an officially recognized province named Sardhana, whose exploits left a dent in the walls of the Delhi empire. The region stretching from Deoband to Aligarh came under its jurisdiction. These victories were meant to be curated in the pages of history.

Meanwhile, loneliness was gnawing at Begum's heart. At this point in life, she had neither a loving husband nor a child. Moreover, there was no one she could confide in or pour her heart out to. Leading a lonely existence and shouldering the burden of an entire province had drained her. She could not entrust even the daily affairs of the kingdom to another person. The endless competition between the courtiers infuriated her. Along with that, the authorities of the army, who had different social circles, constantly tried to put the other down.

In such times, General Thomas's arrival in Sardhana was a ray of hope for the Begum. In a short while, Thomas became her chief courtier and advisor. She discussed every aspect of her *jagir* with him and sought his advice. After all, his loyalty and skills were responsible for enhancing the Begum's status and Sardhana's influence.

Despite his insignificant lineage and lack of education, he had managed to scale new heights in the Begum's army. Undeniably, there was something extraordinary in him. The truth was that Thomas hid a soft heart behind his tough and rigid exterior. He was amiable and understood the intricacies of warfare. For some time, Begum and Thomas got along very well. So much so that people started gossiping about the two. This continued only for a short time though. Both possessed bold and impressive personalities. Later on, the Begum became friendly with a new, young French officer. Thomas moved on with no ill-feelings of jealousy and tried his best to fulfil his given tasks diligently.

Even though Thomas was surprised to see the Begum's growing proximity to Lee Wassey, there was a marked change in the attitude of the Begum. She used to laugh openly at his cheap jokes and anecdotes, strolled with him in the royal gardens and allowed him to enter and leave her bedrooms whenever he wanted. Thomas realized, sooner than the others, that their relationship of desire and passion had scaled new heights and had crossed all limits.

It is said that the Begum was influenced by the personality and charm of Thomas, but she didn't consider him an equal. Some French officers had also promoted Lee Wassey's image to such ridiculous heights, that George appeared to be a lowly man, a man from a humble background. The love triangle between the Begum, George Thomas and Lee Wassey becomes a matter of gossip throughout the province. However, no one knew the entire truth. At one point, the Begum even married George Thomas off to Maria, telling Thomas that Maria was like her daughter and that he ought to love her and take care of her as such only.

It was evident from the Begum's attitude that she was rather fond of George. However, she was reluctant to reveal her feelings to him. He maintained a professional distance from the Begum. Owing to this, their relations remained at a standstill. The Begum was rumoured to be in love with George, but to obviate the possibility of a rebellion with the army, she used to maintain a respectable distance from him. Thus the Begum's love life had become quite complicated. Lee was also vying for Begum's attention. He used to scorn George Thomas. The other French officers also looked down on him because he was Irish. They were of the opinion that George wanted to ensnare the Begum in his love and usurp the kingdom.

The trouble was that these were all either rumours

or gossip. Neither any historian nor any courtier was ever able to confirm whether the Begum was having an affair with the Irish soldier. even though the Begum's background offered the ideal groundwork for the growing allegations of the kind and gossip. People would routinely say things like, 'The Begum is an expert in seducing men of her choice' or 'the Begum's lover could never escape her clutches.' Some even said, 'A dancer is bound to be characterless.' George Thomas was also rumoured to be a lecherous womanizer, who had had simultaneous affairs with countless women. However, no one knew who those women were. It was all rumourmongering.

Time had mellowed Farzana. She no longer cared for the mindless gossip that seemed to follow her everywhere. She did not allow these malignant rumours to deter her from pursuing her dreams and ambitions. According to some people, she had married George to Maria just to be able to dispel the rumours of an affair between her and Thomas. Others said that she had used his marriage as an excuse for getting him to stay in the army.

The talk of the town was that the Begum had completely drowned herself in her love affairs. After the demise of Reinhardt Sombre, her name was linked to several European soldiers. It is important to examine these matters from a multifaceted perspective. After all, the determination of a *purdah*-clad woman to march her army to the battlefield and fulfil stereotypically patriarchal duties was bound to incite gossip and rumours. If she had chosen to remain in *purdah*, she would have had to abandon the throne. Sardhana, which is known because of the Begum today, would have gone to dust. However, she had to pay the price for ruling her kingdom proficiently. The fact that she was a woman added fuel to fire.

There is a rather unsettling anecdote about the Begum. It is said that she ordered her guards to bury the two girls alive, who had dared to seduce officers of her army. Burning in the passionate flames of love, they had set fire to Begum's residential wing in her royal palace in Agra. Incidentally, the Begum was not present when this happened. Upon learning about this, she located the two girls in the marketplace of Shahganj, in Agra. They were brutally flogged till they collapsed. Space was dug to bury them alive. Begum was relishing the sensual pleasures of a hookah when the girls were withering in agony, it is said.

The reason behind such an unconscionable punishment, it is said, was the girls' proximity to General Paulie, who was an officer in the Begum's army. However, this incident has been documented solely in the form of stories and is hardly real. The research which explored her life has claimed that this incident was purely conjecture.

When Begum was in the mood for teaching some lessons to the Sikhs she had deputed George Thomas there. Meanwhile, it was Lee Wassey who spread rumours claiming that George Thomas had started disobeying the Begum and was blatantly disregarding her orders. He also claimed that George Thomas was planning to secede from Sardhana and usurp the province of Tappal. Begum knew that these rumours were fake. The Mughal emperor had advised her to allow George Thomas to be in Tappal.

On the other hand, the Begum was growing increasingly fond of Lee Wassey. When he had first arrived in Sardhana, he could neither speak Hindi, nor English. However, he was so intelligent that he quickly became proficient in these languages and even learned some Urdu. He had mastered the grammar and structure of these languages. This proved to be an advantage for him, enabling him to get closer to the Begum.

George Thomas frequently visited Sardhana. Instead of fulfilling his duties in the armoury, Lee Wassey would spend hours strolling in Begum's palace or her gardens. George Thomas used to watch him cracking jokes with the Begum or sitting nearby many times. The trouble was that the Begum would encourage Lee Wassey's antics instead of disliking his overtures. Although George was never envious of this, he would always wonder how the silly Wassey had managed to ensnare the unwavering and intelligent Begum in his love.

People would frequently doubt the Begum's character. However, no one could confirm whether these allegations were true. The Begum did not pay heed to these rumours. She was only close to Thomas and Lee Wassey, of whom she was increasingly fond. She was sometimes frustrated by the fact that Thomas did not pay a lot of attention to her. Thomas, who hailed from a relatively weak background, felt grateful for all that he had earned in this province. Anyhow, the Begum alone could decide who she wanted to spend the rest of her life with. If she fell in love with a particular officer, no one could stop her from marrying him. Due to this reason, George Thomas decided to never look back with regret. The Begum was his employer after all.

CHAPTER 13

Alliance with Shinde... Lifeless 'Ghulam'

'WE have assembled here today to work on a secret mission. We don't have much time and there is a ton of work to do. Each second should be devoted to this mission. The time has come for us to forego thirst and hunger, and all worldly relations, and immerse ourselves in the service of the nation.'

Mahadji Shinde had started counselling his special courtiers. In history, Mahadji is also known as Mahadji Shinde. He was the fifth and the youngest son of Sardar Ranoji Rao Shinde. Amongst all of Sardar Ranoji Rao Shinde's sons, only Mahadji had survived the third battle of Panipat. The seven years that followed, till the year 1768, saw Mahadji Shinde in a tussle for power. This marked the commencement of his phenomenal legacy, which left a dent in the pages of history. With the help of the Peshwa, he strengthened and stabilized his empire.

On 10 February 1771, the Peshwa's authority was established in Delhi. Mahadji got the prestigious honour to arrange for the sitting on the throne of the Mughal emperor, *to* Shah Alam II on the 6 January 1772. The Maratha empire's influence in northern India, which had diminished considerably after the battle of Panipat, was restored in this way.

Mahadji's demise led to anarchy, which further incited the infamous Anglo-Maratha war. Mahadji had fought against the British, alongside Raghunath Rao (Raghoba), Nana Fadnavis and Shishu Peshwa. After slaying the British in Talegaon in January 1779, he fulfilled his obligation as the principal chieftain of the Marathas by single-handedly defeating them in central India. It was only because of his timely intervention that the Treaty of Salbai was signed between the Marathas and the British. This greatly contributed to his increasing popularity and influence. After the war had ended, Mahadji Shinde turned away from the north. A year after he had managed to establish his authority in Gwalior in 1783, he defeated the Rana of Gohad. He strengthened and expanded his army with the help of a French military officer named De Boigne. He trained the army using French military strategies and taught them the necessary skills to fight against a European army. He also appointed several European soldiers. His army had become extremely powerful. He organized several military excursions and set up camps in Agra and other places. The Mughal emperor felicitated him with the title of '*Wakeel-e-Mutlaq*' and even handed over some administration of the empire to him.

By suppressing several opponents, Mahadji had proved his worth in the Mughal empire. However, after an unsuccessful military expedition to Jaipur in 1787, he discovered that he was amidst a crisis. Nevertheless, he re-established his authority after slaying Ismail Baig in June 1788.

Ghulam Qadir, the notorious tyrant, clashed with Delhi's far-sighted Mughal emperor, who was robbed of his throne, and resettled as the emperor by Mahadji again. By the end of 1791, he had defeated the Rajput clans in Rajasthan too.

The invitation to Mahadji's secret meeting was extended only to a few chosen officers, who were trustworthy. These officers could sacrifice their lives for the accomplishment of this mission.

> *'All of you must be aware of the debacle in Jayanagar. Now is the time to teach those scoundrels a lesson. We must adopt the policy of 'accord- incentive- punishment-discord'. The army must be strengthened because Rajput warriors are ferocious and skilled. They are taught that the earth is their mother. They can go to any lengths to keep their mother safe,'*

Mahadji Shinde said, trying to arouse passion amongst the assembled officers.

In the Mughal empire, the chief of the Marathas, Wazir-e-Ala Mahad Ji Shinde, alone could demand subservience from other rulers. It is said that he was the most powerful axis grounding the Mughal empire. He directly ruled several provinces in India. His influence was all that mattered. Shah Alam II continued to sit on the throne as a proxy emperor of the Delhi empire. A wave of rebellion swept through northern India. However, instead of taking hold of the reins of the empire, the rulers kept banking on Shah Alam's authority to resolve the conflict.

The news was that King Pratap Singh of Jaynagar (modern-day Jodhpur) had revolted against the Mughals. He had refused to perform the ritualistic salute to the Mughal emperor. He had not only declared himself free but several other Rajput provinces did the same. He had dared to take the initiative to unify them under his banner.

After seeking approval from Shah Alam, Shinde decided to crush the rebellion by mounting a military expedition against Jayanagar. Unfortunately, greedy officers and soldiers had found their way into his ranks. To get their hands on the gold coins and jewels in the treasury, they didn't even try to defend themselves from the enemy. In this situation, Shinde's army had to accept defeat and retreat from Gwalior itself. He decided to wait for some help from the South then.

After learning about his lord's defeat, the reliable Nayab Shah Nizamuddin diligently arranged security for the fort in Delhi to keep Shinde safe.

Towards the end of 1787, another calamity befell them. The governor of Saharanpur was Ghulam Qadir, the son of Jabita Khan who was the rebellious leader of the Rohilla tribe. He took advantage of the chaotic political atmosphere by pursuing his desire to usurp the Delhi empire.

After the defeat of Mahadji in Lalsot in July 1787, Ghulam Qadir began penning the script that would ultimately lead to the destruction of the Maratha empire. He strategized how he would strengthen his authority in the fertile ravines in the region under his grandfather's jurisdiction, along with his province in Delhi. On 21 August 1787, Ghulam Qadir arrived in Baghpat with his army. His courage and self-confidence were reflected in his decision to inform the Mughal emperor about his arrival and his expectation of an invitation.

Ghulam Qadir's father, Jabita Khan was defeated by Samru earlier. But now it was Ghulam Qadir's time. The weakening Mughal empire had unknowingly strengthened his cause. According to his strategy, he sailed to the other side of the fort and reached the Yamuna river with his army. Ghulam Qadir Khan was particularly confident about his victory because a senior courtier of the Mughals, their Nazir, Manzoor Ali had joined hands with him and had promised to help hatch this subterfuge.

The Mughal army underestimated the Rohilla chief's army. Shah Nizamuddin sent his small battalion to their stronghold, across the Yamuna river and challenged them to a battle. However, the outcome was one they had neither expected, nor hoped for. The Rohilla army crushed the small Mughal army. This ferocious attack on the trained Mughal army led to the shameful defeat of the Mughals. Countless people were either killed or taken captive. By then, the Mughal commander had learned about Nazir Ali's treachery. He took shelter in Ballabgarh, which was situated twenty-two miles away from Delhi and began to plot the course of action against the Rohillas.

This was a difficult time in Delhi's history. Shinde was stuck in Gwalior and Nizamuddin had to seek asylum in Ballabgarh. Meanwhile, the crafty Nazir Ali had joined hands with the Rohillas, contributing to the Mughal empire's mounting troubles. In a way, the Mughal empire was dependent on the sympathies of the Rohilla tribe. The empire was toppled without any resistance or attempt to defend itself.

One morning, the Rohilla Nawab sailed across the Yamuna river with his soldiers and marched to the head of the devastated Mughal empire. History had never witnessed such a fragile and helpless Mughal emperor before. The helpless emperor began discussing the possibility of amicable relations with his enemies.

The date of 27 July 1788 beholds great historical significance for the Delhi empire. Red Fort's entry gate was also known as the 'Iron Gater' owing to its strength. Before anyone could stop them, Ghulam Qadir and Ismail Baig regally stormed inside. They were flanked by their massive army of two thousand soldiers. A part of the army occupied the shining marble-like floors of the Diwan-e-Khas while the other half wandered in the various wings of the Red Fort. The bearded Afghan Rohilla soldiers leisurely lounged in the veranda, gardens, rooftop and rest houses. They unsheathed their glinting swords, wore their shields and then armed themselves for a mock attack. These tyrannous soldiers had hijacked every inch of the magnificent palace. With every step taken by Ghulam Qadir's army, the Mughal soldiers retreated. The Rohillas did not have to make an effort to impose their authority. The fort was abandoned so quickly that it seemed as though there was no one inside but only a helpless Shah Alam.

Upon reaching Shah Alam's court, the emperor sat feebly on his throne and began wallowing in self-pity. It is said that Shah Alam's nineteen sons were there in the premises of the fort at that time. They were pushed out of the fort and sent to the Moti Masjid, where only the royal family could offer Namaz. At that time, around 1800 servants had been employed in the Red Fort. They disappeared from the lane of Meena Bazar and Red Fort in no time. The ones who remained were told that disobedience would be punished harshly.

The ill-tempered Rohilla ruler now stood before Shah Alam shamelessly. A year ago, he wouldn't have been allowed to enter the palace. Before him was the man whose ancestors- Babur, Humayun, Akbar the Great, Shah Jahan and Aurangzeb had revolutionized history. The massive empire they had established by occupying a majority of the country was a cause of envy for many rulers. Today, this powerful empire had been reduced to a pitiful mess. Rohilla's father, a rebel, was crushed by the Mughals decades ago and his grandfather had bowed before the Mughals countless times. Despite his lineage, he was a shrewd man. He bowed before the emperor. His brown eyes beheld derision instead of respect. He shoved the emperor from the throne and took his seat beside him. The *Hookah* was stuffed with tobacco, and fumes were simmering from it. He puffed noisily, expelling a cloud of smoke in the emperor's face.

He smiled contemptuously and said,

'You are a nobody now. I will be called 'Amir-Ul-Umra' today.'

Shah Alam could say nothing. When he gazed into the Rohilla chief's eyes, he could only see evil. However, he was no longer in a position to retort back to his cruelty and insolence.

'Since you are here now, your command alone will be obeyed,' the despondent Shah Alam spat derisively.

'Who knows if Shinde will even return? He might not have even made it out alive,' he said bitterly.

Shah Alam had a pure heart. He did not hold grudges against others and sincerely cared for the well-being of his people. Shinde was his most trusted courtier and he had set out on an expedition to crush the rebels under his command. The idea of making this cruel tyrant his chief courtier, in place of his most trusted counsellor was appalling.

'You turned out to be the flagbearer of your defiled

race. You have boasted enough about your status and power. But, have you ever considered that the emperor who is blessed with the counsel of extraordinary men like Shinde will ever care for the advice of Ghulam?'

The emperor glared at him furiously.

'Sir, I have no problem with being a Ghulam. But you have also become a slave of this insignificant race now. Time changes unexpectedly and this is our time to shine,' the prudent tyrant insulted the emperor.

Shah Alam stood up. His eyes were red with rage, but the restraints of time held him back. Still, Shah Alam was determined to not allow his evil enemy's ambitions to succeed. He knew that Ghulam was in search of some priceless treasure…

Meanwhile, as soon as the Begum heard that Ghulam's forces had exited across the Yamuna river, she ordered the army to march to Delhi. The Begum's army was battling against Pratap Singh in Panipat at that time. However, it was more important for the Begum to restore the pride and authority of Shah Alam and punish Ghulam for his misdeeds.

In those days, the system of transport and communication was quite primitive. The number of rumours circulating throughout the kingdom was perhaps more than the actual news. However, two things were crystal clear now- one that Ghulam Qadir had captured the Delhi empire and was toying around with the emperor just as one toys with puppets, and Shinde and the Nayab weren't present to oppose him.

It is said that as soon as the Begum heard about this, she commanded her soldiers by saying, 'Head to Delhi!' Dressed in long tight-fitting trousers and a jacket, she mounted a horse, wielded her sword and marched her troops to Delhi. She was actually in Tappal at that time. Because of that, it took her a while to reach Delhi via Sardhana. She was aware of the fact that Ghulam would have dared to attack Shah Alam only with a massive army, prior strategizing and a superior arsenal. She was not oblivious to the possibility of her army's defeat at his hands. However, the question was of sentiments and beliefs now. The Begum respected Shah Alam, and this battle had been initiated based on moral grounds. The slogan, 'Do or die' had its roots here.

Ghulam Qadir not only knew about Begum's power and influence in the court of Delhi but also that she had a well prepared army and was expecting a battle. As soon as he heard that the Begum was marching to Delhi, he became concerned. He sought counsel from his army officers, who were also terrified by the prospect of facing the Begum's army. Finally, it was decided that an irresistible proposal would be extended to lure her.

The Rohilla leader, accompanied by two officers, crossed the Red Fort and reached the spot where the Begum's army had set up its camp.

'Tell Begum Sahiba that the prime minister of the Delhi empire and his younger brother, Ghulam Qadir have come to pay their respects,' the Rohilla chief told a guard.

They were told to wait in a tent nearby. After almost half an hour, the now restless men were summoned inside. Daunting thoughts had been spinning in their heads in that duration.

The Begum was seated on a throne-like chair and was supported by cushions. Ghulam was dressed in a military uniform. A turban was also wound around his head. Four army officers and one minister were hovering around them.

Ghulam Qadir bowed before the Begum but he kept an eye on her. He had heard about her before but had never imagined that he would ever get the opportunity to see her. She beckoned him to sit on an ordinary chair kept at a distance.

'Speak…Ghulam?'

There was a hint of derision and anger in her voice, for she was upset with his antics. She respected Shah Alam from the bottom of her heart and did not appreciate Ghulam Qadir's decision to usurp the throne and the title of 'Prime Minister' with force. She wished to hear Ghulam's demands to understand the workings of his mind.

'Your highness, I wish to propose something in this court. Do I have your permission?' His sparkling blue eyes spoke of sincerity and promise.

The Begum strongly detested Ghulam Qadir. However, they were sitting at a distance from each other. Qadir was unable to comprehend her rage because she did not allow her emotions to betray her. 'What is it that you wish to say?' she said, regaining her composure.

'If her highness has no objection, shall we work together? You can become the ruler of this empire and we can divide the entire country into two halves between ourselves. As you might be knowing, Shah Alam is so weak now that his army will become helpless before our combined forces.'

Begum Samru clenched her fists in rage. Blood was raging down her arteries and her heart was beating incessantly, but she maintained her equanimity. She was seasoned enough to not allow the anger to creep into her face.

'This task is impossible!',she pretended.

'Nothing is impossible, your highness. Leave it to me and everything will unravel perfectly in seconds. You can fulfil Samru saheb's dream of climbing to new heights. This is the only way for his soul to attain salvation, Begum Sahiba!' Ghulam said, appealing to Begum's sentiments.

It is said that treacherous men are perpetually in search of something bad. They can backstab their allies at any time. Such tricksters have no regard for relationships, love or loyalty to one's soil. They are fuelled only by conspiracies, betrayals and greed. Allying with such men was against Begum's principles. However, Ghulam had dared to welcome her, knowing that she had marched to Delhi with the sole intention of slaying him. There was no harm in hearing out his proposal to understand the malevolent feelings he carried in his heart. The only way to defeat an evil man is by being evil.

'How will this happen?' Begum said incredulously.

'Leave all that to me. All I need is your support and your army's cooperation. I would like to request the Almighty to bless our siblinghood.' He touched his ears with his fingers and then raised his hands to pay his respects to the almighty.

Begum's will and hatred did not waver. But, she demonstrated eagerness on a superficial level. She could glimpse a flicker of insolence, betrayal and ill-will in his piercing eyes.

'Elaborate on your strategy!

Two maids appeared with plates of dry fruits, a collection of exotic fruits and rose sherbet. At the Begum's command, they served the refreshments before the guests. She took a glass of sherbet for herself.

'Your highness, I propose…,' the Ghulam said when the Begum interrupted him.

'I want privacy.'

At that moment, the soldiers, guards and maid-servants who were standing in her command made an immediate exit out of the tent.

'Now, where were we? Yes, your rule should remain autonomous, shouldn't it, Ghulam Qadir?' The Begum said, reassuring her uninvited guest.

The Rohilla chief was already pleased with Begum's respectful treatment and hospitality. He began to trust her even more. It was evident from his expression that the pathway to usurping the Delhi throne seemed easy to him.

'Yes, Begum. The plan is that you will lay siege to the fort with your army and I will represent Shah Alam's interests and will negotiate a deal with you. You know the rest…'

Ghulam unfolded his mind and the strategy was finalized.

Ghulam's army was supposed to help Begum's army to cross the Yamuna river. Qadir's battalion of 85 trained soldiers, which was equipped with a tank and modern techniques of warfare, set off at a predetermined hour. No one knew what destiny had in store for him. The unsuspecting predator walked right into the trap.

Once the last soldier of his battalion had arrived, the Begum, with the help of a few trusted soldiers and the threat of guns, blocked all routes for Ghulam to retreat. He felt as though all his dreams had been shattered. He braced himself for a crushing defeat.

When Shah Alam learned about this, tears of joy welled up in his eyes. The Begum had displayed the extraordinary valour that was expected of her. She had demonstrated her loyalty to the emperor at a crucial hour. The emperor of Delhi was not oblivious to the fact that if she had listened to her mind instead of her heart, she would have not only become the owner of a massive fortune but would have also assumed the throne of the empire.

Her loyalty at such a delicate hour reflected the goodness and purity of her heart. Emperor Shah Alam expressed his gratitude by honouring her with the title of

'Zeb-Un-Nissa' which translates to 'My dear daughter.' The Begum publicly declared that nothing would give her greater pleasure and peace than to serve the Delhi emperor. She deployed her army for the protection the emperor and the fort.

Meanwhile, Ghulam Qadir was cursing himself for allowing himself to be swayed by Begum's words. From his camp across the Yamuna river, he sent a message to the emperor. He ordered him to disband Begum Samru's army immediately. If he refused to heed his order, he would have to prepare for war. Shah Alam cast a contemptuous glance at the letter, before tossing it in the bin, where it belonged.

Ghulam Qadir hadn't given up yet. After some time, he geared his army once again and set off on an expedition to the Red Fort. He positioned his cannons in the direction of the fort and ordered his soldiers to commence the shelling. But, before they could proceed, the Begum's army arrived with cannons and other arsenal. They shortly received the news that Shahzada Mirza Jawan Bakht was also marching to the capital with a massive army in tow. Ghulam Qadir was worried now. There was no time to think. If the Shahzada's army arrived, he would be sandwiched between his forces and the combined forces of the remaining soldiers of the Mughal empire and Begum Samru's skilled, trained army which was equipped with cannons and tanks. He was clever enough to contemplate the repercussions of this. He sought counsel from his Nazir and then decided to adopt the strategy suggested by him.

According to the counsel he had received, Ghulam apologized to Shah Alam for his 'impudence' and 'mistakes'. As a peace offering, he returned all the usurped treasure to him and even handed over the prosperous land of the ravines, which was a lucrative source of income for the emperor. The emperor finally accepted Ghulam's apologies and flattery. Royal *khilat* was delivered to Shah Alam's camp across the Yamuna river as a symbolic representation of his acceptance of the peace offering. The Rohilla chief behaved sensibly by leaving Delhi and marching back to his province in Saharanpur.

CHAPTER 14

Gokul Garh Attack... Begum Samru and Ghulam Qadir's terror

MEANWHILE, several smaller provinces had started taking undue advantage of the fragility and chaos that ensued in the Delhi empire. These provinces had ignored paying the revenue and other taxes. Some had even declared themselves independent from the influence of the empire. Najaf Khan was another such stubborn ruler, who had made up his mind to not yield to the authority of the empire. However, the fate of the Delhi province had flipped irrevocably. Shah Alam strengthened his empire with Begum Samru's assistance and decided to crush any rebellious or disobedient province that had dared to challenge his authority.

On 8 January 1788, just a few months before the rebellious Rohillas hijacked the fort, Shah Alam had set off on a military excursion with Begum Samru. Three of the Begum's skilled battalions were taking part in this expedition against the Rajputs. Samru Sahib had personally trained these troops. George Thomas was commanding one of these battalions.

The Gokalgarh fort was surrounded and threats were delivered to the ruler. But owing to the negligence and lacklustre strategy of the royal officers, the Mughal soldiers had gulped down bottles of alcohol and had fallen asleep due to overconfidence. In the early hours of dawn, the Rajput soldiers charged upon these drowsy royal soldiers, who were unprepared for this sudden attack. The frenzied soldiers ran to and fro, contributing to the chaos of the attack. They tried to shield themselves but the vanguard was scattered and the helpless soldiers began to seek shelter in and around the camp. As a result, Shah Alam became a target of the cannons and tanks. Begum Samru's quick thinking not only saved Shah Alam's life but also pushed back and defeated the enemy.

This gorgeous commander, dressed in royal attire, led her army, flanked by clarions, trumpets, horses, elephants and cannons. It was truly a treat for the eyes! The famous Mughal army, considered invincible, was frightened by just the sound of a cannon then. Now scattered, they had deserted their emperor. The fact that Begum Samru's battalion, which was awaiting further instructions, was unwaveringly maintaining the military formation on the left side of the fort, was truly admirable. There was not even a hint of panic or chaos in their ranks. The Begum sent a messenger in Shah Alam's tent to reassure him that the situation was under control and that his safety was their priority. She also told him that administering appropriate punishment to the rebels was her duty. She further added that martyrdom was more acceptable to her than failure to fulfil her duties.

An errand boy was sent to the Najaf clan. He was told that his actions against the emperor were outrageously treacherous and evil. He was threatened that he would have to repent for his sins. However, he paid no heed to these words.

Seeing this, Begum abandoned her camp and stepped inside a carriage so that she could be placed amidst the centre point of her army. She commanded her soldiers to march towards the enemy. As her army advanced, bullets began to rain on them.

Owing to the Begum's strategy, a wave of mindless pain began to sweep through the enemy's forces. Shah Alam began to gain strength. Finally, Begum's army managed to crush the rebels and capture the fort. Most of the rebels were either killed, injured or taken hostage. A few fortunate ones managed to flee. It was evident that in the absence of Begum Samru, this last jewel of the Mughal dynasty would have become one with the earth. This battalion was commanded by George Thomas. The Begum owed a significant proportion of her success in this military campaign to him. With the help of his skilled army and one cannon, he managed to keep Shah Alam safe. Had he not deployed his troops in the emperor's protection, the patriarch of the empire would have surely succumbed to the enemy's relentless firing. Shah Alam thanked the Begum again. He later invited her to his fort to honour her.

The rebels of Gokulgarh were completely crushed. Najaf Khan alone survived. He delivered a message to the Begum. However, the Begum and Shah Alam were both displeased with him.

Upon reaching Delhi, Shah Alam praised the Begum's valour and skill and profusely expressed his gratitude to her for coming to his rescue. In a discourse similar to this, Shah Alam felicitated the Begum with the title of 'Zeb-Un-Nissa.' He gifted her royal gifts even as he bestowed her with the status of his dearest daughter. He acknowledged the fact that if he was seated on the throne of the empire that day, it was solely because of the Begum's efforts. Had she not acted in a timely manner, his rule would have expired.

It is said that George Thomas's efforts in this battle weren't acknowledged fully. However, the Begum was extremely pleased with his commendable display of valour. She had realized his utility. It is said that the Mughal emperor acknowledged his efforts by felicitating him with a ceremonial robe.

On this joyous occasion, the emperor gifted the Begum an important province named Badshahpur-Jharsa across the Yamuna river. Once Najaf Khan had profusely apologized to the Begum and had flattered the emperor sufficiently, she convinced the emperor to forgive him too.

In 1787, the battalion, led by Shinde, was unable to break through the strength of the Rajput province of Ajmer. The influence of the Marathas had decreased in the Delhi empire. To gain more knowledge about the chaotic political atmosphere, Shinde equipped Amba Ji Dhara Rao with a finc arsenal and sent him to Delhi to persuade Shah Alam to provide succour to them. However, his Nazir, Manzoor Ali Khan filled the emperor's ears against Rao. He also persuaded the emperor to rob Rao's arsenal. Fortunately, the Begum arrived just in time. She strongly expressed her disapproval concerning this plan. She then deployed her skilled soldiers, led by French and Portuguese officers, in Rao's protection.

Begum Samru had become a prominent and influential member of the Delhi empire by then. Mirza, who had set up a camp in Faridabad, which was situated on the periphery of Delhi, deployed his most trusted associate Fakir Khair-Ud-Din in the Begum's service.

The Begum set up her court on this occasion. Strapping French, Armenian and Portuguese officers in uniforms were also in attendance. Begum's face was covered by a translucent veil.

'Speak. What is the purpose of your visit?' A sweet, yet firm voice came from behind the veil. The Begum wished to know the intent behind the Fakir's visit without further ado.

'Your highness, you are extremely popular everywhere. Everyone knows how capable you are. You have proven yourself by completely vanquishing the enemy each time.'

'Fakir Khair Ud Din Sahib, this is not the answer to my question. Tell me: how I can be of assistance to you?', the Begums responded pointedly.

Fakir hesitated, but he said,

'Your highness, the Shehzada's heart is melting at the pitiful condition of the kingdom. He wishes to revive the glory that prevailed during the reign of his grandfathers and great-grandfathers, Aurangzeb, Akbar the Great and Shah Jahan. That is all, your highness.'

A veil of silence descended over the court. After a few moments, the Begum said,

'First, tell me, does your Shehzada possess the virtues of courage and masculinity required to perform such a task?'

'By God's grace, you will be able to rendezvous with Shehzada, a beautiful and pure man like none other you might have met before...'

Fakir paused momentarily to gauge Begum's reaction.

A wave of rage swept through her.

'Stupid man! You are certainly a fool. Are you even listening to me? I wish to know if his majesty knows how to wield swords, manage an army and capture provinces, or is he content with playing the flute and tambura?', the Begum screamed.

Fakir was alarmed now. He timidly said,

'Yes, your honour. He is willing to devote all his time to the service of the nation. He will obey all your orders.'

The Begum glanced toward him. Encouraged by her silence, he continued, 'Your highness, a cowardly or egoistical man wouldn't have bothered to remedy the situation. Had he been a timid or lecherous man addicted to prostitution only, I wouldn't have been able to present his case before you.'

These words were unsuccessful in vanquishing the Begum's apprehensions. She disdainfully said,

'From what I have heard, he is a hedonistic and careless man. He is often unable to stick to one task or one plan.'

Despite this, the Begum assured Fakir that her sympathies were with the Shehzada, and the emperor needed his support in those desperate times. To do this, however, he would have to earn their trust and work extremely hard.

It was decided that one of the Begum's illustrious battalions would accompany the Shehzada on his visit to his father, Emperor Shah Alam's kingdom. The Begum would have to persuade Shah Alam that this was necessary for his empire and the fort's protection. Moreover, it was important to entrust the safekeeping of the royal treasury to the Shehzada.

The emergence of the descendants of the Mughal empire after such a long time, especially in this tumultuous period was a godsend for the regime. The elated Shah Alam embraced his son and promised him that the administration of the kingdom would be entrusted to him. It was decided that he would make all decisions regarding the royal treasury and daily affairs.

Yet, the devil of misfortune had latched itself onto the wings of this once-glorious empire. The pivot of Shah Alam's empire was his good-for-nothing Nazir, Manzoor. Emperor Shah Alam trusted him a little too much. The Nazir took undue advantage of this and controlled him like a puppeteer. The Shehzada's arrival had ruined his malevolent schemes, thereby making him jealous. He began filling the emperor's ears. The elderly Shah Alam was unable to discern his Nazir's true intentions. Perhaps he had greater reasons to trust his Nazir over his son. This illustrious empire's end didn't seem too far.

Eventually, the Shehzada distanced himself from the empire. The flame of hope that had begun flickering at his arrival was extinguished now. Upset with his father's behaviour, he drifted away from the empire. Later on, this heir of the Mughal empire died anonymously in Benares. The elder son of emperor Shah Alam, Mirza Jawan Bhakt was leading a simple, solitary existence away from Delhi. When he learned about Ghulam Qadir's antics and the flurry of recent events, he decided to undertake a journey to Delhi, to restore the long lost prestige and influence of the Mughal empire. Emperor Shah Alam was pleased with his son's decision. On 8 December, the prince arrived in Delhi at his father's invitation. He was previously earning a livelihood through the pension of the British.

However, this prince was also a peculiar man. Earlier, on another occasion, he had tried to overthrow his father and take hold of the reins of the kingdom. However, he was unsuccessful in managing the situation. The emperor shrewdly entrusted the task of controlling Agra from Ismail Baig to him so as to keep him at a distance from Delhi. In such a situation, neither Ismail Baig nor Ghulam Qadir was merciful with him. He was compelled to seek protection from the British because of his people's absolute hatred towards him.

The East India Company decided to abstain from intervening in these matters. Cornwallis unambiguously stated that the orders from above had instructed him to refrain from interfering in the mutual discords of the Mughal royals. He decided not to favour any one party and tried to maintain amicable relations with everyone. Later on, Cornwallis travelled to Farrukhabad with Wazir Asif-Ud-Doulah and the Shehzada. Governor-General Cornwallis visited Kanpur from there. Jawan Bhakt was sent to Delhi a few days beforehand. Major Palmer accompanied the Mughal prince as his advisor.

Mahadji never sought help from the British to see through his ploys. On 17 June 1788, Mahadji hoisted the flag of victory after capturing Agra from Ismail Baig.

Begum Samru returned to her province with the feeling that perhaps everything would be well in the empire. However, destiny had something else in store for this dynasty. The Begum wasn't present in Delhi to advise the emperor and the Nazir had alienated the Mughal heir from his father. This empire was now dependent on the wishes of the Almighty. The king and the army were both weak now. In such a situation, no one was particularly surprised when the enemy finally put his foot down.

At that time, the Pathans, led by Ghulam Qadir, supported by the Rajputs, initiated their campaign to acquire Panipat again. They invited the ruler of Kabul to uproot the Marathas from northern India. He was accompanied by his beloved, old lover, the queen of Kabul, who had never left his side. In this situation, Mahadji strengthened his ties with the Sikhs, who loathed the Afghans. They kept them from crossing the Indus for a long time. The Maratha leader, Mahadji was constrained by his preoccupation with protecting Shah Alam. For this purpose, he arranged transportation to safely bring the emperor to his camp in Rewari. However, Shah Alam had now developed apprehensions and doubts regarding Mahadji's capabilities. As a consequence Mahadji was unable to convince the emperor to come along. Mahadji was compelled to leave the unlucky monarch behind and abandon his quest for the peripheral regions. In December 1787, he retreated to the southern parts of Chambal to keep himself safe. This place was inhabited by inactive Maratha soldiers who had been stationed there to protect Agra and Aligarh from invasion.

In the initial three months of 1788, Shinde was unable to find the time to rest. He ordered his army to retreat from Chambal and began preparing to launch a comprehensive attack. He wished to restore his lost glory. Apart from the army sent by Nana Fadnavis he had granted permission beforehand to send a battalion of strapping young soldiers from his birthplace, Jamgaon. Nana's army reached on 16 March 1788. As per his strategy, he launched an attack in the first week of April. With the help of Ranjit Singh Jat, Rane Khan and Macheri's Rao Raja, Ismail Baig was defeated. Devji Gaoli, De Boigne and Raiji Patil together re-established their authority over Mathura. They crossed the Yamuna river and entered the fertile region of the ravines. The Pathans fought valiantly near Agra. However, the joint army of Jeevba Bakshi and Khanderao Hari successfully defeated them.

A terrific battle unravelled on 22 April, near Chaksan. However, it proved to be inconclusive. Ghulam Qadir was compelled to flee to save his life. Ismail Baig was left alone. On 18 June, he lost badly in Dehra, in the suburbs of Agra, on the banks of the Yamuna river. In July 1788, Ismail Baig, a major stakeholder of the Mughal empire, marched his army to Ghulam Qadir's fort, which was located on the opposite side of Delhi, on the banks of the Yamuna river. It was decided that the emperor's treasury and land would be divided in a ratio of two to one between Ghulam Qadir and Baig respectively.

After pledging to remove the Marathas from Delhi, Ghulam Qadir retreated to his camp across the Yamuna river in Delhi. Later on, he returned with two thousand soldiers and forced the emperor to honour him not only with the coveted position of Mir Bakshi but also with the title of 'Amir-ul-umara' and 'Rukn-ud-Daulah Bahadur' by bestowing him the ritualistic robes. On 17 February 1788, he established his authority over Aligarh. Ghulam Qadir was furious with Shinde's victory in the valley of Bagh Dehra on 18 June. Coincidentally, Ismail Baig came across a Rohilla rebel who was also unhappy and helpless because of Shinde.

The Rohilla jagirdar, Ghulam Qadir wanted to weaken the empire, so that he could fulfil his malevolent intentions. He was acquainted with the empire's Nazir, Manzoor Ali, who had once paved the way to allow Ghulam's army to reach the fort with ease. The two rebels revealed their true colours by asking the emperor for the keys to the royal treasury. Shah Alam tried to convince Ghulam Qadir that his treasury was empty. However, Ghulam Qadir refused to listen to him and turned red with rage. He brutally manhandled him and locked him and his family in the prison.

Ghulam Qadir had imagined that Delhi's Red Fort would be well-stocked with sparkling jewels, chests filled with priceless pearls, diamonds, and gold coins. He had dreamt of enormous boxes tumbling with jewels and important documents which would eventually become his possessions. When he was unable to discover the route to this imaginary treasure, he went berserk with rage. The greedy ruler even dug up the floors of the secret chambers in the fort. He failed to realize that the treasure didn't exist.

The fragile, traumatized and subservient emperor, Shah Alam was summoned from prison. He was made to sit on the floor and was subjected to rigorous interrogation. Grey clouds that were menacingly looming in the sky burst open suddenly, resulting in a heavy downpour. To the furious imagination, it seemed as though the Almighty was expressing his disapproval and displeasure towards Ghulam Qadir's atrocious crimes, but Ghulam Qadir was a tyrant. He didn't bother about the moral and ethical implications of his actions.

'I swear by God, if you don't tell me the location of the treasure, I will kill you with my own hands,'

he screamed furiously.

Ismail Baig managed to calm him down to an extent. Out of sympathy for the aged emperor, his old, loyal butler, who had joined hands with the rebels, convinced Ghulam Qadir to lock him up in the Moti Masjid with his sons.

The main supporter of the Rohilla's strategy was Manzoor Ali, the emperor's trusted servant, and in charge of the harem, who was Shinde's arch enemy. The next morning proved to be a harbinger of doom. Shah Alam was summoned to the Diwan-e-Khaas again. Ghulam Qadir reiterated his desire to get his hands on the treasure of his dreams. This was followed by the customary round of anger, screaming and insult. The Mughal emperor maintained his stance that he possessed no treasure.

During this time, Ghulam Qadir Khan commanded his warlord to head to Salimgarh. The fort of Salimgarh, which was situated on an island across the Yamuna river was being temporarily used as a prison. Emperor Ahmad Shah[3]'s successor and elder son, Bidar Bhakt was put behind bars as a captive. The Mughal heir had spent a major portion of his life in prison and was certain that he would grow old there. He could not believe his eyes

3 Azam Shah, was briefly the Mughal emperor who reigned from 14 March 1707 to 20 June 1707.

when he saw himself seated on the throne of the Mughal empire as the emperor of India. The true heirs of the throne had already been deposed.

The Mughal emperor and his sons were deceitfully thrown behind bars in Salimgarh. They were made to starve and even denied water for three days. During this time, the new emperor commenced his reign. He would stroll through the fort and lord over the officers and workers. Not many people were subservient to his rule. On the contrary, a majority of his subjects loathed him.

The huge iron gate was left open for a while. Some soldiers who had been left behind earlier from the invading army were brought inside through this gate. Although a dummy emperor was the real ruler now, Ghulam Qadir remained the true power holder. The empire was cloaked in a veil of terror, barbarity and cruelty. The populace was unhappy. History had never witnessed such brutality before. Each room, casket, and godown, which was suspected of holding wealth was thoroughly searched. Even the rooms in the royal palace, which housed courtiers, officers, servants and the royal chef were not spared from Ghulam Qadir's scrutiny.

Later on, even the Zenana was turned upside down. Nadir Shah and Ahmad Shah Durrani were regarded as domineering tyrants at that time. Ghulam Qadir had crossed limits that were respected by those tyrants. He lecherously harassed and molested the women who hailed from the royal family and other beautiful women around. However, he was unsuccessful in getting his hands on the treasure in the first raid.

Ghulam Qadir ordered his men to inspect the Zenana again. They were instructed to thoroughly search the women's belongings and even remove the tiles of the floor and crack open the walls to unearth the treasure. This time, they were successful to some extent. This success could be credited to their deceitful and manipulative behaviour rather than earnest efforts. The two aged queens of the emperor took the responsibility of searching for the treasure. The condition put forth by them was that a part of the stolen wealth should be credited to them.

The discovery of treasure in the Zenana of such a destitute emperor was truly miraculous. The truth was that the emperor had nothing to do with this treasure.

This was the wealth that had been put together by every woman with or without her husband's knowledge. Since this wealth was associated with the women of the royal family, it was a hefty amount. The women wept loudly as their precious jewels, gold coins and gems were piled in a corner before their eyes. Even devious tyrants like Ahmad Shah Abdali and Nadir Shah had refrained from crossing this boundary. However, Ghulam Qadir had refused to toe the line. There were no limits left to surpass now.

When Shah Alam II denied the existence of some hidden treasure, Ghulam Qadir summoned the princesses of the royal family. Their veils were first lifted and then they were forced to strip. To please the Rohillas, they were made to dance completely naked before their father. Some princesses felt so humiliated, that they decided to jump in the Yamuna river that was flowing nearby. Bursting with grief and rage, the emperor Shah Alam kept his head bowed. However, his answer to the question about the treasure didn't change. He was genuinely unaware of the existence of any treasure.

Although Ismail Baig was fully supportive of Ghulam Qadir in this campaign to loot the royal family, he was jarred and disturbed by his cruelty and the naked dance. He expressed his opposition and anger towards the inhumane treatment of the royal princesses. When his protests were ignored, he removed his army from the Red Fort and set up a camp near the shrine of Nizamuddin. Several Rohilla warriors were also against this, but they did not dare express their views.

It is rumoured that deep in his heart, Ismail Baig did not support Ghulam Qadir's atrocious crimes and brutal treatment of the royal family. However, it was also true that if Baig hadn't supported Ghulam, he wouldn't have had the courage to commit the atrocious crimes that were a black mark in the name and glory of the Pathans.

Ghulam Qadir hadn't scaled the final boundary yet.

The time had come to revolt against his terror. Unfortunately, both Mahadji Shinde and Begum Samru were far away. Mahadji Shinde was camping in Mathura, whereas Begum Samru was entangled in resolving the crisis in Tappal with George Thomas. Owing to multiple reasons, Mahadji Shinde couldn't abandon his camp in

Mathura to come down to the Red Fort immediately. An idea struck him. Shinde sent a messenger to Begum Samru. He urged Begum to rescue the emperor in his place.

Farzana was busy managing the affairs of the new province of Tappal. In those days, Tappal was a mismanaged and crime-infested region. It was often controlled by dacoits and robbers. A hefty sum of money was being devoted to refurbishing and renovating the local fort. The administration, led by the Begum, was brainstorming ideas for maximising the revenue and funding. This was a tedious task since Tappal was drastically different from Sardhana.

George Thomas had a different personality. He yearned to live in thickly forested and arid regions. His frequent clashes with daring dacoits added to the thrill and allure of the entire experience. Begum did not share his views. She was deeply troubled by the affairs of this province. This region had no lord because it had been subjected to countless famines and raids. The political atmosphere could only be remedied with constant efforts, a firm hand and a prolonged stay. After investing a lot of money, the local fort was considered fit for housing. Poverty and low availability of human resources were problems that were deeply entrenched in this region. No crops were produced in the fields, and even the streams had dried up. The villagers were constantly tormented by the fear of being looted.

George was a true connoisseur. He had discovered

the pathway to his future in this province. He pleaded with the Begum who was still apprehensive and hesitant. Tappal wasn't particularly close to Sardhana. The strain of the journey from Sardhana to Tappal had left traces behind in her body. She knew that managing this region alongside Farzana could prove to be extremely challenging. She reluctantly gave into Thomas' pleadings and made him the governor of this province. Shah Alam had given his approval for this beforehand. Later on, the Begum received Mahadji Shinde's message about travelling to Delhi, but matters were extremely uncertain then. The Begum was unable to make up her mind to abandon Tappal to go to Delhi.

Meanwhile, the Red Fort was being dominated by Ghulam Qadir's tyranny. He said to Shah Alam,

'I desire gold jewels, pearls, gems and priceless ornaments. Otherwise, you will leave this fort as a corpse!'

Shah Alam was physically as well as emotionally drained now. However, his honour and self-respect were still intact. Rage was brimming in his eyes. His sudden, uncharacteristic outburst was fuelled by trauma and anger. He screamed,

'My life rests in your hands, Ghulam. Wield your sword and behead me. Anyway, I would prefer to die than spend my last days in your presence.'

Najeeb-Ud-Daulah's grandson, Ghulam Qadir, the chief of the Afghan Rohilla clan was the head of the Pathans. Naturally, his instincts mirrored those of his race. The virtues of shame, pity and honesty had abandoned him. Although he had inherited his conspiring and malevolent tendencies from the infamous warrior of the Battle of Panipat, his grandfather-Najeeb-Ud-Doulah, his grandfather's distinguishing qualities such as intelligence and farsightedness weren't passed on to him. After establishing his authority over his father's province, he executed those members of his extended family, who posed some conceivable threat to his ambitions. His addiction to alcohol aided in accelerating his political ambitions. He was keener on emulating the legacy of his grandfather, Najeeb-Ud-Doulah than stepping into the shoes of his father, Jabita Khan, but he was far from it. His misconceptions drove him to unprecedented heights of arrogance. Perhaps the almighty had created him for the sole purpose of removing all Hindu influence from the Mughal empire and purifying the empire with the help of his gallant Afghan brothers. Until he had forcefully seized every item in the possession of the royal household, the flame of vengeance that was characteristic to the Afghans couldn't be doused. Owing to this, there was no incident in the bloodstained Islamic history which could match the brutality that the royal women of the Mughal empire were subjected to.

These words from the helpless and aged emperor angered Ghulam Qadir. He leapt forward and sat on his chest. Two of his soldiers clasped the emperor's arms tightly. On Qadir's orders, Kandhari Khan scooped out one of the emperor's eyeballs. No one was sympathetic towards the plight of the old emperor who was writhing in agony. When the other eye of the groaning emperor was also pulled out, he began shrieking in pain. Ghulam's barbarity knew no boundaries. He summoned an artist and asked him to paint a picture of him sitting on the emperor's chest and pulling out his eyes.

Owing to Ghulam Qadir's cruelty, Ismail Baig was filled with a sense of remorse and regret. Although his problems were two-fold, he made up his mind to withdraw the support he had extended to the tyrant. Baig sent a message to Mahadji Shinde, recounting Ghulam's brutality. He apologised for his mistakes and his role in helping Ghulam and assured Mahadji that he would unconditionally support the Marathas in their fight against Ghulam Qadir. He also began raising awareness and consolidating power amongst the citizens of Delhi, who were oblivious to the activities that were taking place in the Red Fort.

As soon as he received the message, Shinde began preparing to head to Delhi, even though marching his army in the monsoon season would prove to be difficult. His soldiers weren't ready to leave Mathura unless they got fair compensation. Shinde himself was ailing but he wished to reach Delhi. Despite this, he prepared a battalion with the help of the trusted military officer, De Boigne and sent it to Delhi.

As soon as Begum Samru and George Thomas learned details of the string of events that had unravelled in the Red Fort, they left Tappal. However, they were also troubled by the rain, mud and the dirty water that was characteristic to the monsoon season. But, owing to the sandy terrains of Tappal and the peripheral regions, the flow of water was considerably less. Moreover, during Reinhardt Samru's time, a canal had been constructed in Sardhana which helped reduce flooding. They surpassed all hindrances and speedily reached Sardhana, where they had to divide their army in three battalions. Sardhana's soldiers had set up a contraption in Delhi through the western part of the banks of the Yamuna river. Dressed in uniforms that were bleached a dark Khaki shade, Begum Samru's soldiers managed to reach the borders of Delhi.

Ghulam Qadir had already captured the royal palace of the Red Fort. He was leading a luxurious life there. The women of the royal family were being harassed and molested on a routine basis. Unfortunately, this was done before the eyes of the old, helpless and ailing Mughal emperor, Shah Alam. Bidar Bhakt was insulted and subsequently dismissed. Women and some men of the royal household had lost their lives to shock, injury, hunger and suicide.

On 24 July, Shah Alam reluctantly accepted this tyrant's each and every demand which was hardly genuine and justified. To fulfil his promise, Shah Alam had to hand over his beloved son, Suleiman Shikoh in shackles to Ghulam Qadir. Ghulam Qadir and Ismail Baig lorded over the holy shrine and the royal palace and imprisoned Shah Alam in a small, confined mosque. Any item suspected of being valuable was destroyed and searched for its wealth. This continued for sixty-eight days. The

Red Fort, which had once been the seat of Mughal authority, along with the Mughal family presided by Shah Alam were in the midst of an unprecedented crisis.

After plucking out Shah Alam's eyes on 10 August, young children and helpless women were deprived of food and water for days. The princes were severely caned, the princesses were raped repeatedly and the workers were beaten to death. To locate the royal treasure, the interior of the royal palace and the homes of wealthy merchants were destroyed. During these nine weeks, hellish sights of torture and misery were common in the beautiful Red Fort, the royal palace and the entire campus. Countless noble women were sacrificed to satiate the Rohillas' carnal desires. Slave girls were brutally tortured and eunuchs were killed upon failing to reveal the location of the hidden treasure. Even last rites weren't conducted for the dead. The chateaux of Malika Jamani and Sahiba Mahal were also dug open. The emperor's beloved queens were then stripped before the public. Twenty-one people were killed in this chaos.

A good amount of time had passed. The capital was now abuzz with rumours. Even Mahadji Shinde had learned enough about the string of events. The day was the 28 of September. The armies of Ismail Baig, Mahadji Shinde and Begum Samru surrounded all the exits of Shahjahanabad. This region is presently known as Old Delhi. This military excursion was conducted under the supervision of the Maratha General, Rane Khan. He was quite experienced in dealing with such matters. The next morning, he alerted those troops that were stationed in the important regions of the city.

The last month of September had rolled by then. Although the level of the Yamuna river had decreased, the waters weren't completely tranquil. It was impossible to cross the river to reach the fort. The Begum racked her brains to find a pathway to the fort. Barely twenty-five kilometres from Delhi, in the southern direction, they discovered an intersection in the old city of Baghpat. All the available boats were utilized. Although crossing the river posed some conceivable threat to the lives of soldiers, officers and horses, they were seated in the boat and rowed away.

Shinde entered the fertile region of the ravines with his powerful army. Upon learning about the terrifying events that had unfolded in the empire, Shinde had ordered his General Rane Khan to set off for Delhi to free the emperor from the clutches of the rebels. Begum Samru's army had also proceeded for war. They were determined to not allow Qadir's terror to reign for long now. Ghulam Qadir had realized that his end was near. Holding up the fort effectively meant that he would have to prepare himself for a fierce battle. His army was not equipped or skilled enough for such a war. He decided to hastily pack up all the wealth he could get his hands on and retreat via Meerut. His puppet emperor and crafty Nazir were there by his side.

Ghulam Qadir was fortunate enough to have escaped from the Red Fort in time. His fury of atrocious crimes reportedly lasted from 29 July to 10 October 1788, the day when the arsenal was burnt. General Rane Khan hastily reached the Red Fort and freed the Mughal emperor Shah Alam II from the shackles. He was declared the emperor of the country again. His wealth and pride were restored and doctors were summoned to treat his eyes. Shah Alam formally ordered his army to lay siege on the rebels. The soldiers were instructed to bring Ghulam Qadir alive so that he could be punished for his sins.

The fact that Shinde and Begum Samru took quite some time to rescue the emperor planted a seed of doubt in the minds of those who were critically analysing this situation. Some people go as far as to say that Shinde deliberately reached late. Many reasons have been cited in support of this argument. Till today, no one knows if he was really ailing. However, no one has been able to find a justification as to why this warrior, who loved and respected the empire, would deliberately delay in reaching Delhi. Begum Samru was actually in Tappal. However, couldn't she have left Tappal to rescue the distressed emperor? The answer to this question is still unanswered.

CHAPTER 15

Ghulam Qadir's Chastisement

OWING to the carelessness of the Rohilla soldiers, an explosion took place in the arsenal on 10 October. Deeming it as a bad omen, Ghulam Qadir hastily gathered all the stolen wealth and abandoned the fort. On the next day, Rane Khan, Himmat Bahadur Gossain, and Ranaji Shinde too entered the Red Fort. The starving inhabitants of the fort were fed and offered water, as well as necessities, were arranged for those who lived in the palace. On 16 October, Rane Khan appeared before the blind emperor. He made him sit on the throne and sanctified his authority by preaching the Khutbah.

They chased after the Rohilla tyrants who were trying to flee. However, the Rohillas had scattered completely. The Marathas established their authority over the shrine of Aligarh on 20 October. Rane Khan was busy ensuring that there were sufficient supplies of necessities in the Red Fort and that the victims of Ghulam Qadir's atrocities were attended to. He left Delhi on 3 November to locate the fugitive Rohillas. On 27 September, Ali Bahadur joined hands with Rane Khan to see through the success of this campaign. He carried Mahadji Shinde's message with him which stated that the success in nabbing the dacoits of Delhi should be credited to Ali Bahadur.

Ghulam Qadir, who had fled from the ravines, reached Meerut on 4 November. He sought shelter in a citadel there and fought courageously to protect himself. All routes to Meerut were blocked. He relentlessly defended himself from the strikes of the Rohillas. Finally, on 17 December, the unguarded and helpless Ghulam Qadir crept out of the citadel and took shelter in a Brahmin's home in village Bamnauli, which was located three miles away from Baraut towards Shamli in the south-west direction, with a few of his trusted sidekicks. His two staunch supporters- Mansoor Ali Khan Nazir, and the commander of his bodyguard army, Maniyar Singh were nabbed in Meerut. The Brahmin revealed the location of Ghulam Qadir's secret hideout to Ali Bahadur.

Ghulam Qadir and his sidekicks were caught on 19 December. He, along with the other captives, was first towed to Mahadji Shinde's camp in Mathura on 31 December. For two months, Mahadji Shinde tried to forcefully extract the looted wealth and other information from him. During this time, he also dwelt on the appropriate punishment for Ghulam. Although he was reluctant to execute him, the circumstances compelled him to punish Ghulam severely.

He was imprisoned in a prison made of iron. He was transported to Delhi in a bullock cart. Heavy iron fetters were firmly wound around his hands, legs and neck. His safety was secured by the presence of a thousand equestrians and two battalions. In this manner, he was presented before the blind emperor in the same Agra fort that had been tormented by his brutality some time ago.

It seemed as though Ghulam Qadir's voice was stuck in his throat. He was shivering with fear. Mahadji Shinde was intently watching him. He said,

'I regret seeing the face of an ungrateful wretch like you again and again. Speak: how do you think we should treat you?'

Just like his courage, Ghulam Qadir's speech was also failing him. He glanced at him timidly and then lowered his gaze to the floor.

'Blacken this miserable bastard's face,' Shinde said, answering his question.

Ghulam's face was splattered with black paint. He now seemed to resemble some ghastly animal.

'You like hearing compliments right? Soldiers, slice off his ears!' Shinde ordered his men.

His ears were chopped off. He screamed in agony, but no one sympathised with him. He was then paraded in and around Shinde's camp. Even this wasn't enough to satiate Shine's burning desire for vengeance. He ordered his soldiers to parade Ghulam throughout the city to allow the people to view the repercussions of rebellion, cruelty, deceit and greed.

The inhabitants of the city saw Ghulam in this pathetic condition. He was presented again the next day. His nose and upper lip were torn from his face. He was paraded through the streets again.

On the third day, he was shoved on the ground and was tortured in the same way as Shah Alam: his eyes were scooped out with a dagger. In a pompous procession flanked by drums, he was marched through the city again.

Later on, his hands and legs were severed from his body. His anguished screams could be heard from a distance. Finally, his torso was chopped off. His blood flowed freely through the drains. Shinde then presented his lord, Shah Alam with Qadir's severed ears, nose and head.

The deceitful Nazir, who was a staunch ally of Ghulam Qadir was killed by being trampled upon by elephants. The emperor also ordered his soldiers to kill Bidar Bhakt, who was anointed king by Qadir. Shah Alam profusely thanked Mahadji. He was honoured by being entrusted with the administration of the holy sites of Mathura and Vrindavan. The emperor felt remorseful that the cities of Prayagraj, Benares and Gaya couldn't be handed over to Shinde because they didn't come under his jurisdiction.

Meanwhile, Ghulam Qadir's mother and brothers had gathered all the stolen wealth and had escaped to Kunjpura to seek asylum with the Sikhs. Raiji Patil and Ali Bahadur chased after them and were successful in locating the loot, which Qadir had deceitfully and forcefully acquired from the royal family. In this manner, the regions lorded over by the Rohillas were usurped and Maratha soldiers were positioned there. The Sikh supporters of Ghulam Qadir were nabbed and punished.

The buzz around Ghulam Qadir slowly died down. Although the Red Fort had witnessed countless tragedies, the silence was reigning within its walls now. Begum Samru extended her wholehearted support to emperor Shah Alam II. However, the political situation in the jagir of Sardhana had become unsteady. Although Begum had no qualms about George Thomas' loyalty, she was exasperated with Lee Wassey's indefatigable attempts to fill her ears. So, she authorized a *firman* to order George to return. This can be considered as a *firman* of his dismissal. She had dual objectives behind this. Firstly, she wanted to convey to his enemies that George wasn't out of her reach. Secondly, she wished to acquaint him with his status in society. Unfortunately, she took this decision with her heart, instead of her mind. Lee Wassey's affection was appealing to Begum's lonely being, whereas George Thomas' successful military excursions and admirable governance were being viewed with suspicion and apprehension. Unfortunately, George Thomas wasn't around to defend himself and justify his actions.

According to Lee Wassey, Thomas was deliberately picking out a few of the trusted French officers with whose support he planned to depose the Begum from the throne. He believed that it was Thomas's primary goal to usurp the province of Sardhana. Adrift in the mayhem of these rumours, Begum eventually developed a strong dislike towards Thomas. Driven by some inexplicable force, she summoned Maria, George's wife and explicitly criticised him in a lengthy rant. When George Thomas learned about this, he abandoned the ongoing military campaign in Punjab and returned to Sardhana. He soon realized that the doors to reconciliation were now closed. In such a situation, he left for Tappal with his family and declared himself the owner of this seceded province.

It seemed as though Lee Wassey's prediction had come true. The Begum felt as though the rumours that had been circulating about Thomas had climaxed into this political mayhem. The angry Begum ordered her troops to surround Tappal and capture George Thomas.

A battalion led by Captain Selure was sent to bring George back. Sardhana's army was truly massive. Moreover, George Thomas had no intention of fighting his ex-comrades. Due to this reason, he surrendered without putting any worthwhile resistance.

Despite the entire mayhem, the Begum was influenced by George Thomas. It was also true that she did not allow emotions of anger to affect her. If someone else had revolted, she would have sentenced him to death. However, strangely enough, Begum did not hurt George Thomas. On the contrary, she helped him to escape safely from her jagir. She even handed him the revenue amount collected from the Tappal. It is rumoured that Nizamuddin, a senior officer of the Mughal empire pressurized Begum to spare George Thomas.

The Begum wrested control of Tappal again. Owing to Thomas's governance, this province earned the reputation of yielding good tax revenue.

CHAPTER 16

Qualms About Thomas... Lee Wassey's Love

GEORGE Thomas's resignation effectively meant that Lee Wassey could now monopolize the power dynamics of Sardhana. As his political ambitions grew, he tried to ride to new heights. He began to weave fantasies about becoming the ruler of this province by establishing ties of matrimony with the Begum. Begum Samru was only forty years old. Her stunning beauty could outshine any younger maiden's appeal. The feelings of love were still simmering in her heart. Yet, with unwavering will power she remained steadfast in her goal of not succumbing to some fantasy love story. The question was: for how long?

Eventually, their flirtatious flings turned into a full-fledged relationship. The Begum was clever enough to realize that her decision to wed a foreign army officer could have serious repercussions. Shah Alam, a father-figure, had warned her about hastiness in any relationship. He had advised her that a relationship of this kind would serve as a breeding ground for rebellion. Yet, love is blind.

Anyone who raises questions appears to be an enemy. The Begum refused to listen to her father figure's wisdom.

After much thought, she decided to talk to Lee. He made her drink two sips of the finest wine, which she wasn't particularly fond of.

'Thank you, Begum Sahiba...!'

Lee Wassey bowed to express his gratitude.

The Begum prepared a smaller quantity of wine for herself now. She dismissed all the servants in the room. She wished to speak to him in the privacy of her chambers.

'You should be proud that you were able to scale such unprecedented heights in your career that others can only dream of,' she said.

Lee Wassey took two sips of wine and placed the glass on the table. He reverently said, 'Yes, your highness. I understand that.'

'I don't know if it was because of your fortune or my passion. Now that the thought of beginning a new life together has cropped up...';the Begum said poetically. She had gulped down the wine now.

'Yes, I am extremely grateful...' he said respectfully.

Begum's expression suddenly turned grave. 'Now listen carefully,' she said.

'Yes, your highness.'

'My heart is exceptionally strong; it has never fallen prey to anyone's charms, except that of my Nawab sahib. No one has lingered for long in its chambers. But, there is certainly something extraordinary about you. Find out and tell me why this heart is yearning to be yours?'

The Begum rested her head against the back of her easy chair and closed her eyes. Her lips kept mumbling some unintelligible gibberish. Intoxicated by the wine, she drifted off to a deep slumber. Her body couldn't tolerate excessive alcohol as she rarely drank.

Lee Wassey's joy knew no bounds. He pinched himself just to make sure that he wasn't dreaming. It was the summer season. The Begum's diaphanous attire seemed to conceal her beautifully sculpted body only partially. Her flushed face didn't look any less stunning than a full moon on a clear night. The delicate sweet scent of perfume that wafted through the air and the halo of the dim candles succeeded in creating a romantic ambience. The silence was so profound, that the sound of the heart beating against the chest could be heard. A ghost of a smile flickered across the French warrior's face, reflecting his happiness.

Lee Wassey stood up and took eight steps forward to reach where the Begum had peacefully drifted away. He sat down on a rug and unabashedly gazed at this beautiful goddess, who was loved and revered by everyone. Emperor Shah Alam II himself had honoured her with the status of his dearest daughter. Lee Wassey's gaze trailed from this flawless beauty's feet to her head.

Suddenly, Begum jerked awake. 'You?' she said, draping her veil over her head.

'Yes, your highness. You were perhaps asleep…',

Lee Wassey said standing up in attention.

'Alright. Sit down. You can call me Farzana if you

wish to. You are the only one with this privilege,' she said, smiling slyly. She met Lee Wassey's eyes and it felt as though thunder and lightning had begun to rumble. The strings of his heart seemed to produce melodious symphonies. It was evident from his expression that he was delighted.

Begum had fallen head over heels in love with this strapping young soldier. However, it was unclear whether this army commander was driven by ambition or love. There was, after all, an enormous difference between their positions.

'But, listen,' Begum said, regaining her composure.

'There are certain conditions that you must remember and fulfil sincerely. Even if I forget you must remind me of them. The condition is that this marriage must always remain a secret.'

'You are aware that my late husband is the sole reason behind my position as the queen of this province. He gave me much more than I had ever imagined. Money, wealth, diamonds-gems, this palace, army, this status- all of this is his offering. I am grateful solely to the almighty, to my mother, and to my husband who delivered me from the darkness of my old, lowly life. He relieved me of my misery and changed my destiny.'

Lee Wassey suspected that the intoxicated Begum had entered the lane of memories. The truth, however, was that she was now even more alert to her surroundings. Her ability to discern a person's intent from his words was still strong.

Lee Wassey kept listening to anecdotes about love and life from this beautiful life-sized doll. He had no alternative.

One fateful day, the Begum and Lee Wassey secretly exchanged marriage vows. This marriage was witnessed by only two of their most trusted counselors: Bernier and Selure. Father Gregory officiated this marriage in 1793. The intention behind the Begum's decision to keep this marriage a secret was just to uphold the respect that her army and populace had for her, and also to prevent rebellion. The Begum's fears were not uncalled for because the army viewed the French soldiers with suspicion. Moreover, people respected her owing to her status as Samru's wife. The news that she had exchanged garlands with a lieutenant in her army could incite a wave of rebellion and treason in the province.

Even after taking several precautions, the Begum was aware that the situation could become worse than she had imagined. However, this thought was of no concern to Johanna Nobilis. She had fallen prey to the yearnings of her heart and had allowed herself to be trapped in Lee Wassey's web of seduction. Her inability to understand this can be accounted for as a failure in her glorious career. She failed to discern the indignant and aggressive man who hid behind the mask of decency and gentleness.

Lee Wassey was a talented, skilled, handsome soldier with an impressive lineage. However, his arrogance, unwarranted outbursts of rage and excessive use of expletives ultimately led to his doom. He considered himself a refined gentleman boasting of a prestigious background and high social standing. In contrast, the Begum's image was that of a firm, kind, just, and an empathetic female ruler. She was known for partaking in the joy and sorrow of the commoners and ensuring the well-being of the kith and kin of her soldiers. She was always willing to help others; she would often share meals with her populace. Due to this reason, people always viewed Begum with love and respect. Begum's actions were based on the belief that the love she received from her citizens would uphold her authority. Besides, it gave her an immense sense of contentment to know that the *jagir* was happy under her governance.

Lee Wassey had a contrasting personality. The Begum was unable to understand this because he would put on the mask of a gentle lover with her. Lee Wassey revealed his true colours just a day after their marriage. He disliked the fact that the Begum would routinely welcome those soldiers who he considered inferior. On the other hand, many of these officers were irked that a soldier in their ranks had become Begum's lover and was acting as an intermediary between her and the public. Many officers openly opposed this and questioned the Begum's decision to give a staggering amount of liberty to Lee Wassey.

Finally, the Begum had to open up with him about this predicament. She summoned him to her court and said, 'I wish to talk to you about the *jagir* today. So, this is a more appropriate place to carry out this discussion than my bedroom.'

The sharp intonation of the Begum's voice appeared to be in perfect sync with her personality. She had adopted the cold aloofness that she used to maintain when conversing with everyone else. Lee Wassey was startled, but he composed himself quickly.

'Yes, your highness. I am not surprised that you are talking to me this way. You are older and more experienced than me in every aspect of life. All I can say is that I have tried to know you. And this attempt has been sincere. In simpler words, I have loved you with all my heart. You are my first…and perhaps last love. Every inch of my soul dances to your tune. You reside in every beat of my heart.'

Who doesn't like being treated with love and respect? The Begum was a soft-hearted woman who resembled a doll in blood and flesh. A small, beating heart resided inside her body. That was the reason behind Lee Wassey's presence inside her. However, she was intelligent enough to understand the intention behind his words. She regained her composure. Trying to strike a balance between love and governance, she said, 'I am intelligent enough to know that your love is there. I respect your love with all my heart. However, my love is restrained by my duties. My army, jagir and the emperor of this land are also deserving of my love. If I digress from the path of my duties, how will I be any different from the local lasses? Time neither forgives, nor gives second chances. This is India: the land of culture and duties. People of this country worship ghosts, treat the ailing with talismans and sacrifice animals and believe that fulfilling their relationships with goodness and honesty is their duty. This country is not like your land, where people remain ignorant even after reading the inscriptions on the walls. To rule in such a country, you will have to acquaint yourself with the cultural restrictions and the social atmosphere. Otherwise, you will end up wasting your time proving yourself.'

Lee Wassey intently gazed at the Begum and pounded his chest with his fist, even as Begum's wisdom slipped out of his ears.

'...Believe me, your orders are more valuable to me than my life. I have learned to implement the commands of her highness very well. My Jesus is my witness. Your country and this jagir are mine too. This land is no less important to me than my own.'

Lee Wassey's sweet words did not melt the Begum's heart this time. It was as important for her to express her opinions as it was for her to make him understand.

'Despite your sincerity, I, unfortunately, feel as though tough times are in store now... because of some careless decisions,' the Begum said sternly.

Lee Wassey's astonishment was not surprising. He could not tolerate such harsh words from the Begum's mouth.

'What are you saying, Begum? I am not able to understand. Is some lowly officer filling your ears against me? Some insolent, illiterate, lowly officer...'

The Begum was filled with rage. Trying to keep her

anger at bay, she said,

'Mr. Lee Wassey…you are an educated man…your lineage is pure, you belong to the white race, you have seen the world, you are associated with a respectable family… However, you still have a lot to learn. Bookish knowledge can only thus far. But, to win people's hearts, you need to understand the rhythm of their heartbeats. Only then can you rule over their hearts. There are certain principles that you need to abide by to do this. Having control over your words is even more important than education. Try to keep this in your mind. It will benefit you in the long run. Otherwise, you will have nothing left to lose.'

'And try to instil in yourself the goodness of those you have labelled insolent, illiterate and lowly. No one said anything to me. I just poured my heart out to you. If you don't make an earnest effort to understand this, these flickering sparks of rebellion will consume you and I. There will be nothing left to salvage. It's better if we understand the fragility of time.'

The Begum was trying her best to explain the matter to him. However, Lee Wassey's arrogance had scaled unprecedented heights. Respect extended to an incompetent person turns into ego. It was important for him to contradict the Begum's wisdom with ceaseless arguments, so to avert the possibility of appearing inferior, he said,

'I neither associate with uncultured people nor treat them with equality. Frenchmen are taught to respect the status and positions, not the person. Praising and respecting incompetent people leads to mounting arrogance and ultimately a downfall. This is my weakness. I disagree if you think my actions can arouse flames of rebellion in your jagir.'

The Begum was displeased with Lee Wassey's tone and choice of words. Despite this, she tried her best to make him understand. She said,

'All I know is that a soldier is a soldier only. The subject of status comes later. Everyone bleeds red. Do you know why Samru Sahib was respected so much? He treated everyone equally. He partook in the joy and grief of the commoners. He celebrated all festivals with equal pomp. Sometimes everyone would eat together…'

Despite the anger that was bubbling within her, Begum was able to maintain her composure. Lee Wassey was far behind her in this respect.

'Forgive me, your highness… From what I have heard, he wasn't able to remit his army's salaries on time. In this situation, how could the army of the province have been happy?' interrupted Lee Wassey.

A grave expression appeared on the Begum's face.

'Tell me, which foreigner pays his army on time? The question is of integrity. He never held back from paying any person for his services. He would distribute the money he had got to the army personnel first. Tell me something…if what you say is true, then, why are you so averse to learning from his mistakes? What's wrong with that? No one can make you understand if you are unwilling to understand!'

The Begum took a deep breath.

For some reason, Lee Wassey believed that he was better than Samru Sahib. He wanted the Begum to admit this.

'Why do you keep comparing my status and capabilities to him? What was so special about him?' he said, raising his voice.

The Begum stood up intending to conclude this pointless argument. She firmly said,

'I am not used to being spoken to in this manner. It's better, you understand this soon. This will benefit you. I will not tolerate disrespect in the name of love. And remember, I'm not in the habit of repeating myself again and again.'

Lee Wassey was startled now.

'Believe me, I am willing to tolerate everything in exchange for your support. These are just some bad habits of mine. This warm blood has been running in the veins of my ancestors for centuries. With time, it will dissolve in the coolness of this land. I will always be a loyal friend to you,' he crooned.

The Begum paused in her tracks. She had swallowed some of her anger now.

'Even I hope that the time we spend together fills our hearts with joy and not sorrow. However, I can't withstand the silent stares that are trained on me. That is even more terrifying than war.'

Like a classic European lover, Lee Wassey got down

on one knee and expressed his love. The bitterness of that moment disappeared in thin air. The radiance on the Begum's face made it clear that she was lost in this dreamy reality that Lee Wassey had woven.

The Begum stooped slightly and clasped Lee Wassey's hands with her small, gentle hands. The sweet fragrance that emanated from her delicate frame and luxurious clothes seemed to add a spark to the ambience.

The argument was over for now. However, the matter wasn't resolved yet. Despite the Begum's firm, unambiguous instructions, Lee Wassey did not neglect any opportunity to publicise his relationship with her. Most people were ignorant of their covert marriage. Because of this, the *jagir* was soon abuzz with rumours that the Begum had allowed herself to be trapped in Lee Wassey's web of seduction, and the administration was now managed by him.

These rumours could not escape the scrutiny of the Begum's sharp eyes and ears. She soon realized that these rumours could prove to be detrimental for her rule. But, as they say, love is blind. Love can't distinguish between right and wrong. The Begum was still in love with Lee Wassey. This was the consequence of her love. She had envisioned a rosy future with the love of her life. She advised Lee Wassey to change his behaviour with affection. However, his bad habits and arrogance had gotten the better of him. The Begum's counsel had little impact on him.

CHAPTER 17

Thomas's Growing Influence

AFTER resigning from the Begum's army, George Thomas made his way into the ranks of the Maratha ruler, Appa Khande Rao's army. In 1793, he led his newly-acquired battalion in the military campaign in the canton of Mewat, a southwest region of Delhi. He caused damage to one of Begum's areas because he was still displeased with the treatment he had received in her hands. With time, Appa's army completed several military campaigns. This not only increased the influence and power of the Maratha empire but also led to George's advancement in his career.

Mahadji Shinde's death on 12 February 1794 had a great impact on the Maratha power established in the northern parts of the country. Appa decided to utilise this opportunity to expand the range of his empire by usurping his province. He began dreaming of becoming the emperor of the Delhi empire. The blind and fragile emperor Shah Alam's son, Mirza Akhtar was quick to discern the danger lurking in the shadows. He sent a message to Begum Samru and some other courtiers saying, 'To deal with this situation, start recruiting new officers immediately. The funds will be sourced from the royal treasury.'

On 30th March 1794, a loyal and senior person reached Sardhana to convey this message.

It appeared as though Mirza Bhakt had discerned the prowess of Appa's army, for he took the assistance of the British to see through this mission. However, he was apprehensive that this would cause other Maratha chieftains to stand beside Appa. Because of this reason, he decided to keep the channels of the British open, secretly. He covertly requested help from the Governor-General of India. Meanwhile, Thomas's intentions were making the Begum nervous. She wanted to create an atmosphere to make the British think that Thomas wanted to use Appa to hurt her *jagir.*

The Begum understood that such exchanges should be carried out through a loyal and sincere person. So, she sent Father Gregory to Kolkata for this job. Since Gregory was British, the probability that this mission would be accomplished was higher.

Keeping in mind Thomas's growing influence in Appa's army, the Begum commenced all the preparations. She even ordered some of her special officers to keep an eye on him. General Thomas was oblivious to Begum's intentions and preparations.

After the failure of Father Gregory's mission, the

Begum began preparing to launch an attack on Appa. The Begum wanted to gain the upper hand on the Marathas and teach her enemy, George Thomas a lesson. The Begum was rumoured to have even bribed some Maratha officers to dismiss George. She admitted some Maratha officers in her army to facilitate that.

One morning, she left her jagir Sardhana and set up a camp at a distance of thirty-four miles in the southeast direction from Jhajjar. George Thomas had realised that these actions were driven by the authorities working under the Begum, who detested him. The first name that cropped up in his mind was Lee Wassey's, who was considered to be very close to the Begum. Lee Wassey had been responsible for ousting George Thomas from Sardhana. However, destiny had a different plan. The Begum's army was quite skilled and proficient in clashing with the enemy. However, the region was soon abuzz with rumours that this campaign had been launched by Lee Wassey to explicitly cause harm to George Thomas. This enraged the soldiers in the Begum's army. George Thomas's decency was in stark contrast to Lee Wassey's rudeness. Due to this reason, the vast majority of soldiers in the Begum's army were supportive of George Thomas. The situation became so pathetic, that the Begum had to abandon this military campaign midway and retreat to Sardhana. Little did she know that the problem was about to get worse.

The Begum's army was now controlled by Legois, whom Lee Wassey particularly detested. Legois was inclined towards George Thomas. When he learned that the intent behind this military campaign was to destroy George, he strongly voiced his opposition to it. This triggered a wave of rebellion within the army. Legois was friendly with George Thomas. He had tried to reconcile the Begum with him countless times.

On the other hand, Lee Wassey's disdain for Legois was not concealed. He convinced Begum to demote him. She allowed herself to be swayed by his words, forgetting that Legois's valour had helped accomplish countless military campaigns. The army's supervision was now entrusted to a junior officer. Several senior officers tried to make the Begum see the repercussions of this. Heavily influenced by Lee Wassey, she ignored them. This had some obvious impacts; a rebellion stirred in a large swathe of the army.

Frightened by this unexpected turn of events, the Begum postponed her plan to attack Thomas. The soldiers were ordered to retreat to Sardhana. However, the spark of rebellion kept growing in size. The army now refused to obey the Begum's orders. The soldiers who had once been her strength, on whose basis she had demonstrated extraordinary military valour, who had protected her without caring for their own lives had now begun to defy her authority.

CHAPTER 18

Begum's Anxiety and the Lover's Flight... Suicide

IT was quite natural for the Begum to feel anxious and concerned about this sudden change in the army's attitude towards her. The conspiracies in the army's fold, secret meetings and defiance of her and her husband's orders concerned her greatly. The Begum had raised and developed the *jagir* of Sardhana just as how one nurtures a child. However, matters were slipping out of her grasp now. She had understood that it wasn't safe for her to stay in Sardhana any longer. The rebellious army could go to any extent to hurt her and Lee Wassey.

They tried again. The British Resident, Palmer spoke to the Maratha chief. The plan was that the Begum would surrender the position of commander of her army to the Marathas. She would also have to pay a sum of twelve lakhs. In return, the Marathas would ensure that the Begum was able to leave Sardhana safely. To keep Zafaryab away from this conflict, the Begum would have to pay a cess of two thousand rupees for the rest of her life, every month. The Maratha leadership wanted to hold Lee Wassey hostage as a prisoner of war for an extended period. A secure shelter was ensured for the Begum in the French colony of Chandernagore. However, this arrangement proved to be inadequate. If this had not happened, Lee Wassey would have gained complete protection and autonomy in the Hugli region of Bengal because of his French roots. Chandernagore had become a French colony in 1763.

However, in a battle with Nepal in 1794, the British wrested control over it again. The French power established there was toppled in 1816, but it continued to be a French enclave till 1950 when owing to public support the seventeen major population clusters of this region were dissolved after India gained independence. It was governed by Pondicherry's French Governor till then. Had the Begum and her husband decided to seek asylum here, they would have gained the protection and sovereignty thanks to Lee Wassey's ethnic roots.

The rebels installed the late Samru Sahib's first wife's son, Zafaryab on the throne. This task was performed by one of the rebellious battalions of the Begum's army. The helpless Begum could do nothing but watch these incidents unfold. But, the next moment, secret messengers came to inform her that some enraged, rebellious soldiers of the army had anointed Zafaryab as the head of the province of Sardhana. As soon as the Begum learned this, she began preparing to flee with Lee Wassey. On the Begum's orders, he contacted Lieutenant-General Macguvin, the nearest army officer from the East India Company for help. However, Macguvin's train of thought had taken a different route. He was apprehensive that helping the Begum and her husband, who had gotten into a conflict with senior army officers, would give the British a reason for annoyance. Owing to his scepticism, he abstained from replying to Lee Wassey's letter immediately.

When there was no reply for the letter that had been delivered on April 2, the Begum realized the true reason why Macguvin had refused to support them. She reiterated her request for succour from Macguvin. A letter was also sent to Governor-General Sir John Shore. However, by the time the reply to this letter would arrive, Sardhana's condition would have gone from bad to worse. Without any delay, the Begum decided to secretly leave Sardhana forever. Later, a letter arrived from the court of Calcutta, granting her permission to dwell in Calcutta and the peripheral regions. The restless Begum sent another letter to the Governor-General, reminding him that she was in dire need of help.. The reality was that this letter from the courts of Calcutta never reached the Begum.

Meanwhile, a battalion from Begum's army was urging Samru Sahib's son, Zafaryab to take hold of the reins of the throne of Sardhana in place of the Begum. They believed that as General Samru's only legitimate son, he had the sole legal and moral right to the throne.

Zafaryab was reluctant at first. He was aware of his

inadequacies and lack of experience in the intensive fields of politics and diplomacy. He also knew that he would be unable to compete with his step-mother's level of governance. However, after constant persuasion and assurance by the army officers, he agreed to become the ruler of the *jagir* of Sardhana.

Around this time, the news that the Begum had fled with her lover, Lee Wassey had begun to spread throughout Delhi. Zafaryab mustered his courage and commanded a battalion of his army to capture the Begum and her lover and bring them back to Sardhana.

The Begum's secret message system had become very strong by then. Even before she learned that Zafaryab had begun marching to Sardhana with a battalion, she, Lee Wassey and a few loyal workers fled hastily. In the pitch darkness of midnight, the Begum's entourage travelled to the Gangetic region. She wished to reach the region governed by Nawab Asif-Ud-Doulah and seek help from him. The Begum had gathered all the valuables at that time. She had one lakh rupees in cash and jewels worth the same amount. She had left her remaining assets behind. Even so, misfortune refused to leave her side even now. She hadn't even covered a distance of five miles from her province when the rebellious soldiers almost caught onto her tail in the Khirva village. Lee Wassey was riding a horse some distance behind Begum's carriage. He rode close to her and spoke, in a loud and firm voice,

'Do you remember your promise, Begum Sahiba? It would be better for us to commit suicide than be caught at the hands of these incompetent rogues.'

The Begum drew back the curtains of the carriage and gazed into the eyes of her lover-husband. In the darkness of the night, she could see the spark of true love in his eyes; the unconditional love that desires to leave all worldly affairs behind and become one with the soul. Tears welled up in her eyes. She smiled and gave her consent.

'See, if you are not with me, I would prefer death. I have prepared the altar of death beforehand.'

The Begum unveiled a dagger that was tied at her waist. This dagger was not only sufficient to rob the enemy of his life, but also to sacrifice themselves, if necessary.

Lee Wassey sighed in relief and urged the drivers of the cart to speed up. His attempts to do so were futile because the rebels were closing on them.

By this time, it was evident that Lee Wassey's fickle love for the Begum had transformed into everlasting love. He began to believe that the power and status he had acquired were only because of the Begum's actions, and not his capabilities. He wanted the Begum to have faith in the last moments of their life that his love for her was pure. This was the truth. Lee Wassey had had countless opportunities to abandon the Begum amid this crisis. He could have escaped the clutches of the rebels even at this point. However, leaving the Begum in such times would be nothing but absolute cowardliness.

The clatter of the hooves of horses had become

louder now. The rebellious army had almost caught up with the Begum's cart. Suddenly, shrill sounds of despair echoed from the Begum's cart. Lee Wassey rushed to the carriage in the dark in a frenzy. He was stunned to see that Begum was bleeding heavily and was lying in the carriage in agony. It appeared as though she had stabbed herself to escape the clutches of the rebels. The cries and screams of the slave-girls were making the atmosphere even more desolate.

Begum's blood-stained body agonized Lee Wassey. He had no time to think. Still, he prodded the Begum. She was nearly dead. The carriage was filled with a loud mournful wail the very next moment. As per the promise he had made, Lee Wassey positioned his revolver against his temple and shot himself.

He died in the nick of time. The soldiers involved in this event were the true culprits, who had pretended to be his slaves till the previous day and had ceaselessly flattered him. It was as though their dream had come true today. They insulted Lee Wassey's corpse in every possible manner. They rained down kicks and punches and crushed him completely.

Meanwhile, the Begum had tried to kill herself. Perhaps, the Almighty was not pleased with this action of hers. Despite bleeding puddles, the wound inflicted by the dagger wasn't deep enough to rob her of her life. The dagger hadn't struck a crucial part of her body and had instead glided over her ribs. This certainly led to blood loss and even rendered her unconscious. However, she was rescued and revived in time.

When the Begum regained consciousness, she discovered herself in fetters. It was Begum Samru's turn to be insulted by the rebels now. They had robbed the Begum of her money and jewels and were taking her back to Sardhana. Upon reaching, the Begum was taken to the old fort. The period of distress and torture had just begun for her.

She was tied to the mouth of a cannon kept in an open field. She was continuously kept in this state for a week in the scorching weather. Passing crowds would regularly curse and belittle her. She was deprived of food and water also. Begum would have succumbed to these atrocities long ago, had it not been for a nameless maid-servant, who fed her in the darkness of the night and tended to her wounds.

The Begum's incompetent step-son, Zafaryab's desire to usurp the throne was realized only because of sheer luck. He had become the ruler and owner of Sardhana. He was not oblivious to his incompetence. He was unable to conceal his happiness. Overjoyed, he drowned himself in celebrations and parties that he was known for. Deep down, he knew that this wouldn't last long. His situation would remain uncertain until the Britishers recognized him.

Keeping in mind that the Begum had amicable ties with the British, Zafaryab tried to give the impression that the Begum was displeased with the rebellious Lee Wassey's antics, and that he, Zafaryab, had heroically rescued her from the clutches of the rebels in the nick of time. Rumours that the Begum had entrusted the administration of Sardhana to Zafaryab to thank him for his assistance soon spread like wildfire. The reality was completely different. The Begum was being held hostage by the same step-son she had once convinced the Mughal emperor to title 'Zafaryab'.

A six-page letter addressed to the British Commanding officer, Lieutenant Colonel Weyar, from behalf of the Begum said,

> *'Sir,*
>
> *You must have read about my situation in the newspapers, which was caused by a French officer named Lee Wassey, to whom I mistakenly entrusted my jagir's administration. Without consulting me, he began dismissing those officers and soldiers who had supported me through thick and thin for decades. Eventually, the entire battalion began rebelling against him. In the dearth of any other solution, Lee Wassey positioned the barrel of his revolver against his temple and shot himself. In these circumstances, I have decided to entrust the administration of my province to my dearest step-son, Zafaryab. After all, a competent and capable son is the most valuable asset one can possess.'*
>
> *'My son is an intelligent man, who can never be defeated. His capable administration has yielded success. Each task has been performed diligently as per my liking. He has also succeeded*

in mending and strengthening ties with the rulers of those provinces that were previously our enemies. This has further reassured me of his competence. I would be delighted if my son is honoured and awarded a worthy designation.'

The British Administration had suspected that this letter was fake owing to multiple reasons from the very beginning. Their suspicion proved to be true.

CHAPTER 19

Arrest and Acquittal

AT that time, the Begum had only one loyal officer on her side. His name was M. Selure. He initiated several efforts to extract the Begum from this terrifying situation. However, she remained in captivity. Certain privileges that were ordinarily given to prisoners were soon extended to her. This itself was a cause of relief for her.

In the initial days, the Begum was tied to the mouth of a cannon. She was kept in this condition for a week and was even deprived of food and water. Begum felt as though she wouldn't be able to make it out alive. She was kept in the view of the common people, where she was insulted and belittled daily. The Begum would have perhaps died owing to this treatment, had it not been for the sympathy of some workers, and a maid-servant, who secretly fed her. Some army soldiers believed that the mistreatment extended to the Begum was immoral. At least she was alive. She could still try to escape this situation and regain control over her lost provinces and authority.

Months passed away in this tussle. After a lot of contemplation, the Begum realized that contacting George Thomas was her best bet to get out of this situation. She knew that his heart was pure and he had respected her when he was working under her command. The bitterness that had crept into their relationship was directed towards Lee Wassey rather than her. Now that Lee Wassey had been eliminated from the political scenario, there was no harm in mending their ties. She had already sent a message to George Thomas beforehand.

The period of the Begum's capture, which extended from October 1795 to July 1796 was filled with torture, despondency and grief. The Begum's willpower did not shatter even in this hour. The scars that now tainted her physique did not affect her determination. Contrarily, Zafaryab did not make use of that time to strengthen his authority. He was content with maintaining the status quo and immersing himself in the luxuries that came along with authority. Upon the advice of his crafty counsellors, he kept the East India Company in the dark and declared himself the ruler of Sardhana. He wanted to give the impression that the Begum had voluntarily surrendered her claim to the throne in his favour. A few senior British officers were able to discern his malevolent intentions and realized that the letter was a counterfeit.

After much contemplation, the Begum summoned her favourite maid-servant, Nigar. She looked around to ensure that no one was watching them. Then she said,

'Nigar, no one is more important than you today. You are all I have. The people who lived in my house, on my money have averted their gaze and joined hands with the enemy. You are perhaps the only one who understands me.'

Nigar was able to ascertain the emotions then ruling the Begum's heart. Overwhelmed, she said,

'Begum Sahiba, God forbid I lie, they are no different from what they were yesterday. It's just that everyone strives to save himself. I will serve you as long as I am alive and my prayers will only be for your well-being.'

The arrow sailed and hit its mark perfectly. The Begum wished to understand everything first. Nigar's game was either driven by her loyalty or her greed. Had she joined hands with the enemy, she would end up revealing the plan to them. Otherwise, she might have been caught aiding the Begum and would have become the harbinger of trouble. However, Nigar knew a lot of things that the Begum might have wished to make her understand. She had proved her worth by performing the seemingly ordinary task of feeding Begum in captivity.

Begum asked her something important now,

'Tell me- did the messenger reach my George Sahib…?'

Before Begum could speak any further, Nigar leaned towards her to whisper in her ear,

'You have appointed me for this job, Sahiba. Nigar breathes a sigh of relief only once the task has been completed. The messenger has reached your Sahib. Now, just wait and watch.'

Nigar's confidence filled the Begum with boundless joy. She could have kissed her face and granted her any boon that her heart desired. She felt assured that Nigar was still loyal to her.

'Your Sahib, Mr Thomas will be arriving in a couple of days. Believe me: you will soon become the ruler and rightful owner of this province again. The faces of the rebels will be blackened. I know this for sure. Then, these imbeciles, who are wallowing in the lap of luxury will be buried here...'

It appeared as though Nigar had become quite friendly with the Begum. Perhaps that's why she was repeatedly referring to George Thomas as 'your Sahib'. Her eyes were shining with a rare emotion and they seemed to say, 'No need to be secretive with me, Begum'. She was unconditionally loyal to her at a time when even the most trusted courtiers had turned their backs on her.

Although the Begum was relieved to hear this, Nigar's tone and style of speaking disquieted her. However, she was intelligent enough to know when to speak and when to ignore her emotions. The Begum welcomed the maid's news with a gleeful smile.

'Your highness, tell me something...,' Nigar said. Begum's gaze was trained on Nigar's question.

'What did you write in the letter that made George Sahib forget everything and readily agree to restore your province? This decision of his threatens his life as well as position. Everyone knows that had you not decided to attack his province, this army wouldn't have rebelled.'

The Begum was aware that Nigar's position was no longer that of an ordinary servant. It was excessively important for her to become an envoy to decrease the possibility of something unexpected happening. She said, 'Listen, Nigar: I respect George Thomas from the bottom of my heart. The conflict was a result of some of my mistakes, some of his and a lot of ours. You must be knowing how quickly misunderstandings spread and grow. My letter must reach George Thomas. I have sent him a message stating that our enemies might poison and kill me.'

Although Nigar was shrewdly clever, she wasn't intelligent or knowledgeable enough to understand the intricacies of diplomacy and politics. She kept smiling quietly.

To reassure her further, Begum said, 'I even added that the future of the *jagir* is in danger...the wrong sorts of people are eyeing it. Anyway, I do not bear any racial enmity towards him. It's only us who care about the wellbeing of the *jagir*.'

Nigar readily agreed with Begum. She hastily collected the vessels and walked away.

The Begum, in fact, had told Thomas in her letter that she had pinned all her hopes on him. He could understand the situation himself. Even if he had to pay something additionally to the Marathas, he was ready to do so. He would have to help restore the *jagir* of Sardhana to her.

The series of incidents that followed later proved that Begum knew how to comprehend the emotions of other people. She had hit its mark. George Thomas had been oblivious to the atrocities and injustice that the rebels were committing against her in captivity at that time. This was beyond his imagination. Upon reading her letter, he was filled with displeasure and rage. This even aroused some suppressed feelings of affection that lay within his heart. He was determined to extract her from this situation now.

Thomas's heart had melted after learning about the Begum's plight. He was certainly a nice man. His relationship with the Begum had remained quite a pleasant one. A proportion of his success could be credited to her. He devised a plan to help the Begum. The planning was kept a secret to prevent Zafaryab from knowing this and causing any harm to the Begum. He kept aside his animosity towards the Begum and promised Bapu Shinde, the Maratha Governor of this upper region of ravines a sum of rupees one lakh, twenty thousand from the Begum to help make this campaign a success. By engaging in a dialogue with Zafaryab, Thomas tried to elicit some information from him, and after some initial success, he decided to take the next step in this campaign. This entailed marching a battalion and setting up a camp in Khatauli town which was located at a distance of eight kos[4]

4 One *kos* is equal to about 1.8 kms.

from Sardhana in the south-east direction.

Thomas issued a proclamation in Sardhana stating that the Maratha Governor had demanded that the Begum's province of Sardhana be returned to her. Any opposition to this would meet with severe punishment. He also announced that if the Begum was physically or mentally harmed, the Maratha governor would not only clash with the undisciplined army and punish the rebels but also demand monetary retribution for their crimes.

This proclamation brought forth the same results that Thomas had expected. A battalion of the army deposed Zafaryab and held him hostage. Preparations for the coronation of the Begum were commenced. However, Thomas knew that this army couldn't be trusted. It had revealed its true colours by rebelling once; it could do so again. Without wasting time, he set off to Sardhana. In line with his apprehension, a small rebellion had taken place in favour of Zafaryab. They had begun preparations to reinstate the Nawab on the throne.

In such a time, Thomas considered it unnecessary to start afresh. He crossed the border of Sardhana with forty of his trusted cavalrymen. Zafaryab's supporters initially thought that the equestrians were few in numbers and they could be easily defeated and captured. However, he had already arrived with 400 soldiers , in due pomp and splendour. Chaos ensued in Zafaryab's army. He and his army men thought that the entire Maratha empire had encroached on Sardhana. This was not true. These soldiers were part of the ensemble of George Thomas's skilled and trusted warriors. Although the Maratha army did arrive later, the soldiers and the army deployed in Zafaryab's protection dropped all arms and surrendered.

George Thomas hastily located the Begum, who had been kept in captivity till that time. He was saddened at seeing the Begum in such a pitiful condition. As soon he glanced at her, he greeted her,

'Salam, Begum Sahiba. I extend my greetings to the Begum of Sardhana. Hope she will respond too.'

Tears welled up in the Begum's eyes. She said,

'Salaam, George Sahib! I am relieved to see you. I don't know how to thank you. You are like an angel in disguise. Whatever I say will be less than you deserve. The history of this land will remember you forever.'

George Thomas's strategy worked. His army laid siege to Sardhana and other surrounding places. All his soldiers remained on high alert. George himself began unfolding the ropes that had kept the Begum tied up. Tears were flowing down the Begum's cheeks. Her heart swooned with relief at the sight. George was busy completing the task that had earned the Begum's gratitude.

The ropes were freed off at last. George held the Begum's hand. He made her sit on a chair kept nearby. He took his seat on a chair that had just been kept by a servant.

He then respectfully said,

'Your highness, what shall I do next?'

The Begum was speechless. She was surprised by the fact that she had been rescued. She considered this a miracle. She was having trouble believing her senses. But, this was the reality.

'What more can I ask, George Sahib? After the Almighty, you have given me everything. I will be indebted to you for as long as I live. You freed me, saved my jagir and turned my hopelessness into an optimistic dream. I should be serving you. Command me, sir, what can I do for you?'

George Thomas was a soldier at heart and a vassal in mind. He said,

'Begum Sahiba, I am your servant. Servants don't command. Rather, they fulfil commands.'

The Begum was gradually regaining her equanimity. Although this period of captivity had taken a toll on her physical health, her mind was still sharp. She said,

'Don't say that, George Sahib. You are the closest ally of this jagir. In your absence, this jagir would have collapsed. You are my closest friend. You are India's friend. You are first a Nawab and then an army officer. You are even better than I; you know how to rule over the hearts of the people. Everyone loves your capability, kindness and compassion. You reside in every heart that beats in this land.'

George Thomas did not have any delusions about his status. He believed in speaking truthfully and honestly. He said, 'Your highness, despite everything, I am still a foreigner like the Portuguese, French and British warriors. Everyone knows that foreigners only work for themselves… only to secure a livelihood.'

The Begum ordinarily had a better understanding of these matters. However, she was brimming with gratitude that day and was reluctant to waste even a single moment in praising her favourite officer. She said, 'I know and understand everything. I have seen all of them: Mughal emperors, Marathas, Jats, Sikhs, Rohillas and alien adventurers too. You are undoubtedly better than all of them because you are compassionate, loyal and bound by moral and ethical values'.

George smiled quietly. He, like anyone else, liked to be praised. However, he was still loyal to one emotion: self-respect.

'Let's go, George Sahib. Let's leave this dreary, desolate place. Please assist me in laying out the future of my jagir,' Begum said pleadingly.

'Certainly, let's go Begum Sahiba. But, you can lay out the future perfectly by yourself. You are completely safe now. Your authority has been restored. No one can even dream of laying a finger on you. Please permit me; my heart doesn't allow me to stay any longer. I must leave.'

The Begum was rendered speechless. She had pinned all her hopes on George. Sardhana had descended into the bottomless pit of hopelessness that year. The task of bringing the jagir back on track, dealing with the rebels, and remitting the dues were looming overhead. It was also important to teach Zafaryab, a puppet in the hands of the rebels, a lesson. She gathered her strength and said, 'Don't say that for God's sake. Return where? This is your country; this is your land.'

'Certainly, Begum Sahiba. But I must leave. I have to finish some work so that I can head back home with my head held high. I yearn to return to pay my respects to the soil of Ireland where I was born and spend many happy childhood days. I wish to relive those days. Yes, I will devote some more time to this land, which earned me my identity. It taught me to discern the intentions of people and pave new pathways.'

Those emotions coated Thomas's words .

'What are you saying? This jagir is dependent on your support alone. This land is yours. It's no less than your country,' the Begum said, reasoning with him one more time.

'Certainly, Begum Sahiba. I can't deny that. All my success can be credited to this soil. I am not ungrateful. Nor can I forget your goodness. The fate that befell you, or what you did to me were all turns of the wheel of fortune; no one is at fault. But, I am tired of being an army officer. The clatter of the hooves of horses, the dust of the cannons, corpses and bloodshed have become daily affairs. I don't want this life anymore. Somewhere deep within, I am hurt. I don't know how long I will be able to bear the strain of this tumultuous life. That's why I wish to give some time to this land which earned me my identity. Not everyone's dreams are fulfilled; millions of hearts conceal shattered, unfulfilled dreams. There is some unfinished work that I have to deal with. Manage the affairs of your jagir while I finish some tasks that await my attention.'

The Begum felt worried and disappointed by George's utterances. The shock of losing out on his support stung her. She knew that he had been unconditionally loyal to the jagir, even after being inflicted an insult. He was also compassionate and trustworthy. She had never encountered anyone like him before. There was only one thing more that she wanted to ask him.

'What will happen to your army, your officers and your children, George Sahib?'

'The army, soldiers and property were never mine, to begin with. They can be usurped by the enemies in sight at any time. If possible, can I request you to assist me in ensuring the well-being of my children? I would be indebted to you if you could raise them and strengthen their roots after my departure from this noble land. They do not wish to tread on my soil, my land even after persuading…,' George murmured with a heavy heart.

The Begum immediately said, 'Your children are like my own. Let them stay here. They will become princes and princesses. You needn't worry about them. Trust me.'

'I am relieved, Begum Sahiba. I don't even know if I'll ever return. I will forever be indebted to you,' Thomas said firmly.

'Don't say that. I owe you a lot. I will be burdened by gratitude for the rest of my life, George Sahib,' Begum said respectfully.

They discussed some other matters too. Thomas advised Begum about several army personnel and strategy. He also discussed political affairs and brainstormed ideas for public welfare schemes. The Begum had an idea to design a church that would have become the defining feature by which Sardhana would be known in the future.

During the time when Begum was being taken to the mainstream from isolation and reinstated on the throne, a war council was holding a discussion too. At that time, M. Selure was the only officer amongst the thirty European officers taking part in the council, who could make his signature on the official documents. The remaining were either completely illiterate or could write their initials only.

CHAPTER 20

The Begum's Return

THIS incident took place in the year 1796. After spending two months in captivity, Begum became the ruler of Sardhana once again. This was an unimaginable, thrilling and extraordinary experience for her. She was deeply grateful to George Thomas for this. Although Thomas had respectfully declined her offer, he still dreamt of ruling an independent kingdom… province, owning a capital and a fort, of being a sovereign. He wished to accomplish all this through his own efforts. He did not want the Begum's help in that.

The Begum remitted a part of the amount that had been agreed to Maratha chief, Bapu Shinde in return for reinstating her on the throne. She promised to give the remaining amount that had been decided upon. The Begum met the Maratha chief and paid thanks to him for his active help.

The Begum reorganized her army again. M. Selure

was made the new commander-in-chief. He was the only top brass who had not only refused to join the rebellion, but also had tried to persuade his fellow officers to refrain from rebelling.

The scales of fortune had tipped away from Zafaryab now. He was arrested and imprisoned in a wing in the Begum's mansion in Delhi. He succumbed to a fatal illness in 1802 while in captivity. There were rumours that he had been poisoned but no one was able to ascertain the truth. Later on, he was buried beside his father, Reinhardt Sombre in the Roman Catholic cemetery of Agra.

Although the Begum was resentful of Zafaryab's antics, she loved him deeply from inside. She could glimpse the shadow of her late husband Reinhardt Sombre in him. She stood by the side of his real mother in this hour of grief. She went to Delhi to meet Zafaryab's mother and assured her of her support and presence in those difficult times.

She also convinced her to live in Sardhana with her daughter-in-law, Juliana and 12-year old granddaughter, Julia Annie. Julia was a lively, loving and beautiful child. She was able to befriend the Begum quickly. Her arrival acted like a spark in Sardhana. She became a source of joy for the Begum. She was adept in the English language and soon became proficient in horse-riding too.

The Begum noticed that Julia had inherited many traits from Reinhardt Sombre. Her facial expressions and style of speaking mirrored his. The Begum loved Julia dearly and tried to fulfil all her desires. Whenever the

Begum had to go to Delhi for political affairs, she would take Julia along with her.

Thomas remained active in the State of Hansi for a few years after reinstating Begum on the throne. He ruled from the fort here. He sowed the seeds of an entire city and employed people to help them earn a livelihood. He tried to gain an upper hand over the provinces in Rajasthan and Punjab in accordance with his expansionist policies and the orders of the Marathas. He attacked countless provinces by himself and sought compensation for damage. But after a while, when he was surrounded by enemies, he was forced to give away the throne and surrendered the province. He decided to return to his motherland, Ireland. He entrusted his wife, Maria and his children to Begum Samru. She accepted this responsibility with pleasure, as she promised and fulfilled it till the end of her life. She had made some provisions according to which George's wife, children, sons-in-law were to be given a pension after her death.

In the winters, Begum Samru would wrap herself in a green silk European style robe. She would throw on a bright, delicate yellow coloured Kashmiri shawl over it. She looked beautiful and alluring even in old age. Many people wondered why she liked this dress, whose fabric had started fraying with time. Only the ones close to her knew the truth. The dress looked royal and princely from a distance and it had become the Begum's signature outfit.

In correspondence, the wife of a British officer wrote in 1809,

'In contrast to the elaborate customs and rituals that are prevalent amongst the royal women in this country, Begum Samru always dons a bright coloured turban. Her footwear and jewellery are a subject of discussion. But this only happens when the Begum has dressed for an occasion which requires public appearance. She ordinarily prefers simplicity. The turban adds substance to Begum's character. It helps overshadow and draw attention from her petite frame.'

During her lifetime, the Begum's stables were included in the ranks of the best stables in the country. According to Miss Dene's description,

``We have seen exemplary horses in her stables. She has recently built an English style carriage in Calcutta which is pulled by four horses. I had the honour of sitting with the Begum in this carriage. It included moulding of bright yellow and silver paint. Soft purple cushions embedded with silver-coloured starry sequins were laid out in it. The frames of the windows were made out of silver. Its laces and chandeliers were also built out of silver strands. The wheels were blue in colour and complimented the colourful carriage beautifully.'

Considering Begum Samru's diverse interests, it wasn't surprising to view the spectacle of a band under the supervision of a musician, M. Anthony. After Anthony's death, the Begum took the assistance of her ally, Ranjit Singh who was a music lover. He had employed several musicians to pursue and advance music in his kingdom.

Begum Samru's personal life was like a secret book which only a few had access to. This was because of the Begum's tabooed background from which she had scaled new horizons and also because of her personality. Even when her popularity was at its peak, she frequently shied away from excessive publicity. She preferred to stay in her jagir itself. Just like in her husband's times, she continued to maintain distant ties with the Delhi empire, despite the fact that Mughal emperor Shah Alam II was grateful to her and regarded her as his own daughter. In her personal life, there is no evidence of any kind of dialogue with another person of royal lineage.

Although the Begum used to keep herself with her army in the battlefield, she always kept her veil in the court and in other public events. If she had to meet someone, she would present herself through a mesh. All dialogue would be carried out from behind the curtain. However, there was no kind of barrier used while conversing with British or European authorities. Begum was in a way conforming to the saying, 'When in Rome, do what Romans do.'

During her councils, mealtimes or team meetings, educated women from all walks of life would also be present. Her male servants were forbidden to serve at that time. Despite regular interactions with elite Europeans and senior officers, her lifestyle and rituals-traditions remained Indian. When the women departed after the meals, the Begum could be seen gurgling on a hookah. She would begin indulging in sensual pleasures only after all guests had left.

The Begum would usually organize a grand feast during Christmas. A number of British officers from Meerut, Delhi and the peripheral army cantonments would be invited to this three-day-long festival. According to one description,

> *'Marquees were installed in the gardens of the palace. These tents, equipped with all necessities, were used by guests. All their needs and desires were taken care of. There was no item of luxury that wasn't in the guests' reach. They were served the best-imported liquor and delicious cuisine. The Begum would often mingle and interact with her guests on this occasion. But, she never dined with them at mealtimes.'*
>
> *'The Begum's palace was flooded by senior officers and their families. This European style feast witnessed the Begum hosting the wives of the officers. The garlands emitted the fragrance of tuberose flowers and were woven with golden ribbons. As soon as she took her seat, the front gates would begin to open on the beats of the fading music and a group of beautiful girls would steal the hearts of the assembly with their dance.'*
>
> *`Immersing one's emotions, sight and being into*

> *the one-inch long ankle bells worn by these girls, which swayed with the beats, speed and music was not that easy. This spectacle was beautiful to watch. Dance is composed of such rituals and dignities.'*

Praising the Begum's kindness and hospitality, an officer said,

> *'The Begum was not only friendly but also took special care of her female guests. Every time she bade them goodbye, she would give them a shawl woven out of Kashmiri silk, some other apparel made of silk, or jewellery worth 20-30 gram gold coins.'*

CHAPTER 21

A Mysterious Woman

IT is a known fact that the Begum hailed from a lowly background and she had received nothing in inheritance. The fact that she had prospered and ruled a principality for more than half a century was nothing short of miraculous. Her understanding and decision-making skills were better than that of the elite rulers and officers in some matters.

Although Begum Samru was known for the lavish hospitality she extended to her guests, she ordinarily led a very simple life. A significant chunk of her time was devoted to ensuring the well-being of her populace. She was a determined and hard-working woman, who feared nothing. Begum believed in performing all tasks by herself. She would delve deep into the intricacies of any subject, weigh the pros and cons, and then make a decision. She had never taken decisions in a rush. She believed in herself and the justice system. Her intelligence was astonishingly acute. Begum's strength and decision-making skills would amaze even the most qualified statesmen. Many men wondered at her quick responses and decency.

On 19 October 1803, General Lake invited Begum Samru to come to his camp alone, because he wanted to discuss a secret mission with her. The Begum rode to this camp, which was situated twenty-three miles from Bharatpur in the east direction in her carriage. Dinner was being served at that time. Upon receiving the news of her arrival, General Lake personally went to welcome her. In a sudden move, he tightly hugged Begum as soon as she stepped down her carriage and ignoring the amazed stares of the people around them, kissed her full on the lips. This action of his was repulsive and inexcusable. The Begum's security persons were also upset by this. The Begum, a far-sighted woman, decided not to make a big deal out of this and managed the situation as best as she could. She pulled herself away from General Lake and said, in a measured tone, 'Look, how a father's love is unravelling for his daughter today…'

The matter was closed.

A British woman wrote this about Begum Samru in her memoirs,

> *'The Almighty has blessed this lady with extraordinary innate powers whose synchronization with the mind and heart is rarely found, especially in a woman. The local people say that politics and diplomacy run*

> *through the Begum's veins. They are supported by all, befriended by none.'*

A scholar of that time who lived during Begum's reign analysed her character and personality,

> *'First of all, she was a woman. Moreover, she was short. However, her soul was purer than anyone else's in the entire kingdom.'*

The Begum was always conscious of treating everyone respectfully. She was kind to even those who were inferior to her. She would ensure that she got the same respect from all of them. A British Resident once complained to senior British authorities of Delhi when the Begum refused to give him an audience. But the Begum knew that going to his court and presenting herself would be unnecessary and against her self-respect. Owing to that reason, she never met him.

Similarly, a string of misunderstandings unfolded between the Begum and the then ruling Mughal emperor, Akbar Shah, the son of emperor Shah Alam II. He allowed Begum to come to the Delhi darbar on an elephant but demanded that the elephant bow before him like the elephants of other jagirdars. Initially, the Begum went to Delhi twice and accepted this insult quietly. But, later on, she decided to disregard it. Eventually, she stopped visiting Delhi's Red Fort, which had once been her favourite place.

CHAPTER 22

Skilled Commander

IN the 18th century, several adventurers made India their land of choice. Samru Sahib was one of them, who prospered in the background of the strategic power struggle in India. This was the period in history which witnessed the reorganization of several armies. The Mughal empire was being threatened by small principalities. Due to this reason, the Mughal empire had become very fragile. This condition was at its peak from Mughal emperor, Muhammad Shah's death in 1748 to the reign of India's new Governor-General, Lord Wellesley in 1805.

It is neither extraordinary nor surprising that the proficiency in warfare of an unknown foreigner named Reinhardt Sombre enabled him to earn his place in the pages of Indian history. However, the fact that his wife, Samru Begum became the recipient of this courage and grandeur and replaced her husband was certainly extraordinary. This was because the Begum neither had a military background nor could she boast of a royal lineage. It would have been impossible for her to receive training in these matters. She was well-versed with the intricacies of *Mujra* and the graceful renditions of *Kathak* along with the varied genres of music because of her early dwelling in the brothel. People expressed their astonishment over the military successes of this dancing girl, Farzana, a veiled woman now and bowed before her. The Begum had become popular as the commander of Indian and foreign officers, and of ordinary soldiers. She had acquainted herself with the very instincts of her soldiers, officers and the army. She also exercised stringent discipline. The army respected her immensely.

She was a fearless warrior with an unbreakable will. The Begum led her army proficiently; something she had been trained to do in her childhood. Colonel Skinner, who was working in the Maratha army, had watched her lead her army in several wars. He once mentioned,

> *'A beautiful young woman could be seen leading her army on the battlefield and challenging the enemy to attack her. Her fearlessness, military proficiency, courage and uniqueness can surprise anyone.'*
>
> *'However, after brokering a bond with the British government, she was only seen on the battlefield in Bharatpur last time.'*

Major Archer wrote the following about the Begum's role in the British attack on Bharatpur,

> *'This happened in the year 1826. The British*

> *army was some distance away from Bharatpur. The army's commander-in-chief had issued an order stating that the army or commander of any Indian province will not take part in this battle. However, this order disturbed Begum as she had planned to set up her tent in Mathura itself.'*
>
> *'Begum said that she needn't obey the fool's orders. If she did not participate in this war, the entire nation would think that old age had weakened her and had made her a coward. She took part in the battle and fought gallantly.'*

The consolidation of Begum's army was meticulously planned. Her artillery was led by an officer holding the position of a Major. After him, the artillery was supervised by one Captain and three Lieutenants. All these officers were ordinarily European. The Indian officers were deployed for various tasks after them. They consisted of three Subedar-Majors, eleven Subedars and Jamadars.

The soldiers were an equally important part of the army. Forty-two havildars, thirty-nine amildars, and ninety-seven laskars were employed. One artillery unit was composed of 432 soldiers. 172 soldiers in total were kept as reserves.

The cavalry units were consolidated according to certain standardized ratios. Two captains and one Lieutenant led this army. They were both European. In the cavalry army, working Indian officers were employed as risaldar Majors. Four risaldars and four jamadars also served in the army. Apart from this, sixteen policemen and sixteen chiefs were employed. 432 cavalry soldiers of various ranks were also a part of the army. A total of thirteen soldiers were in reserve.

In the troops that served as Begum's bodyguards, one European captain and two lieutenants were always kept alert. The Indian representation in this troop was that of one Subedar Major, four Subedars, and four Jamadars. Other commissioned officers included sixteen Havildars and Amildars. 192 soldiers of different levels and ranks were also on alert in this troop.

The additional officers consisted of quartermasters who were responsible for keeping the ration stores well-stocked. A surgeon or doctor was employed to treat the injured in the wars. This doctor was also mostly European. A Hakira was also employed for the Indian soldiers. A person was employed for pouring water and ensuring a ready supply of water. A messenger was also considered necessary for communication. Along with this, a driver was employed to drive the bullock carts.

Miss Dene, the wife of a British officer, visited Sardhana in 1809-1810. She wrote the following about Begum's army,

> *'A Colonel-Commandment gave us a tour of the army cantonment. The Begum had established this temporary dwelling for her army. Several facilities were provided explicitly for the families of the officers. Tall, muscular Rajputs, who were considered to be skilled warriors, were usually*

> *employed as soldiers in the army. They were also known for smoking poppy and their arrogance and egotistical attitudes were legendary.'*
> *'Their attire, which extended to their legs, was blue. A red turban and an armlet were also a part of their uniform. Their weapons would always gleam dangerously and large cannons would always be kept loaded near the gates of the royal palace.'*

It is said that the Begum was quite concerned about the expenditure of her army. A large part of her province's income was devoted to the maintenance of the army. This was because the Begum credited her prestige and influence to the army. Due to this reason, she considered this expenditure to be worth it.

The strength of the Begum's army would grow and decline with time. The book *Ibaratnama* reports that when the Begum prevented Ghulam Qadir from capturing the Red Fort in 1787, her army consisted of four regiments and 85 cannons.

The Begum was very generous in paying her soldiers their salaries with timely disbursement. She had divided the salaries of the army men at three distinct levels. The first level included general salaries, the salary in the second level was given only during wartime, and the third consisted of allowances which were given only to those soldiers who participated in wars in other principalities. In those days, a colonel was paid a sum of thousand rupees, a captain was given eight hundred rupees, and a lieutenant was paid five hundred rupees every month. A commander was given 162 rupees, a subedar-major 115 rupees, jamadar 48 rupees, and equestrians 55 rupees monthly.

Owing to the restrictions imposed by the British army in 1805, half of the army -three battalions and a part of the artillery were kept on alert according to their wishes. Out of these, 251 people in Meerut, 195 in Muzaffarnagar, and 62 people in Saharanpur were constantly on alert. Around 250 and 265 soldiers were sent to Karnal and Gurugaon. After imposing restrictions, the British authorities began to use the services offered by Begum's army. This was because these soldiers were skilled and highly disciplined.

After the Begum's death, when the British commissioner selected and counted soldiers from her army, the strength of the troops was found to be 4485. At one point in time, the strength had exceeded 6000.

CHAPTER 23

The Begum's Magnanimity and Gratitude

BEGUM Samru was an innately compassionate person. She never disregarded those who had helped her in difficult times. After all, her friendship with Thomas went a long way back. How could she forget him!

Had it not been for George Thomas, neither Begum Samru nor the Principality of Sardhana would have existed as they did that day.

When George Thomas came to free the Begum, one-half of the rebels began quaking in fear upon hearing his name. The other half heaped praise on him and eventually began supporting him. The fact that Thomas's army was much smaller than Zafaryab's magnificent forces and insufficient for such a military initiative was revealed later.

George Thomas remained immersed in his military campaigns till the time he was surrounded and defeated by the joint forces of the Marathas and Sikhs. He wanted to emancipate himself from this military life and return to Ireland. However, he was unable to fulfil his dream of bowing to the land where he had been born and raised. On 22nd August 1802, in Berhampur, Bengal, George Thomas succumbed to a fatal illness. He was merely forty-five years old at the time of his death. Frequent military expeditions, a hectic lifestyle, struggles and conspiracies had aged him. He had left behind the principality of Hansi. Enemies were closing down on Begum Samru and her health was deteriorating. Despite this, she fulfilled her promise by unconditionally supporting Thomas's elder son, John. She officiated his marriage to the daughter of an Armenian officer, Aga Vanoss, with pomp and ceremony. In her will, Begum left forty-four thousand rupees behind for George Thomas's family.

The Begum had realized that tying the knot with Lee Wassey, a French officer in her army, had been her biggest mistake in her personal as well as public life. She vowed to never allow lust or love to become an obstacle in her path again. She stayed true to this vow till her very last breath. She had also realized that the rebellion in the ranks of her army had not been purposeless. The rebels had acted out of respect for their old leader, Sombre and their admiration for George Thomas. The Begum's affair with Lee Wassey had tainted and caused harm to both of these.

The Begum expressed remorse and regret over this incident for a long time. She vowed to be doubly cautious and careful in the future. After this, Begum made extra efforts to remain faithful to the memory of her first husband, Reinhardt Sombre. Till the time she was alive, she abstained from discussing her secret affair with Lee Wassey, which only a few people knew about.

At the time when Samru chose Sardhana as his jagir, the British crown was in the process of establishing its authority in Bengal. They weren't able to expand their influence in northern and southern India. Warren Hastings had barely scraped the surface in disrupting the unity and organization of southern kingdoms, which the British crown speeded up to combat the increasing competition in 1779, when East India Company's presence was insignificant.

Mahadji Shinde was perhaps the only ruler who was whole-heartedly supporting the British. In return, he was getting assistance to train and strengthen his forces. Not only did the number of territories subordinate to him increase, but he also came to be known as the 'kingmaker'. British officers wanted to maintain strong ties with him because he was extremely powerful and could help the crown if the need arose. These amicable relations were maintained during the reign of his successor and adopted son, Daulat Rao Shinde. Lord Cornwallis and John Shore maintained those relations like their predecessors.

The Begum maintained friendly ties with the British. Her friendship with them was out of choice, not due to circumstances or pressure-related. When the need arose, she stood by British officers and British owned principalities. An army officer named Colonel Stuart who was posted in Anupshahr was taken captive by Sikh insurgents. These Sikhs would operate in gangs and would travel on horses. Often, they would illegitimately enter different principalities. They would rob and capture the wealth and residents of different principalities. They had not only slain an enemy from a Rajput principality but had also held Colonel Stuart hostage. This outrageous operation was led by a Sikh leader called Bhanga Singh. He wanted to get the British to agree to some of his conditions in exchange for Stuart's life. Upon hearing about this, Begum initiated a discussion to resolve this conflict. She acted diplomatically and warned the Sikhs to treat the hostage well while delivering a threat to them through her lawyer. Stuart was eventually released in exchange for fifteen thousand rupees. The Begum also took the trouble to personally travel ten miles to bring him to her principality.

This act of kindness and compassion succeeded in influencing Begum Samru's allies and the British. To express their gratitude, the British sent fifteen thousand rupees, some priceless gifts and a letter of thanks for her help. Stuart was so moved by her, that he started considering her as his sister.

Later on, Sir John Shore took the Begum's help to nab certain fugitive soldiers in Kanpur and Fatehgarh. The British were grateful to the Begum for her help. After Hastings became the Governor-General, Britain decided to not interfere in the affairs of the Indian principalities, especially Begum Samru's. The British kept to themselves and abstained from going to war. They supported only those principalities that were subordinate to them. Military expeditions were only launched if there was a threat to the peace and sovereignty of the principalities subject to them.

When Lord Wellesley became the Governor-General of India in 1798, the British crown had established its authority in many principalities. This was owing to their hidden politics.

India's new Governor-General had a monomaniacal obsession with strengthening the empire. He also wanted the small principalities of India to become subservient to him. Later on, he wished to utilise the strength of his alliance with the principalities in India to combat the threat that Napoleon posed to Europe and shatter the latter's dream of becoming the most powerful person in the world. To fulfil these objectives, Hastings had begun the task of integrating Indian principalities with the British empire. This was also done to use their armies to gain access to other resources.

It is said that the discovery of naval routes in the Mediterranean Sea and the Atlantic Ocean by brave sailors like Columbus and Vasco da Gama was, for Europe, like winning a lottery. . These routes allowed Europeans to travel to India, China and America with ease. However, the expedition carried out to these regions wasn't out of benevolence or an intention of preaching a faith. The lecherous gaze of western European powers, who cared little for humanitarianism, were fixated on the natural resources and wealth that these countries possessed. Their greed fuelled their competitiveness. After the Portuguese and the Dutch, the British authorities attempted to amass this wealth. French warriors also demonstrated their skills and valour in the same task.

History has witnessed that the conclusive Battle of Plassey enabled the British to grow their roots on Indian soil. After allying with one jagir that day, and befriending some other Nawab another day, the British managed to make India bow before its flag. The British began the practice of stripping the wealth of royal palaces, which resulted in the revolt of 1857. Deceitfully, or sometimes even unnecessarily, the British would hang men, or tie them to the mouths of cannons and blow them off. By wreaking havoc, the British managed to sustain their rule in India.

The success that the British had wrought in comparison to the Dutch, the Portuguese or the French could be credited to their good fortune and well-planned military strategies. This was a result of the Industrial Revolution, which had begun in Europe. The British were able to overpower other European countries because of their diplomacy and entrepreneurial tactics. The Industrial Revolution was furthered by the decision of English leaders, and members of the middle class to impose restrictions on the king's authority and establish a parliament. In the sixteenth century, the Pope's clerical dominance drastically decreased after the rise of Martin Luther and the establishment of the Protestant faith. The seventeenth century saw the rise of political awareness and vigilance in the middle class.

Increased repression led to the rise of dissonance amongst the middle class, which ultimately led to the beheading the British monarch Charles I. After this, the power wielded by the succeeding monarchs decreased and the middle class thrived. Despite this, the British did not establish democracy because their influence was rapidly growing in other European countries. They desired a puppet government to rule ruthlessly in the countries they had colonized or nations whose rulers they had corresponded with. This strategy sustained authority. During crises, kings were forced to help the puppet governments to save themselves. The British had an uncomplicated policy- irrespective of whether it was a state or a religious authority, all opportunities to extract benefits would be seized. If the colonized state became an obstacle, the government there would be toppled. This policy of the British helped them win over the middle class not only in India but also in several European nations.

CHAPTER 24

Diplomacy

BEGUM Samru witnessed the expansion of the British empire in different regions of the country. These developments had begun to disquiet her. The fact that new principalities were rapidly being conquered and integrated into the British empire troubled her. The British authorities were conducting two separate campaigns to conquer Indian principalities in northern and southern India.

Internal conflicts within the Maratha confederacy were at their peak, leading to chaos and disunity. The Peshwa was involved in conflicts between Shinde, Kolhapur and the women of his family. The Begum's far-sighted vision predicted that a battle between the British and the Marathas was inevitable. She would have no choice but to pick a group. Opposing the East India Company would be suicidal for the principality of Sardhana. They would leave no stone unturned to destroy her land completely. Anyway, the Maratha General, Perron had been hostile towards her as she had maintained a sort of not so friendly attitude towards the Marathas. Perron was in search of an opportunity to pick a fight with and defeat the Begum.

In 1800, the Begum visited Agra to thank Mahadji Shinde for helping her break out of her step-son's captivity. She knew that the actual emperor of Delhi was not Shah Alam, but Mahadji Shinde. Mahadji extended to her the respect she expected. This was a time when both of them needed each other. On 23rd September 1803, Mahadji Shinde broke his waist in a battle with the British, in which the Marathas lost badly. In this battle, the Begum sent five out of her six battalions led by M. Selure to support the Shinde dynasty. In this battle, popularly known as the local Waterloo, British estimates claimed that around 1200 Martha soldiers had been killed. Later estimates suggest that the death toll for the Marathas crossed to about 6000.

In this battle, the Begum's soldiers alone had given a tough competition to the British. Despite losing, they were the only ones who managed to save their lives. The Begum had understood that locking horns with the British was suicidal now. The time to resist the British had passed. Unlike her husband, who had engaged and hidden from the East India Company for a significant chunk of his life, the Begum was a glib diplomat. She was determined to whole-heartedly support the British. The seeds for that were sowed.

To fulfil several aspirations, the Begum had started mingling and siding with the British. In January 1802, the Begum wrote letters to the Governor-General, assuring him of her loyalty and friendship. In August 1802, she wrote another letter to the Governor-General, Lord Wellesley in which she told him that her troops were at the British's disposal. In return, she only asked for protection. This historic letter was a testimony of Begum's conformity and the East India Company's diplomacy. The letter said,

> *From Begum Zeb-Un-Nissa to Lord Wellesley.*
> *Date (on the envelope), 4 Rabi-Us-Sani, 1218 H.= 4th August 1802*
> *Received: 9th September 1802*
> *'Before assuring you of my servitude and expressing my desire to meet you, I wish to say that I have written a letter to honourable Lieutenant-Governor Mister Wellesley in the past also. The purpose of this letter is to discuss the departure of General Colleen from Daulatrao Shinde's residence and General Perron's decision to dismiss Colonel Sutherland from his service. It's possible that this was brought to your attention, or you read about this secret news in the newspapers.*
> *General Perron is aware of the fact that I am a well-wisher of the East India Company administration and certain western officers are hostile towards me. They constantly hatch*

conspiracies and traps to worsen matters that concern me and my province. They wish to influence my army, just as they did with the Maharaja's soldiers. It is certainly true that they haven't achieved success in their attempts to fulfil their political ambitions. To maintain discipline in my army and among other soldiers, I have implemented the same rules as the East India Company. However, after the death of my step-son Zafaryab Khan, I am left with no heir. Keeping in mind the progress India has made under the governance of the Honourable Governor-General, I request the Company to accept and capture my assets, armaments, stores, all my possessions, my well-wishers and allies and their wealth. Whenever you tell me to, or whenever it is required, I will send the necessary documents with my signature to confirm that my wealth is now in the possession of the Company. Apart from this, the honourable Governor-General can ask for my services anytime. It would be my utmost pleasure to fulfil any such demands in the present or the future.

Keeping all this in mind, I have deployed Hakim Mir Mohammad Jafar Sahib, a trusted officer and a resident of the presiding administration in the service of Bareilli's Lieutenant-General. Hakim Sahib will explain everything to his highness. Kindly let me know about any decision

> *that you take regarding my wishes, which uphold my respect, reputation and opinion. If his highness wishes to say anything else, he can contact me through Respected Lieutenant Colonel Henry Wellesley.'*

The British neither accepted nor rejected the Begum's offer.

On 1 February 1804, in a different letter, the Begum tried to strengthen her ties with the British by explicitly allowing them to use a battalion in her army, that was stationed in southern India, in their military campaigns in that region.

The British administration expressed its delight over the proposal but was unable to accept it because it had stalled its military excursions because of diplomacy issues. The deteriorating political conditions of Tipu Sultan, the Nizam of Hyderabad and other rulers in southern India from 1798 to 1800 affected the already hostile relationship between the Marathas and the British. The Marathas used to demand tribute from the southern kingdoms. This was no longer possible because of British dominance. The impact of this was a continuously increased tension.

Finally, on 22 July 1803, Lord Wellesley decided to make use of the Begum's proposal. For this task, he deputed the Commander-In-Chief, Lord Lake. On 7th September 1803, Lord Lake asked the Begum for some military boats, and also asked her to withdraw the battalions which were working for the Shindes so that they could be made available for their use.

Before the Begum could issue orders to implement this, the battle began and the battalions she had already deputed to the Marathas gave the British a good fight.

This was a very tumultuous period in history. During this time, the British captured Delhi. Their influence grew in the peripheral regions also. The Begum secretly proposed that as the representative of the British administration, she would remain the ruler of Sardhana and other regions in the Doab.

Lord Lake asked the Begum to get her friend, and ruler of Lahore, Ranjit Singh to abandon the regions of Saharanpur that he had captured. Although some parts of Saharanpur were under the Begum's jurisdiction, this was a temporary arrangement.

It appeared as though Lord Lake had mapped out the future of the British through the Begum. Wellesley intended to pay the Begum a reasonable monthly allowance and integrate her principality into the British empire. The allowance would be determined by the revenue that the principality procured.

According to Wellesley's policies, the entire region of the Doab should have come under the British. However, this was difficult to achieve under the leadership of General Lake. After doing an in-depth analysis of Begum's power and influence in that region, he proposed to assign the Begum a different principality in exchange for the one under her command. Lord Wellesley approved this.

The conversation went as such-

Wellesley: Do you know which is the best land, with the best people in northern India?
General Lake: Although the entire country is like a gold treasure, the Doab and Punjab are the most fertile. The inhabitants of that region are also very laborious.
Wellesley: You identified correctly. That's why the administration wants all superior things and places to be under its watch and control. What do you think?
General Lake: Yes, your excellency! I agree with you. Let's usurp Begum Samru's jagir first. It's not easy to have a woman govern such a large principality. We can improve her administration. We can strengthen our army and treasury using her.
Wellesley: The idea is good. But, it won't be appropriate to evict Begum just like that. She has a lot of influence in that region. The people idolize her. We must work out a plan carefully. We will have to give her some other principality in exchange and talk to her respectfully. The consequence of not doing so could be a full-fledged rebellion across the country.
Lake: Yes, sir. Has his highness thought of anything to implement this idea?
Wellesley: Yes. There is a plan; you will be informed about it when the time comes. Just behave with caution. It's like putting your hand

in a hornet's nest…

Lake: Yes, sir. Don't worry.

After slaying Shinde's armies, and establishing his influence in northern and southern India, General Lake turned his attention to the other side of the Yamuna river. He wrote a letter to the Begum on 29 October 1803, asking her to present herself immediately.

In the council, he asked her to surrender the Doab region that was under her control to the British empire. In return, she would be given a piece of land on the other side of the Yamuna river, which she could use to establish a sovereign principality. Contrary to the British administration's expectations, the Begum readily agreed to take up this offer because she knew that she could play a major role in assisting the British with this action. To complete the formalities, the Begum was asked to meet Delhi's administrator and military authority, Ochterlony who was in charge of drafting the contract that would officiate the transfer of ownership.

On 12 November, the Begum reached Delhi and met Ochterlony. Just a week after receiving this gift, Begum wrote a letter to Lord Wellesley. In this poignant letter, Begum not only expressed her acceptance of the transfer clause but also raised some important points. She desired that the land being given to her should be joint and it should compensate for the royal palace and buildings she had constructed in Sardhana in three years.

Although the British government had a lot of land under its control across the Yamuna river, it was difficult to take objective decisions because of the frequent rebellions that had arrested this region.

Despite this, Wellesley wrote a letter to the Begum on 23 December 1803 in which he not only reiterated the terms of the offer but also urged her to sign the documentation required to transfer her jagir to the British so that she could receive her newly-assigned land in exchange. It had only been three months since the battle of Assaye, in which the Begum's battalions had given a tough fight to the British, even though the Marathas had lost. The situation had altered drastically since.

Governor-General Wellesley wrote a long letter to the Begum assuring her that the size of the land allotted to her on the left side of the Yamuna river would be equivalent to the size of the land she surrendered to the British and would be qualitatively better. The East India Company promised to provide funds to the Begum in case of any revenue shortage because of a delay in transfer of the ownership of the jagir. The only condition that the British put forth in exchange of the jagir was access to the Begum's army if the need arose.

Although this letter did not appear to be deceiving, the Begum intuitively felt suspicious of the British administration's terms. This was perhaps because the Begum had seen the East India Company conveniently forgetting about their promises. In such a situation, it was difficult for her to rely solely on Lord Wellesley's words and not suspect that he was trying to deceive her and usurp her jagir.

From what the Begum had understood, as soon as she gave up Sardhana, she would be given the new piece of land. However, she was dubious when she saw that no efforts were being made to do so. On 3 February 1804, Begum wrote a letter to British administrator, Ochterlony.

Through this letter, she expressed her disappointment over the British administration's policies regarding the transfer of ownership of a *jagir*.

In a nutshell, the Begum wrote that after leaving her jagir, her property and the love of her people, how would she be able to call another land home? Was it right for the British administration to abandon the jagir, which had always been friendly to it and had always supported it in the time of need in this condition when they couldn't even understand where to take shelter after surrendering their jagir? This was nothing but outrageous injustice.

The Begum was so disappointed with this offer that she wrote-

> *'My brothers,*
>
> *Do you realize that after leaving this jagir, I will have to find a home for my family and those dependent on me? My principality is inhabited by a thousand incapacitated people, many of whom are blind or lame. I will have to find a place for them to live too.*
>
> *Since the time I took up the administration of this jagir, no ruler has dared to speak to me in such a disrespectful manner. I have welcomed*

the British with open arms and have helped them to my fullest capacity each time. Because we are from the same background, I hoped that you would honour my efforts over the last thirty years and the help that I have extended to you. I realize now that the matter is different.'
'If you consider this behaviour friendly, I am willing to receive all kinds of 'respect' from you. If this is happening to me, I wonder about everyone else's condition. Brothers... it would be better if you held my hand and evicted me from my jagir! Neither is this world so naïve nor am I so disabled that I won't be able to live without you. I don't mind spending the last days of my life in anonymity and solitude, in some lonely corner.'

Lieutenant-General Ochterlony felt stunned when he read this letter. Begum's displeasure would complicate the transaction. He began reconciliatory dialogues with her and assured her that the British would resolve her concerns. He further told her that the presiding administration had no desire to harm her and the British administration's enemies were trying to drive a wedge between them and the Begum. He gave the Begum the letter that she had written to the Maratha rebel ruler, Jaswant Rao Holkar, who was the biggest obstacle in the path of the British in those days.

Although the Begum did eventually derive some consolation from Ochterlony's words, her scepticism sustained itself for a long. On the surface, she was satisfied with the meeting she had had with the British and returned to her jagir. However, the seed of doubt that the British administration had planted in her mind simply refused to leave.

She not only wrote a letter to Ochterlony to assure him of her approval of the offer to surrender her jagir but also voiced her outrage concerning the allegation that she had been conspiring against the British with Holkar.

In one half of this letter, she wrote,

> *'I have been accused of secretly writing letters to Jaswant Rao Holkar. You must be knowing this and I can assure you that no one has accused me of being a traitor in the forty years that I have ruled. Since I consider you a friend, I hope that you will investigate and find out who forged the report.*
>
> *I will send you the letters I received from Kabul in the original seal cover. I don't know what is written in them...I don't want another false allegation that I am now conspiring with the ruler of Kabul also.'*

CHAPTER 25

Allegiance

AT that time, the Begum's allegiance to the British was wavering. Senior British officers knew that. It was true that the Begum had close ties with the neighbouring principalities. The ruler of that province, senior courtiers and messengers would frequently visit Sardhana. However, this did not mean that the Begum was secretly conspiring or scheming with them.

It was true that the Begum had sent her troops to the aid of the British when they had been relatively weaker. Scholars claim that if Lord Wellesley had steered clear of unnecessary diplomacy, he wouldn't have had to get involved in several unnecessary battles, which were a complete waste and led to the loss of lives.

The British administration headed by Lord Wellesley regarded the Begum as their well-wisher. Everyone knew that the rumours were baseless. Governor-General Lord Wellesley himself claimed this. But those rumours, coupled with a delay in allocating Begum a new province in exchange for Sardhana, along with the false allegations questioning her loyalty, had planted a seed of doubt in her mind regarding the ulterior motives of the British.

When the English soldiers arrived in Delhi, they saw a camp of soldiers installed there for protection. They initially put on a charade of moving forward hand-in-hand with all the principalities. The Begum was also assured that she would be ruling in Bawni (a district to the south of Hansi). The judiciary, army and ultimate authority would be in her hands; she would be able to rule autonomously. Three months later, however, the British administration changed its tune. In the middle of that year-1804, Holkar allied with Ranjit Singh and the Sikh rulers in the lower half of Punjab. The campaign they ran together proved to be cumbersome and challenging for the British. But because Holkar's army was neither organized nor disciplined for this battle, it lost to the British troops led by David Ochterlony. He had saved Delhi. When General Gerard Lake heard about this, he began withdrawing from Punjab without further ado. He intended to evict Holkar. This battle was fought till the time Holkar had no choice but to flee.

Holkar immediately set off for Sindh. He gifted Maharaja Ranjit Singh priceless goods of gold and silver, thus befriending him. When General Lake heard about this alliance, he officially announced that he was at war not only with Holkar but also with the Sikhs. The enemy was proven weak in this war. The administration desperately needed the Begum's help. This was because the Begum could not trust Holkar and his allies' capabilities. Due to the strategically advantageous geographic position of Sardhana, neither the Sikhs could think of attacking Delhi without her active support, nor could Delhi run a successful campaign in Punjab without taking the Begum into confidence. Maharaja Ranjit Singh of Lahore was regarded as the main enemy of the British in this equation. Despite being illiterate like Shivaji, he was a powerful warrior. However, unlike Shivaji, he wasn't far-sighted, patriotic or daring. The presiding administration had bolstered him and his Sikh allies by persuading them to not pay homage to the Marathas. They had further reassured him by saying that they were there to protect his interests. They were simultaneously deterred with threats of being involved in military struggles of being overthrown. They were also told that they would benefit from joining hands with the British.

The British administration became panicky after it learned about the alliance between Jaswant Rao Holkar and the Sikhs. They were apprehensive that this alliance would bring forth some serious repercussions. They weren't even close to Holkar in terms of military proficiency. The British realized that if Holkar wasn't crushed soon enough, it would become impossible for them to rule India. They did whatever they could-betrayal, conspiracies, gossip, lies and baits, to stop him from allying with other principalities.

Holkar wanted Begum Samru to whole-heartedly

side with him. For this purpose, he sent a special message to her. The conversation that took place from beyond a curtain, with the messenger and Begum went as such-

> *Messenger: Holkar Sahib requests you to join our campaign to chase these foreigners out of our country. We should all work for the well-being of our principalities and country.*
>
> *Begum: Does he need some sort of help from Sardhana?*
>
> *Messenger: Please give his highness the four battalions that you had earlier made available to the Shindes, and openly participate in this joint campaign.*
>
> *Begum: All that is fine. What I want to know is- how will you behave with me during the campaign; what will be my status or role in this?*
>
> *Messenger: You will be treated by his highness just the way you were treated in the courts of Shinde. We must ensure that your honour is upheld.*
>
> *Begum: But I have heard differently…I am also curious to know if you have even thought about the consequences of losing to the British. What will happen to my jagir then?*
>
> *Messenger: This thought is just a fancy. They won't be able to compete with our army's numerical strength, morale, and courage.*
>
> *Begum: I must examine the flip side of the coin too. Today, Delhi, Agra and Aligarh are*

subservient to them. Even the emperor himself is getting his pension from them...the scales of fortune are tipped towards them, and you are misleading yourself.

Messenger: But the government should see how unhappy the principalities are in their rule. All they do is collect taxes. They don't care about the joys and sorrows of the people. Robberies are happening in broad daylight, dacoits are roaming free, and women are being raped. They are blissfully oblivious to everything...even you know that!

Begum: But, is your Sahib any less? You looted and burnt all the places you passed. Despite being a part of this country, you committed such atrocities. Do you remember the Pindariya? They flourished under your rule, didn't they? Weren't these scoundrels, who mercilessly looted villages more barbaric than the presiding government? The Marathas lost the confidence of the people by supporting them. Had it not been for the British, we would have been at the mercy of those cruel Pindariya. Submissively give up your hard-earned money to them- what kind of justice is this?

Messenger: What you are saying may be true. But, everyone should forget these things and move on. You can see how they are rapidly usurping principalities with some of the other excuses. If someone thinks that their jagir will be safe, they are fooling themselves. At least the Marathas were Indian. Even though they robbed people, the wealth kept circulating within the country. The foreigners are going to drain all our resources. They are shipping the stolen wealth across seven seas. The nation is on the brink of destruction. We can empower ourselves by uniting for a common cause.

Begum: You are assessing their loot…? Are you going to tell me now that your highness is even more powerful than the Shindes?

Messenger: Certainly, your honour. His strength has grown because of everyone's support. Your aid will dampen the British's morale.

Begum: Tell me- what will be my relationship with your emperor, Salamat?

Messenger: Everyone is gathering because the scales of fortune are tipped in his favour. There should be at least one guardian. No one is more accountable than him in these tumultuous times. Only those people who are still helplessly imprisoned in the palaces of their fathers and grandfathers can understand his pain.

Begum: Alright. I am with you. However, it would be better if you could bring the courts of Bharatpur, the principalities in Lahore, and the landowners of the hilly regions around. I will make arrangements by then. Four of my

> *battalions will be at Holkar's disposal in time. One more thing—this alliance should remain a secret till the time the date of declaration of war is finalized. Remember that if a Maratha even glances towards my jagir, I will be forced to forget about this friendship.*

The messenger bowed and the Begum bade him goodbye with a gift and the ritualistic departure.

The complication of the situation did not allow this arrangement to come into effect. Later on, the Begum decided to maintain a safe distance from both sides. She appeared to be supporting the British but secretly engaged in dialogue with their enemies. In this manner, she got the best of both worlds. She leaned towards the winning side each time. During this time, Holkar and Ranjit Singh made several attempts to get the Begum to publicly support them. They exaggerated their capabilities and preyed on the weaknesses of the British army. They also added that they were about to receive military aid from the principalities of Jodhpur, Jaipur and Kota. News about Begum Samru's interactions with the enemies reached the British. They were considered very seriously also.

In October 1804, the Sikhs occupied Saharanpur. G. D. Guthari, an honest and sincere collector was taken hostage by the tyrannous Sikh commander Sher Singh. The Begum decided to rescue Guthari. However, this action of hers brought forth unpleasant consequences. Through her influence, the Begum freed the British collector's district from the clutches of the rebels. This action had two benefits- A senior British officer was rescued, and the British administration was convinced of the Begum's loyalty to them.

British authorities were worried that the delay in allotting the Begum a new piece of land in exchange for Sardhana had upset her, which could cause the Begum to not only support the rebels but also actively take part in the campaigns against the government. The Begum was rumoured to have allied with Ranjit Singh, the arch-enemy of the British, who had promised to pay her one lakh monthly and also give her a fort. The truth was that the Begum had no interest in leaving Sardhana because she wanted to prolong negotiations with both sides until the Battle of Deeg concluded. On 24 December 1804, the British succeeded in capturing the fort of Deeg. The Begum softened her attitude towards the British then. However, she refrained from reviving the friendship that she had had with them earlier. She continued her policy of interference rather than support in Lord Lake's work.

When the rebellion in Saharanpur had reached its peak, General Ochterlony requested the Begum for cannons and tanks, important weapons and logistical help. Ochterlony said that this would allow the Begum to prove, once and for all, that she was supportive of the British administration. This would also help in dampening the morale of the rebels and the British government would be able to firmly establish itself. Considering the fragility of the situation, the Begum hastily granted Ochterlony's request. As expected, the British government greatly benefitted from this aid. It was Ochterlony's turn to repay the favour now. He discussed this in the letter he wrote to the Governor-General. Ochterlony also added that to ensure that the Begum remained loyal to the British administration, she would have to be assured that her jagir would remain in her hands for as long as she lived. This wasn't a big trade-off in exchange for retaining control over such a large country.

Despite this correspondence and the seriousness of the delicate situation, the Governor-General was either ignorant of the ground reality or deliberately did not want to resolve this conflict. Ignoring Ochterlony's proposed course of action, the Governor-General issued an order to begin the procedure to free Sardhana from Begum Samru's rule and evict her army from the Doab region as soon as possible. The Begum would be permitted to temporarily live on in her jagir only if some unforeseen situation occurred. The Begum would first have to provide evidence that she had reduced the strength of her army, and had replaced all French officers with British ones.

Scanning through the letter sent by British secretary, N. B. Edmundston to Delhi's former Resident Lieutenant- Colonel Ochterlony on 15 February 1805 helped understand the situation better. He wrote,

> *India's Governor-General Sahib Bahadur is satisfied with the news that he has received from various sources that Begum Samru is working*

on her policy of indecisiveness. This allows Jaswant Rao Holkar to believe that she is with him. In this situation, her hostility towards the British doesn't hold any importance. The public may start believing that Begum is against the British. This will also make it look like the side which is gaining power will demonstrate its influence on her.

Naturally, success will enable Holkar to sustain the autonomy and freedom of his jagir in the doab region. It looks like the Begum was involved in the unrest that is spreading in the doab. Unfortunately, Sahib Bahadur Governor-General Sahib is still oblivious to this. Learning about this will speed up the process of integrating the doab region into the British empire and relieving it from its owner.

Governor-General Sahib Bahadur will not be content with the suggestion that if the Begum's wishes are not obeyed, she can side with the Sikhs and other principalities and emerge as a threat to the British empire. That's why this decision needs to be taken speedily. Before removing her army from the doab region and positioning it here, it is important to do an unbiased evaluation of her political influence.

In the current situation, the Governor-General has no desire to encourage the contract that was signed in 1803 that she would be given an equal part of the banks of the Yamuna river in exchange for her jagir. The circumstances of this time do not permit this course of action. However, Governor Sahib wants the Begum to understand that using her army to maintain peace and stability in the Doab region will make room for the possibility of the reinforcement of the contract. She must also be told that if she commits any acts of betrayal, she will not only lose her claim to her jagir in the Doab but also be deprived of any new jagir by the Yamuna river.

The Begum may hold up the fort till the time the Commander-In-Chief arrives to capture her jagir.

If there is a need for any changes in the contract, the Commander-in-Chief will have the right to process matters according to his intellect. His decisions will be respected. If the Governor-General decides that the Begum should remain in her jagir in the doab region in these tumultuous times, he will ensure that she knows that her jagir will remain with her till she dies. But in this situation, she will have to reduce the strength of her army and replace all French officers with British ones. The Commander-in-Chief will decide if it's wise to reduce the battalions based on the situation at hand.'

The emergency or unprecedented event that has

been mentioned would have only been possible if Lord Lake's military campaign in Bharatpur happened to be unsuccessful or a new rebellion stirred within the Maratha empire. Because the Bharatpur army lost to the British in 1804, the Governor-General's prediction about an emergency was proven wrong. The Begum's jagir was also left untouched.

The British Governor-General Wellesley's rigid attitude towards the Begum harmed the British administration. Their malevolent expansionist policies which involved usurping smaller jagirs not only sowed the seeds of loathing for the Governor-General but also distanced her from the British government. The Begum was quite experienced in such matters. However, it was difficult for even her to believe that the Governor-General would fulfil his promises. It won't be wrong to say that the Begum had no faith in the Governor-General's words.

Had Governor-General Lord Wellesley not been ordered to return, he would have surely gotten his hands on her jagir. It is difficult to tell whether she would have received any other jagir in return. In that case, the history of this Doab region would have been entirely different.

In July 1804, Lord Cornwallis was made the Governor-General of India for the second time. His policies and principles were clear: he believed in resolving matters with dialogue, counsel and alliances. He demonstrated this in his second tenure as well. The Begum turned her attention to the condition of the Doab region and Sardhana.

General Gerard Lake gave him a briefing on the events that had unravelled in the past. This was the same Commander-in-chief under whose leadership the rebellion in Ireland was suppressed in 1798. Thereafter, he was appointed as the Commander-in-chief of British India. Lake defeated Daulat Rao Shinde in Aligarh in 1803 and Yashwant Rao Holkar in Farrukhabad in 1804. He was now irritated by the joint forces of Holkar and the Jats in Bharatpur. The valour and ruthlessness of the Jats frightened him. Lake was a successful propagator of the 'Put your foot down and rule' policy amongst the Indian principalities. That's why he was successful in persuading Bharatpur's king, Ranjeet Singh to support the British rule in India and agree with the conditions put forth by them. Lake's diplomacy had worked wonders in this region. Even he knew how hard it was to get Bharatpur on his side.

Lake also pressured another king named Ranjeet Singh, who ruled in Lahore and had strong ties with the Begum, to remove his army from several regions in Saharanpur. Lake believed that it was necessary to create an atmosphere of trust and peace to ensure that British rule remained strong in northern India. To do this, he wanted to initiate a dialogue with Begum Samru, gain her trust and make her believe that the administration was bound to maintain the sovereignty of Sardhana. In exchange, the Begum would be expected to ensure that the British administration remained stable and strong.

After analysing this situation and the dialogue that

had taken place, Lord Cornwallis realized that to keep the Begum on their side, he would have to allow her to autonomously rule in Sardhana with the present conditions in place. Thereafter, the letter that Lord Cornwallis wrote to Begum on 29 August 1804 is an important document embedded in the pages of history. The letter said-

> *I am pleased to know that after being placed under British control, your attitude towards the British has softened. I would like to personally thank you for deploying your army in rescuing Saharanpur's collector, Mr Guthari with promptness and dedication and welcoming him with kindness and warmth.*
>
> *These circumstances have enabled me to establish amicable close ties with your administration and the subjects living under your rule. I must keep this in mind while staying within the limits of my power and building an atmosphere of peace and satisfaction for you.*
>
> *I have reasons to believe that the Governor-General before me knew that it was difficult for you to part ways with the jagir that has supported you for so long. That's why he decided to not integrate your jagir into the British empire, despite your approval.*
>
> *After carefully examining the situation, I am delighted to tell you that the British administration trusts you completely. I give the*

approval to allow you to keep your jagir, with all its soldiers and officers as before. I also have the authority to expect you to not only maintain a distance from those who destroy the harmony of this nation and plant seeds of doubt but also help us in stopping them from doing this in the areas under the company.

To explain and elaborate on all points I have mentioned in this letter, I have sent Mr Guthari to Sardhana.

According to the conditions put forth by this letter, the area of the Doab region which was a part of the Begum's jagir would remain under her control for as long as she lived. The Begum's army would have to always serve the East India Company. The Begum would have to do all that was expected from a loyal friend. She would also have to abstain from maintaining ties with any principality that went against the company's interests.

It ensured that the Begum's rights or status were not compromised in any way. Her constitutional powers and authorities were upheld just the way they had been in the past.

It was decided that Begum would decrease the strength of her army to half- the size she needed for her safety and revenue. She would have to give up the other half of the army to the British on her expenditure.

The compromise that was agreed upon through Guthari Sahib can be interpreted this way-

The regions of the Doab that belong to Zeb-Un-

> *Nissa Begum will remain with her in the same form as it was before the Company for as long as she lives. It has been decided that Begum's army will be in the service of the East India Company. In every matter, Begum will support the company the way a good friend is expected to. She will also not be permitted to maintain ties with any other power or administration, or any power that is friendly or hostile towards the British, either personally or through an agent or letter. The only alliance that she is allowed to have is with the British East India Company.*

Through this alliance, the Begum was given administrative powers of her jagir. The Begum gave her approval by signing the documents that sealed this contract. Although the Begum became a sort of the sovereign of Sardhana in 1805, this alliance marked the end of her political journey. She remained confined within the borders of her jagir. She had realized the matter and she turned her attention to domestic matters and completely devoted herself to the wellbeing of her people. The Begum's priority was to look after those who were dependent on her for their livelihoods. After Begum's demise, they would end up in a helpless, orphan-like state. It was important to ensure that the Begum's death wouldn't impact the lives of those who had themselves supported her or those whose parents had supported her throughout her life. Seventy villages located at a distance of fourteen miles from the borders of Delhi in the Badshahpur-Jharsa region, the Bhatgaon village in Sonipat pargana, the Bhogipura-Shahganj area in former Akbarabad (modern Agra) and a staggering plantation all were covered under her territory. She had greatly expanded her *jagir*. This was a result of her proficiency and ace management.

Her *jagir* in the Doab region was held in high regard; no one could compete with it. This area was irrigated by the Jamuna and Hindan rivers from one side and the *Krishni* and *Kali* rivers from the other side. The soil of this region was extremely fertile. Owing to this, all kinds of crops-whether cereal, cotton, sugarcane or tobacco- all grew well. The Jats who predominantly inhabited this region were considered to be hardworking and mild-mannered. Their high compliance for paying taxes was admirable.

The Begum did all that she could to improve the lives of those who lived in her jagir. When she took up administration in her hands, the condition of her people was pathetic. People would use the land to trade drugs instead of growing crops. Either this land was losing its fertility or being converted for other purposes and where it had become easier for wild animals to seek a habitat. A subordinate officer working under Lord Auckland happened to shoot a leopard in the jungles in Muzaffarnagar. The inhabitants of the uprooted villages did not have sufficient incomes to pay the taxes. Incidents of robberies and dacoities had become increasingly common. The travellers passing through this region often became victims of the dacoits. People from other lands would steal the relatively prosperous animals of farmers from other territories. All in all, the situation was hardly peaceful. Shah Alam II was the emperor in name only. Even his courtiers seized all opportunities to get involved in conspiracies against him or get their hands on the stolen loot. The farmers were affected the most by poverty.

In this situation, the Begum promptly decided to establish peace and stability in her jagir, and come up with policies to reinforce the well-being of her people. Measures were taken to ensure peace in the region stretching from a part of Muzaffarnagar to Aligarh. The Begum proposed certain policies that would boost agricultural production since farming was the primary source of income for the majority of the population. Harmonious and inclusive administration were some ideals that guided the Begum's policies. Efforts were made to improve irrigation. It was decided that farmers would not be excused from taxes and royal dues during natural calamities. The Begum would personally tour her jagir to understand and solve the problems of the people. She also assisted in constructing wells in the villages. The Begum gave financial aid for the construction of four wells in a village named Kandera. She also built strong roads in Bamnauli. These efforts pleased the people, creating an atmosphere of joy and contentment. The farms in this region were lush green, whereas the farms in the areas under the East India company were still dry and infertile.

The government records of that time state that around 319 people lived in Sardhana, whereas the total population of Meerut itself was only 293. This can be interpreted as evidence of Sardhana's prosperity. The Begum was known for improving the lives of people and ensuring their safety. It is said that even the Mughal empire marvelled at the extraordinary success of her jagir, which was known for its farms that always yielded a good crop. Firstly, all farming resources were funded by the administration, and secondly – there was no threat of any oppressive policy. Because of this, the jagir flourished. Unlike the British who relied on police repression and tax collection, the Begum focused on ensuring the wellbeing of the people.

Philips Antony, also known as Antony Sahib, also played a major role in the Begum's team. He was assigned the task of making the barren, uncultivated lands fertile and structuring the outlines of gardens and parks. The Begum and the populace were pleased with his contribution in making Sardhana a green jagir. Several authorities of the company were irked by the prosperity of Begum's jagir and constantly disparaged her to malign her image. On 1 August 1834, when Frazer, a company agent, complained that the Begum was unable to rule her jagir properly because of old age, the Governor-General at that time reprimanded and ordered him to expel this thought from his mind and abstain from interfering in her jagir.

CHAPTER 26

Art, Architecture, Literature and Music

THE Begum was relieved of major concerns after she had given her written approval to be the sovereign of Sardhana till her death. She now began devoting all her attention to the Catholic Mission. Although the number of Christians had shot up, there was no church in the region for them to worship in. She decided to build a resplendent church, similar to the St. Peter's Basilica in Rome. The Begum proclaimed that once the construction was concluded, the establishment would be counted in the list of the most beautiful architectural wonders in the country. A sum of rupees four lakh was invested in this task.

When this church was completed it served as a unique example of the craft of architecture. It was thrown open to the general public in 1822. It was named Saint Mary Cathedral Church. In 1830, she also built a separate prayer house, which was named after Saint Paul. This church and the Begum's palace were inspired by Italian architecture. The main highlight of this church was an 18-foot tall memorial which pictured Begum Samru in her court. In the painting, the Begum was surrounded by European as well as Indian courtiers. Diwan Rai Singh, a forefather of India's future prime-minister Jawahar Lal Nehru, was also depicted as a courtier.

The name of the Italian artist, who had carved the premium-quality stones i was Adamo Taolini. This handiwork was first transported through the waterway from Italy to Calcutta, and then from the Ganga river route to Calcutta and later Meerut. It was finally loaded on a bullock cart and brought safely to Sardhana. This church had been established for the convenience of Indian Catholics. Later on in 1834, the Begum built a beautiful church in the Meerut Chawni region to allow Catholic soldiers to worship there. The Begum paid the priest, Father Macdonald, who was employed in that church, the sum of a hundred rupees every month.

The Begum was interested in art and architecture too. She viewed these fields and the people involved in them with reverence. The art of photography emerged after the Begum's time, although efforts were being made in several countries, especially France and Germany, to develop this technology. In 1820, an artist from Delhi named Muhammad Azam made several paintings in the palace. These paintings reflected the cultural changes brought about by the East India Company. Some featured fusions of both European and Mughal culture. These paintings were primarily made for the Dutch, the French and the British officers of the East India Company. The Begum was also eager to ensure the preservation of art. Her palace displayed paintings which focused on her life and legacy. One of them depicted Begum Samru amidst Indian and European officers. The central position given to her and the hookah that accompanied her were used by the artist as symbols of grandeur and power. Even more important was the position given to the male officers in this painting. The rolled-out carpet, pillars visible in the background and the colossal doors encrusted with glass shards express a lot.

The Begum had portraits as well as landscape paintings made by renowned artists. Jeewan Ram, a reputed artist of that time made several stunning paintings on the Begum and Sardhana. He was perhaps the only artist who had successfully managed to make realistic as well as hyper-realistic paintings of the Begum and her people. His hands possessed such flair that he could recreate a carbon-copy of any person's eyes, nose and face. His paintings, which kept Sardhana at the centre, were all marvellous. The Begum whole-heartedly praised his art. Apart from the royal palace in Lucknow, these paintings have been preserved today at the Oxford Institute in India.

These paintings not only depict the Begum's legacy, but also portray councils that took place with Lord Combermere, who played a major role in the collapse of Bharatpur in 1826. Dyce Sombre, General Allard,

Sir Charles Metcalf and Colonel Stuart also had their portraits made. This was the same Colonel Stuart who had been kidnapped while in command in Anupshahr in 1790 by the Sikh leader, Bhanga Singh. Begum Samru had intervened later on and had paid a sum of fifteen thousand rupees to free him. The art gallery at the Oxford Institute of India also featured a portrait of Julius Caesar Scotti- the first Bishop of Sardhana. The Begum was known for being a patron of music; music and dance were her primary hobbies.

The first palace built by the Begum in Delhi in a European style, in which she had lived for a long time, was truly extraordinary. It was an excellent example of her power and influence in the nineteenth century. Its construction involved both the principles of European architecture and aspects of Muslim culture. The elaborate feasts, entertainment, gardens and decoration arranged by the Begum in the palace for British, French, other Europeans officers and elites hailing from royal Indian families were often a topic of discussion. No compromise was made in the quality of the church and palace in Sardhana during construction.

People say that the Begum's palaces in Delhi and Sardhana provided different outlooks for men and women. The Begum's views were clear on this subject. Her outlook towards society and women expressed her views.

Begum Samru was constantly making efforts and taking initiatives to preserve literature. Poets were treated respectfully in her court. She was well-acquainted with both Farsi and Urdu. Her pronunciation in those languages was pure and accurate. Her manner of speech would mesmerize guests. The Begum had also drafted some policies to award Farsi and Urdu poets.

Harchand, an Urdu scholar and writer, has been mentioned several times in texts concerning Begum's courts. He had penned several prose compositions and poems in Urdu. He frequently took part in several Urdu poetry gatherings and competitions. Samru Sahib's first wife's elder sister's son also professed a keen interest in poetry. He would write poems under the pen-name of 'Sahab.' While he was certainly incompetent in dealing with politics and administration, he had a flair for the Urdu language. He was well-acquainted with metre and radif which were some techniques used in Urdu poetry. In one of his poem, he referred to Ali and said,

'How can men be expected to understand
the mind of Sahib Ghulam Haider,
when the greatest scholars failed.'

In other words, when the most prodigious scholars failed to grasp the likes of Sahib Ghulam Haider, an ordinary man would naturally fail. Zafaryab was known for being a preserver of poetry. Owing to that reason perhaps, several renowned poets had been composing odes in his honour.

Naseer, the teacher of the famous poet, Zauq wrote a long poem praising him. Begum Samru's royal poet, Farasu wrote several compositions for the Begum. When he wrote during Hindu festivals, he ensured that he included words from the Hindi language. His poems on spring and Indian festivals were very famous. Besides Farsi, he was also acquainted with the Arabic language. His poetry reflected his knowledge about politics and his grasp of the language.

Farasu's poetry often depicted the Begum's valour. Military campaigns, courage, swords, archery, proficiency in arms, camps, beauty, decoration, kindness, justice, empathy, and armies were some topics that were frequently highlighted and discussed in his poems. These poems also prayed for the Begum's happiness and long life. Farasu's poetic take on Mughal emperor Shah Alam's decision to honour Begum with a title was discussed widely. The Begum respected Farasu so much that she included him in her convoy when they ventured out for recreational hunting.

The book Gumbad-e-Gotinuma is a compilation of 250 odes and verses written in the honour and praise of the Begum and Zafaryab. Another compilation named Jam Jamshed Numa has been divided into seven parts. The poems in this provide insights on various subjects. In these seven topics, education of children, youth, message for the elderly, address to love and lovers, Sufism and ways to know the lord and remain close to Him, and some love stories have been included. However, Farasu's scornful commentary and lewd descriptions in some texts have been brought to light. Collections of Hindi couplets and Urdu verses penned by him have also been found. Farasu wrote a long poem chronicling the capture of Bharatpur's fort. In the present, he is included in the list of talented poets in the intermediate stage.

O' heart don't complain so raucously
Do not unveil royal secrets in public
The heart still longs for a kiss
Someone heartlessly clips out my shrubs

Farasu was among the few people who were allotted a monthly pension by Begum. He was entitled to receive two-hundred rupees every month.

Lala Gokul Chand was the Begum's special secretary. He wrote a lot of verses in the Farsi language, highlighting the Begum's personality and achievements. A majority of his compositions praised her. The famous poet, Mirza Rahim Baig was an inhabitant of Sardhana. Besides other compositions, his book, '*Fakr-e-Shoara*' was discussed widely in public spheres. Similarly, Heera Lal, a resident of Kasbe Badaut, located near Farzana was the first and only Hindi poet at that time. He wrote '*Chandraprabha Charit*' in 1825.

John Thomas 'John', Sardhana's Abdullah 'Oj', and Kothana's Ghulam Jameer 'Karam' all became famous under the Begum's rule. Dyce Sombre, the grandson of Reindhart Sombre alias Samru was also talented in Urdu and Persian. Several Urdu memorandums have referenced his poems.

The Begum had a keen interest in taking part in various festivals and in the hustle and bustle of fairs. She made adequate arrangements for Hindu, European and Muslim festivals.

CHAPTER 27

Will, David and Father's Strained Relationship

THE Begum had become old now, but she was not inclined to leave the matters of inheritance of her province to fate; she wanted to resolve this as quickly as possible. In July 1807, she wrote a letter to the presiding Governor-General, Sir. John Barlow and acquainted him with her will. She wanted the British administration to give financial aid to a few of her wards every month. The problem was that John Barlow's term in India was about to end. Due to this, he was unable to arrive at a decision on this matter at that time. He wrote a letter to Lord Minto, the new Governor-General, telling him to take up the Begum's request. He clearly stated that considering the Begum's friendship with the administration and the help that she provided to them, her request was completely reasonable.

Later on, Lord Minto also did not feel that there was anything inappropriate with this request. Acclaiming the Begum's behaviour towards the British, he wrote a letter to her on 4 August 1807, giving his approval of her request.

On 17 December 1831, the Begum registered her will. According to this, David Ochterlony Dyce and Colonel Clemens Brown of the Bengal artillery were made responsible for executing her will. But three years later, the Begum got her will translated from English to Persian, so that she could get it sealed in the presence of the presiding Magistrate of Meerut district, some of her leading army officers, and a few European citizens. As stated in her will, she handed over all her assets to her adopted son, David Ochterlony Dyce, who was given the surname of Sombre as per the rules.

It wasn't as though the Begum loved David alone among all others. She was particularly fond of some of his peers too. Her architect, Major Antonio Reghellini's son was one amongst these children who had been raised in the British fashion. This Italian officer had tied the knot with an Indian woman. The Begum adored their three-year-old son. She had once gifted him clothes embroidered with gold and a hat encrusted with pearls. Unfortunately, however, when Antonio Reghellini got into the Begum's bad books for some reason, her love for his child faded away. Later on, this child is mentioned nowhere in the pages of history.

Apart from David, there was another child who was the focal point of Begum's love and attention. His name was John Thomas. He was the son of one of her most popular officers, George Thomas, who she had wedded with the daughter of one of her local officers. The Begum owed George for freeing her from her stepson's captivity and reinstating her on the throne. Had it not been for George Thomas, the Begum wouldn't have survived. He was deposed from his principality of Hansi by the joint forces of Sikhs and the Marathas and French armies. Next year, he passed away without being able to fulfil his desire to return to Ireland. At that time, the Begum fulfilled her promise by adopting John. In her will, the Begum considered John her adopted son, besides David. The Begum and John Thomas were similar in that they preferred to wear Indian clothes. David, on the other hand, chose British style clothes over Indian ones.

As the children became busier, David's star began to shine brightly. It appeared as though David was eager to grab every opportunity to disparage and trod upon John on special occasions. In his attempts to do so, he would frequently misbehave with his father-in-law, who was an officer in the Begum's army. It is rumoured that once he even tried to trap John's relatives in some lowly conspiracy. This was done to ruin the Begum's impression of John.

The Begum loved David Ochterlony Dyce not only because she saw shades of her late husband in him but also because of some other reasons. Firstly, David was her son in the eyes of the law. Secondly, he was extraordinarily clever and bright. David was born on 18 December 1808. He was the son of Juliana Sombre, wife of Reinhardt Sombre's son from his first marriage with elder sister. He was born in the lap of luxury. The Begum was pleased with the political situation at that time, there was peace and prosperity in the jagir, the people were happy, and her ties with the British had also improved. A sense of stillness and tranquillity had descended upon the jagir's administration and subsequently in the Begum's life. In celebration of his birth, the Begum had announced that taxes would be reduced. The province was abuzz with festivities, music and dance were adding a spark to the region, and the poor and helpless were given gifts.

After officiating the will in 1831, the Begum entrusted the day-to-day administration to David. She made time for herself to immerse herself into spiritual and philanthropic work. The Begum's personality was indeed strange. She was very liberal and encouraging about devotional and charitable initiatives. However, the domestic, as well as state budget, was approved by her. Only after her approval, could any expenses be made, irrespective of how small the expenditure was.

After some time, the Begum began entrusting a greater amount of provincial work to David. Begum's attachment to David excited the jealousy of the eminent people in her jagir, her courtiers, and especially her brothers-in-law. But, it wasn't as though the Begum's love was completely unbridled. As David drew closer to becoming the Begum's successor, she kept reminding him that his life decisions were in her hands, not his. Although, this wasn't particularly threatening and can be interpreted as the height of love. Upon being summoned, it was important for him to arrive immediately, lest he bear the brunt of Begum's wrath. She would routinely test his allegiance and dedication to her and the jagir.

David wrote in his diary that the Begum had once summoned him and threatened him with dire consequences if he ever betrayed her. She would often poison those who had become treacherous. To acquaint him with her power and influence, she once forced a maidservant to drink poison at her orders. The sight of her agony was seared into David's consciousness. The Begum advised him to not trust blindly and be cautious in his conduct so that he could live and rule for long. She told him not even to trust his closest courtiers, relatives, sisters, wives and to take decisions by himself. A clever man is always aware of the conspiracies and poisonous advice being given to him.

The first political incident that left a lasting impression on David was an untimely and uncertain stand-off, where Britain was not only at war with almost every country but had also locked horns with all the principalities in India. When David was just eight years old, the Battle of Gurkha was being fought in Nepal, which was quite close to Sardhana. The Begum believed that the Gurkhas would gain nothing by directly engaging in warfare with the British. She wanted the Gurkhas to retain their strength through diplomacy, to negotiate the retention of sovereignty even after losing the battle.

Meanwhile, Begum Samru's former lord and ally, the Maratha empire was engaged in continuous warfare with her current superior, the British. The frequent conflicts between the two groups climaxed into the Anglo-Maratha war which took place from 1817-19. The soft-hearted eleven-year-old David had witnessed the unnecessary bloodshed brought about by the strife between Indian administrators and the British, leading to the destruction and dissolution of countless smaller principalities. This can be juxtaposed with the war between Britain and Burma from 1824 to 1826, which was concluded not only by bloodshed, but also the British government's triumph in usurping a significant chunk of Burma. The 18-year-old David concluded that Indian soldiers had contributed a great deal to the prestige of the British army.

With his carefree yet intelligent vision, David had watched countless principalities being annexed by the British on some pretext or the other. Young David was saddened by the ridiculous excuses and techniques used by the British to depose permanent and temporary Indian rulers. There was no rule or mandate in favour of this action. In this situation, he was apprehensive about how long Sardhana would be able to maintain its sovereignty and autonomy. The presiding government could alter its policies concerning even stalwart principalities like Sardhana at any time. He did not want to meet the same fate as the other rulers.

This was still a relatively distant possibility. In the strife between Begum Samru and his father, Dyce, David was required to pick a side, and this was an even more pressing issue. Since childhood, David was tied to the Begum through love. Despite such a natural and spontaneous relationship, it was difficult to say that the Begum was happy with him. From time to time, the Begum would test his loyalty to her and keep an eye on his behaviour and activities in public. This continued even during the years of his youth.

In contrast, David's father, Dyce, was keen to ensure that David was attached and spiritually associated with him, rather than with the Begum. In this relation sealed by blood, he did not want anyone else to interfere, irrespective of the possibility that David could become the rightful heir to the throne. Fortunately, David had become wise enough to understand these situations in depth. He would have to create a balance between his blood ties and lawful association, and his allegiance to Catholicism and Protestantism. This was more difficult to achieve than the balance that had once been successfully established in the interests of the Mughals and the British. David wrote about this in detail in his diary. It was up to him to deeply understand the relationship between these opposite forces and their mutually opposite interests. It was equally important to maintain the balance between the two sides with the diplomacy that he was perhaps lacking. It is undoubtedly unreasonable to expect a boy of his age to possess a deep understanding of such matters.

In the passing years, George Dyce frequently reminded the Begum that after her, the jagir of Sardhana would fall into the hands of his family. By 'his family', he was referring to himself and his wife, and after them by their son, David and their daughters. This troubled the Begum as she disliked Dyce. However, the sequence of events that followed weakened Dyce's claim. Dyce's mother-in-law, Aloysius passed away at the age of forty-five in 1815. His wife and David's mother passed away in 1820, at the age of thirty-one. In July 1825, the reluctant Resident Ochterlony, who was the British government's pillar, and Dyce's patron and distant relative was forced to step down from his post in Delhi. Shaken by this, the ailing Ochterlony was housed in the Begum's palace in Meerut and was provided with all necessities and luxuries. However, his condition kept deteriorating, until he passed away. Delhi's new Resident, Baron Metcalf was a veteran in politics and expert in Indian administration because this was his third tenure here. The message he sent to the Begum regarding the uncertain status of Sardhana was ambiguous. He first proclaimed that Dyce's claim was more legitimate, but later whispered, '*Don't let him get his hands on Badshahpur...*'

Dispirited with Metcalf's contradictory suggestions, the Begum began to maintain a respectful distance from him. However, it had become important for her to keep an eye on him. It was difficult to tell what was going on in his mind. Despite this, the altercations between Dyce and the Begum were mounting. Dyce had lately expressed his opposition regarding the appointment of the army's leading officers in the Begum's presence. Dyce was the Colonel-Commander of the royal army, whereas the Begum had managed to become the Commander-in-

Chief with her efforts.

David was educated well. His early education was done at home itself, under the guidance and supervision of scholarly educators. Later on, he joined the Delhi College to seek higher education. David became well-acquainted with the Persian and English languages. He had become an expert in performing his work and in matters of politics. This handsome, dark-coloured man was extremely intelligent. He was not only kind but also had a soft heart. All those who came in contact with him became his followers.

What more could the Begum want? As she drew closer to her end, David's virtues managed to steal her heart away. Gradually, she entrusted almost all the daily administration to David. The Begum's love towards David became the reason for the growing jealousy amongst the elites in the jagir.

On one hand, Begum was worrying about the future of her people and jagir, on the other, she could see that the darkness of the end of her life was slowly descending. She was going through bouts of despondency. The vivacity and action with which Sardhana had been ruled were now putting restraints on the activities of her long public life. Clouds of sadness were looming over her palace also.

David's diary chronicled the four years, in which he became her successor and how she passed away. He described how he had always remained in her frame of vision during this time. Old-age and other problems associated with it began to burden the Begum. She was innately strong-willed; however, this situation had begun to irritate her. This behaviour of hers deeply affected David. Along with this, discussions about her progressing age, administrative prowess and other discussions amidst the other potential successors gave rise to sentiments of jealousy not only in Sardhana but in Delhi, Meerut and other places too. David was ill-prepared to deal with them. To understand and restrain them, it was important for him to gain some experience and dig deep into their personal histories and backgrounds. He would have to behave in a certain way with them.

CHAPTER 28

The End of an Era: Boundless Prosperity and Kindness

THE Begum had immersed herself in the construction of the new palace in Sardhana named 'Dilkusha Kothi'. However, it wasn't in her destiny to spend time in this magnificent palace. As days passed by, the disease's grip tightened on her. David has described these days in his diary. His father-in-law, Solaroli, who was living in Sardhana on Begum's mercy and who David had appointed as the City Magistrate and Revenue Collector with the Begum's approval, wrote the following in his diary 'The foul odour emanating from the Begum's body was sufficiently offending to deter a person from approaching her.'

It can be inferred from David's diary also that he thought that her end was near. He also encouraged her to 'confess' if she wanted to do so. However, the Begum declined the offer every time by saying that she had nothing to confess.

Finally, a high fever trapped Begum in its claws. Since its arrival, the fever had refused to depart, even after proper treatment. After lingering in the lap of the fever, a moment came on 29 January 1836 at 10 pm, when her body became still. Her voice also deserted her. This period was followed by a gentle stillness, as Begum Samru's soul escaped from the earthly confines of her body.

This happened at half-past six in the morning of Wednesday 27 January 1839.

It is rumoured that a fakir named Shakir Shah had predicted Begum's death at this time years ago. This fakir lived in Meerut. One day, he suddenly professed the desire to go to Sardhana. His divine vision had enabled him to see that the aged Begum was seriously ill, and the possibility of her making it out alive was low. When he set out on this journey from Meerut, he was not in a condition to travel with ease. Although the distance between Meerut and Sardhana wasn't particularly long, travelling on foot could prove to be extremely difficult for someone with such a frail body. He passed away even before Begum Samru's death. He sent a written message to the Begum, which said,

"It came for you, but swept me along."

As the fakir breathed his last, he told those around him that Begum's life would end in exactly five years. Saying this, he passed away.

When the Begum heard about this, she built a memorial to honour and remember Shakir Shah. It is said that exactly five years later, Begum Samru breathed her last in the exact place predicted by the fakir.

When the Begum died, she was the owner of an astonishing amount of wealth. This included several palaces and gardens, in which she would frequently stroll. Any person who has seen these palaces could infer that Begum had an extraordinary vision and flair for architecture. The monuments and buildings that had been constructed under her rule are evidence of her knowledge in this field.

All across the globe, especially in Europe and America, the newspapers discussed Begum Samru's life and legacy and analysed various aspects of her life in detail. Clippings on her lifestyle and wealth were published in the news for several days. However, the detailed editorial published by a local newspaper named 'Meerut Observer' outraced all other news. This editorial shed light on the Begum's age, the highlights of the half-century that she had ruled for, her friendship with the British administration, the invaluable inheritance left behind for David, mourning rituals that had been carried out in her court, an atmosphere of mourning, the grief of the maid-servants of the palace from behind the curtains, and preparations for conducting the final rites. The editorials published by other newspapers had sourced their content from the 'Meerut Observer'.

It is interesting to note that not even a single foreign newspaper published that the distinguished administrator was a follower of Catholicism. After this information was published in a Calcutta newspaper, copies of it were sent to Washington and other places, after which this fact was included in the editorials about Begum Samru. These newspapers also discussed the astonishing wealth and assets of the Begum, which had been inherited by David. In this manner, David became popular in Europe and America as the wealthy successor of the Begum.

Although everyone had been waiting for this moment, members of the court of Sardhana were feeling dazzled and overwhelmed. David did not raise any opposition, except for the time when Sir Robert Hamilton, Magistrate and Collector of Meerut seized the gold wands that were a symbol of respect towards the soldiers of Sardhana. Hamilton then firmly, and angrily reminded David that,

> *'I am responsible for taking care of all the matters of concern here. Remember that your status is that of an observer. Understand that I alone will give all orders!'*

David knew that Hamilton was simply following the orders of the senior British officers, and the terms of the contract. Understanding the seriousness of this situation, he even gave up the music box to Hamilton that had been one of the Begum's prized possessions.

The palace in Chandni Chowk in Delhi was famous by the name 'Palace of the bangle-makers.' This area, located right in front of the Red Fort was gifted to the Begum by Mughal emperor Akbar Shah II in 1809 when this place was just a beautiful garden. It was once surrounded by scenic gardens. When Begum undertook the construction work, it was included amongst the initial colonial architecture. This mansion, built in a Gothic style, was decorated with trees bearing fruits and flowers. The lush greenery of this region was enhanced by shady trees, a majority of which was comprised of Lotus conifers. The first floor of the palace was demarcated by colossal, Greek-style pillars, with a front door that was of double-height. One could reach the door by climbing two identical staircases. In virtue of being located opposite the Red Fort, which was the highlight of Chandni Chowk and the stronghold of power, it was easy to infer this palace's strategic and political importance. It can also be viewed as a symbolic representation of Begum Samru's proximity to the administration. The Begum would use this palace to conduct ceremonies in honour of her guests. Akbar Shah himself was sometimes her guest.

After Begum Samru's death, her adopted son, David Sombre, sold this palace to a British bank in Delhi in 1837. A part of this palace was used as the residence of Beresford, a manager in the bank. During the revolt of 1857, there was massive strife between the Indian and British soldiers here. During this time, Beresford and his family were murdered. After taking this palace under their control, the British administration used it to imprison the last Mughal emperor, Bahadur Shah Zafar after accusing him of supporting the rebels. Later on, the administration allowed the Imperial bank and the Lloyd Bank to use this magnificent palace. Even today, the name Lloyd Bank is inscribed in the upper half of this palace.

Presently, a popular market called Bhagirath Mal has been built around that area. The gardens that previously existed have all been demolished. After the British left India, several people tried to buy it. In 1922, Munshi Shiv Narayan bought it. However, the owner of this magnificent palace never stayed in it. Initially, Bhagirath Mal rented out the twenty-five luxurious rooms surrounded by gardens in the outhouse for marriage functions. Later on, he converted the entire area into a centre for professional functions. This region was named Bhagirath Palace Market after Seth Bhagirath. Today it is known for being one of the most popular electronic markets in Northern India. A part of this region is famous for selling medicines and surgical items.

This once beautiful palace is in ruins today. However, its ownership has shifted frequently. Some parts of the palace are being used currently by the country's two main banks The State Bank of India and Central Bank. One of the branches of the bank, located in Chandni Chowk is also called 'Mini Reserve Bank.'

The Begum owned a garden located near Bharatpur and a well-organized residence. According to the royal records, the 1900 Beegh land, which had belonged to Zafaryab, was signed off and made a part of Begum's possessions.

In Agra, Begum owned three gardens and one market.

She had a beautiful garden and a colossal home in Meerut. Begum had frequently lived there, before the construction of the new palace in Sardhana in 1834. This mansion, located in the southern half of the Meerut Palace today and south of the erstwhile Begum Bridge, was called 'Begum Kothi'. This palace served as the headquarters for supervising the consolidation work after Independence in 1947. The district authority stipulated in 1985 that this palace was to be protected and conserved, however later a government division constructed a multi-storeyed building on it.

The Begum built a church nearby, which is known as the Baptist Mission Church today. She also constructed a special prayer house for members of the Presbytery Christian denomination. In 1834, she built a Catholic Church in Meerut for British soldiers and officers. After expanding in 1862, this church is identified as a Cathedral today.

The Begum constructed a beautiful mansion for herself, at a distance of five miles from Sardhana. She visited this palace just to experience a change of air. She also had another magnificent residence in Jalalpur.

The construction of a palace in Sardhana, built in the Anglo-Indian style, had been concluded just a year before Begum's death. An Italian officer named Major Reghellini had been tasked with designing and constructing this palace. This architect also constructed Sardhana's renowned church.

This palace constructed on top of a thirty-foot basement was named 'Dilkash Kothi.' The area occupied by this palace and its adjoining garden was spread over seventy-five acres. It was secured by a boundary wall.

The magnificent and attractive front gate was called 'Sher Gate'. A splendid court hall in this palace was prominently discussed. In the Dilkush Kothi, above the basement, there was a beautiful garden.

Later on, Dyce David Sombre's widowed wife, Lady Forester, had this palace auctioned through her legal counsel. Agra's Archbishop bought it for only fifty thousand rupees. The twenty-five oil paintings in the court had already been bought by the government. At present, two oil paintings, one depicting the Begum's court and the other portraying Begum Samru add to the charm of the royal palace in Lucknow, the capital city of Uttar Pradesh.

The house that had been used earlier for the Begum's personal use was also beautiful. The Begum spent a significant chunk of her life in this mansion, built in the Indian style. It is rumoured that this palace had been existing before the construction of the Begum's residence in Sardhana. However, the Begum had later renovated it according to her liking. The basement, that the Begum lived in to avoid the scorching heat during the summers, is still present today. It is said that after the construction of the Sardhana palace, Begum gifted this mansion to Solaroli, an Italian native, who exercised influence in her court and was David Sombre's brother-in-law.

Some distance away from this palace is the royal graveyard. This was mainly built as a heartfelt tribute to Zafaryab's daughter, Juliana Annie and her adopted son Dyce Sombre's mother. The elite who had played a major role in the Begum's life were later buried here.

The main market of Meerut, known as Begum Pul today, had been a necessity. The Begum had taken the initiative to build it.

The Begum had also established a new city near Meerut, which was named Begumabad. Although the extended region, Modinagar is the property of industrialist Gujarmal Modi and his family, it is an outcome of Begum Samru's planning scheme.

Sardhana's Saint John's school proved to be useful to the Begum's residence for some time. Dyce Sombre decided to run this school to train priests, although later on, the usefulness and impact of the school were heavily debated. It was later converted to an institution to educate the local Christian children. Right in front of this school is the Saint Mary Cathedral and its adjoining campus, a girl's school.

On the right side of Saint Mary Seminary, the Lady Forester hospital has been constructed in an old building, which was the Begum's property. The Begum allocated funds for the construction of this hospital in her will.

There is another building on the other side of the road, in front of the Begum's palace. This was the home of the architect Antony Reghellini. That's why it is also known as Anton House. This building was also purchased by Agra's Archbishop for just four rupees. It is presently used for running a primary school.

To prove her steadfast faith in Christianity, the Begum gifted am amount of Rs 1.5 lakh to the pope, Gregory

XVI on 12 January 1834, so that he could use them for religious work. This sum is worth 13,700 Pounds today.

The next month, on 18 February 1834, the Begum gifted a similar amount to a church in England, which was availed through Kolkata's Begum Samru Trust. One part of this fund was used for the expansion of the church, and the other part was used to help the poor and needy in Kolkata.

The church was instructed to use the interest earned from the money donated to the Trust for its proceedings to ensure the security of the income. Before her death, Begum Samru had established a detailed code of conduct for this trust's functioning and had made her adopted son, Dyce Sombre, the supervisor of this Trust.

The Begum arranged for the upkeep and maintenance of the church in Sardhana after her death with the interest she earned from the Trust funds. A significant chunk of that income was used for the maintenance of the Roman Catholic College in Sardhana. The Begum set aside money for the poor and needy living in Sardhana and the peripheral regions through a fund.

The Begum also made provisions for the upkeep of churches in Agra, Bombay, Calcutta, and Madras in the fund. Although she had devoted a huge part of her property and cash income for the upkeep of churches and other Christian institutions, she also took care of general infrastructure. Till the end of her days, she drafted several policies for the wellbeing of the general public such as ensuring the construction and maintenance of the bridges and roads.

Death is the ultimate truth of life. It surpasses everything else. After succumbing to an ordinary illness, the Begum's final rites were performed after she breathed her last in her bedroom in Sardhana's royal palace. At that time, the Begum was around 85 years old. She had ruled as the Begum of Sardhana for nearly 57 years. Sardhana's Bishop Julius Caesar Skoti remained by her side till the very end. He stayed awake all night at the palace. Finally, he gave the Begum the last massage.

Sardhana was subdued. A veil of mourning had descended all over. At nine-o'clock, her dead body was brought from her bedroom to the main assembly hall. The assembled people paid their respect to their matriarch with moist eyes till eight o'clock in the morning. After this, the Begum was buried following the rituals in Christianity.

This incident is embedded in the pages of history in the following words-

> *'All preparations had been made by nine. A funeral procession led by Christian soldiers and senior Indian officers brought the Begum's body under a canopy. Along with her son, David Sombre and bodyguards, the Bishop and other officials of the church were also paying their last respects to Begum. The local Magistrate, Hamilton and the main officers of the palace followed them. The Infantry and equestrian army were behind.*

> *On this final journey, men riding four horses were distributing cake and other material to the assembled mourners. This entourage, flanked by the soldiers, reached the main gate of the Cathedral. The Begum bid farewell under the leadership of Captain Campbell. The final rites concluded by lowering the Begum's coffin, which was placed in the centre of the Cathedral.'*

In this manner, the act of lowering the Begum's coffin in the earth marked the conclusion of the golden era in Sardhana's history.

'Meerut Observer' published a detailed description of Begum's death and her last rites. This editorial also described the state of those who were dependent on her and her subjects after her death.

> *"Along with the boundary walls of the royal palace, crowds had huddled to pay their respect to their matriarch. The number of mourners' present was rapidly increasing. Not a single corner of the street was empty. Yet, everyone was engrossed in his grief and silence. It appeared as though silence had also decided to drape the white robes of mourning and stand by the mourners..."*

> *'The atmosphere was filled with a shadow of grief, incessant sobbing, mournful cries, and snivels. It was increasingly despondent, and yet languid. Conversations between those who had lost something with the Begum's death cut in at*

> *regular intervals. Ritually, only the relatives of the deceased were supposed to not eat anything. However, no fire was lit in the homes of her dependents and subjects that night."*

It is said that till the last moment the extraordinary Begum lived, her mental strength and agility remained intact. In December 1830, French traveller, Victor Jacquemont wrote the following about her,

> *'She is better, almost like a walking-talking Mummy, who still deals with everything by herself. She listens to two or more of her counselors at the same time and resolves all problems by making appropriate decisions."*

But, after Begum's death all that had become history. Her subjects were unable to discard the beautiful memories of the golden era from their hearts, which Begum Samru had turned into reality. There was no end to the list of welfare schemes and policies implemented by her.. The curtain had fallen while the play was still in progress. Although the protagonist had departed from the play, the stage was still standing upright. The life of Begum Samru, also known as Farzana or Zebunissa, was now confined to the pages of history. Although Sardhana's political condition and progress are marginal to the overall history of the country today, the Begum's soul continues to dwell in the minds and hearts of those who cherish Indian culture. The more we try to understand the Begum, the more we are enamoured by her legacy.

The Begum was buried below an altar on the left side

of the Church, which is marked by an enchanting statue of 'The Mother of Fazlon' today. However, on 24 May 1870, she was dug up and her remains were buried on the left side of the big altar because the coffin that had come from Italy for her was much too big to fit into the spot she had been buried in earlier.

Begum continues to sleep in that same place today. She is remembered every Saturday when the priest prays for her soul. Once a year, a Mass is held to pray for the well-being of her soul.

The conditions might have changed, the era has passed, certain mannerisms and practices have also become extinct. However, history has never encountered another Farzana or Begum Samru. Even after nearly two centuries, Begum Samru continues to dwell not only in the pages of history but also in the hearts of the people. The Begum's heart was just like an ordinary woman's. While it was brimming with emotions, it could become cold and strong when the need arose.

Even though the wheels of fate never halt, women like Begum Samru become milestones in the endless passage of history. She might have drifted off to the land of the dead, however, she lives on in the memories of her historical triumphs.

CHAPTER 29

An Evaluation

BEGUM Samru's life might have been a mystery for most people. However, she has found a place in the hearts of those who live in the environment created during her rule. She was known as the daring Indian woman, who had written a glorious chapter in Indian history.

Begum Samru has a very unusual personality. She did not keep a fixed image of anyone in her mind but adjusted her relationship with people according to the situation at hand with time. One could never predict when and in what way her behaviour towards another person would change. The person who was treated with reverence in the court one day could very well fall out of Begum's favour the next day and could be replaced by another previously inferior person. The local authorities were well-acquainted with this aspect of Begum's personality. However, they did not have any objection concerning this. On the other hand, certain European officers posed a challenge.

The Begum was like a divine goddess for orphans, widows and the homeless. She was a walking-talking epitome of courage and wisdom for her soldiers and her subjects. Many people accuse the Begum of conspiring with the British to protect her jagir, instead of opposing them and throwing them out of the country. These allegations are true to some extent. But, the Begum had her vision. She had understood that the local principalities were fighting a losing battle. The Mughal emperor himself had become extremely weak and powerless. The British army was well-trained and disciplined. The Begum herself was too old and too shrewd to be willing to sacrifice herself on the battlefield. The fact that she had watched a powerful king like Ranjit Singh bow down before the British and accept each of their outrageous conditions heightened her reluctance to oppose them.

Begum Samru's childhood memories had a significant impact on her thought process. As she recalled the financial and social problems that she had faced as a child, her determination to not suffer again became stronger. She possessed an astonishing intelligence, far-sightedness and high emotional quotient. She was an enterprising politician and prudent diplomat. She not only relished power and control but also possessed a deep understanding of the possible consequences of any decision taken by her. She was intelligent, kind and empathetic. The Begum possessed the ability to understand the root causes of the tension that was a direct result of her work. More importantly, she was able to turn adverse situations to her advantage.

A cornucopia of energy nestled within Begum. Whether the task was managing the affairs of the jagir or keeping an eye on the proceedings of the army, or executing policies and resolving matters through dialogue- the Begum would personally dissect the problem till she had reached the root cause and then take appropriate decisions. She was efficient, intelligent and shrewd. Old age did not affect her intelligence adversely.

Unlike some of the other outrageously wealthy people of that time, the Begum kept a tight rein on her expenses. The Begum's expenses were practically negligible compared to the owner or ruler of a jagir. The fact that there were more than fifty lakh rupees in her treasury at the time of her death shows that she managed her jagir extremely well, and unlike other royal families, kept a distance from any extravagant royal expenditure.

After converting to Christianity, the Begum retained her Islamic roots only in her meals. She remained true to her new religion in all other matters. She enjoyed meeting new people and throwing parties in her palaces in Sardhana and Delhi. Whenever the British General, Gerard Lake was in Delhi, he professed a desire to meet her. The Begum would invite selected few guests with their families for dinner. Once the women had left the dinner table, the Begum's *hookah* would begin smouldering. She would smoke the *hookah* till the last spark, till it had completely extinguished. She never left a half-burnt *hookah* in the hall.

In British scholar Thomas Bacon's opinion even though the Begum was very old and short, her body language and grace hinted that she must have been extremely beautiful in her youth. She admired her small hands and feet. Whenever she felt that they would be praised, she would intentionally display them. Her facial expressions and manner of speech were pure and refined. Anyone who happened to speak to her would become an admirer of her. . She seemed to believe that coffee and tobacco would preserve her through old age.

Kanaiyalal Maniklal Munshi, the famous novelist, educationist, activist and politician who served as the Governor of Uttar Pradesh from 1952-57 delivered his opinion about the Begum in the following words,

> *'Begum Samru was the only unconquerable female ruler in that period when most principalities were spiralling downwards. She lived her life intelligently. Moreover, the land was taken care of so that it remained fertile and gave a good yield. Her subjects were as prosperous as any principality permitted at that time. Discussions about her kindness were commonplace. She did what she had made up her mind tor, irrespective of whether it was the establishment of a palace, the construction of a Church or finishing tasks related to public welfare such as building roads or buildings for the public. It was strange to even think about public welfare at that time…'*

The Begum was a true visionary. It was her thinking, according to which special tents were set up outside the palace to meet any visitors. During festivals or any celebrations, she would welcome special guests in the hall of her palace. However, she avoided presenting herself in grandeur and maintained a simple appearance even while greeting guests.

When she used to attend social gatherings, she was elegant. Sometimes, she would be seen travelling on the back of an elephant in her entourage. Sometimes she would also ride a horse, or travel in a palanquin. When she was seated on a horse or elephant, she would take special care of her hat and veil. In informal meetings with British dignitaries, she would crack jokes with the help of her interpreters. They would break into fits of laughter, many times. However, the Begum would always ensure that the boundaries of decency and civil behaviour were maintained.

Talking about the Begum's love life, no one except Lee Wassey could claim to have gotten close to the Begum. Lee Wassey's suicide brought about a radical change in Begum's life, and she immersed herself in a life of modesty and simplicity. Before that, a German army officer, Paulie, followed by a French General, Montogri, and George Thomas tried to confess their feelings to Begum. However, there is no independent source, which could claim that any one of them even got close to doing that.

It is also true that the Begum's luck was poor in matters

of heart and love. The chain of events linking her love affair with Lee Wassey and the disastrous consequences they brought forth provides a unique insight into this aspect of the Begum's personality. . However, certain parts of the life of the Russian Empress, Catherine the Great almost resemble the Begum's life.

It is unfortunate that people overlook the benign emotions of motherly love nestling in the Begum's heart and tend to search for romantic elements in her relationships especially with European officers, but those elements were largely missing. It is certainly true that the Begum deliberately sidelined Reinhardt Sombre's first wife and took her place. However, she had always maintained friendly relations with Reinhardt's family. She saw to it that her husband's first wife and her step son were kept in comfort, even in luxury, even though the latter had supported a rebellion against her and had imprisoned her for nine months. She cared for Zafaryab's wife and children as her own.

Along with her adopted son, David, Begum took good care of both his sisters. This is evident from the fact that the Begum married both of them to senior army officers and provided funds for them after her death in her will. She did this even when David suspected that one of his sisters, Georgina, was not his real sister, and was the daughter of his father's concubine. Whenever there was an argument, she said,

'Why do you people fight? Weren't you born from the womb of the same mother?'

The Begum loved her adopted son, David Sombre so much that she alone took care of him after his birth. It's not been mentioned anywhere that his father ever looked after him. All he did was keep an eye on the Begum's jagir.

Lord Combermere's A.D.C Major Archer had the following opinion about the Begum-

> *'This pause in her long life, and the place she had secured for herself and her jagir amongst other powers in this duration, bears a lot of similarity to our Queen Elizabeth in terms of the respect she earned.'*

The Begum wasn't arrogant and had no desire to remain in the lap of luxury. Had she done something like this, it would have not only become the central focus of all gossip and discussion, but also the shadow cast by a tainted image on her jagir would have made it difficult for her to earn the public's respect and ensure that discipline was maintained.

Begum Samru respected all religions equally. She would always take care of Hindu and Muslim institutions and ensure that their purity and sanctity was maintained. She was extremely compassionate by nature. The sorrows of others would sadden her. In such situations, there would be no limit to her charity and generosity.

On any occasion when female British guests were present, the Begum would not bid them goodbye without giving them a gift. She would never hesitate when giving a Kashmiri shawl, silk garments or jewellery. But, she was against extravagance. That's why she kept an eye on all sources of income and the smallest expenditures. Her style of administration and diplomacy were so nuanced that it seemed as though she was born to be an administrator and diplomat. She would appropriately fit the pieces of her next move in such a manner that the enemy's malevolent and treacherous intentions would be revealed. She possessed a personality and qualities that are rarely found in one person. One of them was knowledge about other people's behaviour since she believed in taking decisions based on reality and practicality. She would conduct her friendships and diplomatic affairs systematically and efficiently. She was able to manage her jagir with proficiency even in situations of distress. All of this is sufficient to understand the extent of her capabilities.

The fact that in her lifetime, the Begum protected Sardhana from conditions of anarchy and maintained law and order is itself admirable considering the circumstances of that time. Unexpectedly, everyone obeyed the rule of her power, entrepreneurship and courage. Because of this reason, she played a leading role in Indian history. She lent a compassionate and concerned ear to her people, and not only maintained a correspondence with other rulers and dignitaries through letters on a routinely basis but also kept an eye on those subordinate to her. Law and order were maintained in the jagir. Any anarchical activity or any person engaged in criminal behaviour was severely punished. Any courtier or authority in her jagir also did not dare to engage in any illicit activities or protect any criminals.

This was the time when the entire country was traversing a period of political and diplomatic instability. During this time, legendary politicians in the political field were trying to fulfil their political aspirations. These included capable Governors such as Richard Colley Wesley, Lord Minto, Charles Cornwallis, George Hilaro Barlow, Lord Hastings, William Pitt Amherst, and William Bentinck as well as popular Residents such as David Ochterlony, Metcalf Martin, and William Fraser. During this time, the Begum encountered army chiefs such as Arthur Wellesley and General Lake who were courageous, skilled as warriors and proficient as politicians. In the history of British India, never had a ruler maintained such close contacts with an assortment of intelligent and skilled officers as the Begum had done.

The Mughal emperor Shah Alam II hadn't awarded the title of 'Dearest Daughter' without any reason. When the powerful Sikh leader, Baghel Singh set up a camp in the vegetable market to capture a big part of Delhi, the entire city trembled with fear. Baghel Singh didn't stop there. He started collecting taxes from those who came there and marched over to the Red Fort with his army. The Mughal emperor's army was very small and weak in comparison. On 11 March 1873, Baghel Singh anointed the leader of the Dal Khalsa, Jassa Singh Ahluwalia as the emperor without any resistance from the Mughals. In this situation, Begum Samru travelled from Sardhana to Delhi, to help negotiate a deal between her sworn brother, Baghel Singh and the Mughal emperor. According to the terms of the negotiation, the administration would be returned to the Mughal emperor. The Sikh leader was assured that Gurudwaras would be constructed in those seven holy spots in Delhi which were associated with Guru Gobind Singh, and the old Gurudwaras in those areas would also be restored. For this task, he was permitted to allocate 35.7% of the collected taxes. This compromise, dispelled the grey clouds of danger that were hovering over the Mughal empire, and preserved the Mughal emperor's authority. The architect of this agreement was Begum Samru.

The places captured by Baghel Singh in Delhi are popular by the names of Malkaganj, Hauz Khas, and Sabzi Mandi today. The Begum also convinced Baghel Singh to send his entire army back, and leave only four thousand soldiers to help ensure Delhi's safety and aid in the task of tax collection.

Mahadji Shinde also always trusted Begum. She lent a lot of help to his son, Daulat Rao Sindhia, however, bitterness managed to creep into their relationship during the time of Ambaji. She also managed to maintain good relations with those who kept their distance from others in the heat of political rivalry. She had managed to lead her political career forward with intelligence, and hard work, and reach the finish line after traversing an uneven and jagged road.

After drafting the contract with the British administration, Begum maintained her friendship with them and kept cordial ties with them. She was always ready to bow and accept defeat in not only important matters but also smaller, more trivial disputes, even when she knew that she was right. She was intent to keep the emotions of amity and cooperation alive. The truth was that the Begum had established ties of friendship with the British with sincerity from the bottom of her heart, while the British were operating cautiously and diplomatically. This is evident from their correspondence with Begum through the post.

Despite establishing ties of friendship and cordiality, the British weighed each of the Begum's demands, even those which had some sentimental value for her, in terms of their benefits and consequences, according to their policies and then took a decision. She wanted Dyce David Sombre to be her successor after her death and asked the British administration to award him a suitable post or title. However, her request wasn't fulfilled because the British government had an expansionist policy, and there was no provision to include a local citizen in the army. One of the key policies of the British administration was to integrate the local principalities into their sphere of influence. In this situation, the Begum was promised the ownership of only her personal property and assets.

Even in this situation, the Begum did not regret her failure. She began devoting a significant portion of her time to community work and spiritual pursuits. If ruling for a long time is considered a measure of success for an administrator, then the Begum was extremely successful in this respect. Excluding the nine-month-long interlude, the Begum ruled Sardhana for 57 years. She earned a spot in the hearts of the people, ensured the safety of the region in which she was ruling, and upheld harmony and progress. In contrast, the public and other principalities kept opposing and revolting against the British in different ways. They might have claimed otherwise, but the truth was that the general public disliked them. They would always be prepared to launch another wave of rebellion against the administration. In contrast, the Begum's subjects were content with her rule and remained busy with their daily chores and livelihoods.

There is no mention of any instance where the Begum might have tortured or punished a farmer for not paying taxes on time. She kept the principles of humanitarianism and empathy in mind when she ruled. The Begum believed that if she opposed British policies when they were flourishing and scaling new heights in India, her fate would be similar to that of the other smaller principalities and jagirs. Along with her jagir, the subjects of her principality would also suffer. Her decision to join hands with the British can be considered an act of betrayal. However, the consequences of challenging the British army would include unnecessary bloodshed and the British occupation of Sardhana. This would have kick-started the era of unimaginable harassment and exploitation. This would have also destroyed the agriculture, industry and businesses set up in this region, and detrimentally impacted the condition of the people and stability and peace in the jagir.

When David took up the administration of Sardhana, he overlooked the Begum's policies on tax collection and adopted the British style of coercion. He had been given a British style education and like them, he believed in the superiority of his policies over others'.

However, it is unlikely that David was capable of introducing changes in the system without seeking the Begum's approval. David had written about these reforms and the Begum's approval of them is recorded in his diary. The Begum was probably pressured to do this by the British administration.

Till that time, the Begum had always collected taxes keeping in mind the circumstances of that time and the convenience of her people. However, the British system of tax collection that had been implemented was exploitative. Now the taxes were worth Rs 6,91,388, which was a significant increase in comparison to the taxes collected before. In 1833, David wrote in his diary that the revenue earned from taxes collected that year was ten lakh rupees. But later on, there was a cataclysmic famine in India. There was also an increase in communal tensions at that time. A major portion of agriculture was in the hands of Jat farmers. The better farmers amongst the entrepreneurial Jats gradually displaced the natives of Tagaon. Now there were five well-established Jat families for every one Taga family. In this manner, 3700 Tagas lived here against the 17,000 Jats. These two tribes had always borne enmity against each other. Diwan Harbans Singh who was responsible for assessing the tax revenue and was also the head of the collecting team and Magistrate of the subdivision of Barnawa was himself a Taga. Displeased with his partial treatment and casteist outlook, the Jats brutally murdered him in 1825. His son, Rao Singh who became the Diwan later also operated on the principle of vengeance, even though the Begum did not have any such policies. The region in which the land of the 27 farmers was located went out of the Begum's jurisdiction.

The British administration should have been happy now that the Begum was implementing their rules and policies with strictness. However, this did not happen. They got the opportunity they had been waiting for since long. While the Begum was registering a gift deed for her adopted son, David, in 1834, the local authorities were busy filing complaints of discrepancies and illicit things which were allegedly taking place in the Begum's jagir, in the court of the Governor-General. Allegations of engaging in corruption and bribery were heaped upon the honest and sincere tax collector in the Begum's jagir. They also said that old-age had rendered the Begum incompetent and that she could die soon. They additionally claimed that her successor wasn't qualified or experienced enough to manage the jagir. They opined that the British government should take over the Begum's *jagir* and run the administration of it before the situation got worse. However, the Governor-General took a firm decision in Begum's favour.

The authorities still tried their luck against the Begum. In 1834, Delhi's resident, William Fraser wrote a letter to the Governor-General, urging him to issue the orders. The letter said,

> *'Because of physical weakness and old-age, the Begum's life span is becoming even more uncertain with every passing day. In these circumstances, when the life of such an old person is constantly at risk, what will be the government's role.'*

This letter further dwelt on what the course of action would be after Begum's demise. The Governor-General's reply to this was crystal clear,

> *'In such a situation you will have to immediately begin the process to officiate the transfer of the jagir and ensure that no person other than the authorized officials can collect taxes.'*

Sir John Elliot had surveyed Begum's *jagir* in his youth and had been greatly influenced by her multi-talented persona, style of ruling, decency etc. After her death, he had these words regarding her,

> *'There is a lot of debate and discussion about the Begum's character amongst the people, but she was undeniably and undisputedly an enterprising and brave woman. She should be respected for protecting emperor Shah Alam II so many times and for the various initiatives that she undertook. If she is found guilty for some crimes that haven't yet been discovered, then we should remember that countless rulers have been accused of committing grave crimes*

in the same set of circumstances.'

Despite all this, the Begum's personality continued to evoke the same level of astonishment and wonder that it did then, if not more. It wasn't easy for a woman to establish her sovereignty over Sardhana's *jagir*, take control of all the property, wealth and the army, after the demise of her husband, Reinhardt Sombre in 1778. That too when the son of her husband's first wife emerged as the legal and natural heir to the throne. Even later, Begum Samru, was always cautious of any challenge to her sovereignty. Zafaryab managed to depose and imprisoned her for a brief interlude. However, he wasn't as intelligent, brave or skilled a diplomat. Because of this reason, his regime did not last long and came to be known only after death.

Despite the strong and amicable ties that the Begum had with the senior authorities of the British administration, the British public had a general dislike for her. For them, a number of anecdotes about the Begum were a subject of gossip. They claimed that she had earned her unfathomable wealth by exploiting the poor. However, the real reason for this enmity is the Begum's unshakable faith in Catholicism. Interestingly, those who were associated with the Roman Catholic church also disliked the Begum because she had congenial relations with Protestants.

The Begum's habit of suspecting everyone, always being cautious and not trusting anyone can be understood from her inborn and imbibed perspective.

CHAPTER 30

Conflicts between David and his Father

THE Begum had made David the owner of a significant portion of her property, wealth and assets. She had also kept a sum of two lakh rupees in cash for him. However, the Begum had specified in her will that David would remain under the guardianship of a legal counsel, and he would be able to use this wealth only after he crossed the age of 30 years. Till this time, he would have to live off the interest he earned. The authority to invest David's inherited wealth would remain with a counsel named Colonel Brown for these years.

On 18 December 1831, David turned twenty-three. Two days before this, on 16 December, the Begum had signed on the Persian and English will of this inheritance. The Begum had earmarked half a crore rupees to be invested under government securities for David a long time before her death. That wealth amounted to a sum of 47,88,600 in coins. Along with this all of Begum's expensive gold and pearl, gem-encrusted jewellery, jewels, expensive furniture at home, all apparel, even priceless horses, elephants, and every other thing that hadn't been mentioned separately became David Sombre's property. Besides Sardhana, the expensive lands, gardens, and all other invaluable assets in Delhi, Agra, Bharatpur, Meerut and many other places, had all been left to David Sombre.

As under the terms of the will, David could never dare to claim ownership of either any money or property from the Begum while she was alive, he knew that the Begum could change her will if she wanted to, anytime as per her mind. She lived for four years more after drafting her will, during which time, David remained fully obedient to her.

The only part of the Begum's assets that David could not get his hands on was the Badshahpur-Jharsa region and the regions of Bhogipura-Shahganj in Agra which was captured by the British along with stores of weapons after the Begum's demise. David had opposed this. Although he did not register any official claims in writing, except for the representations that he wrote to Queen Victoria after he was refused.

The Begum had built a splendid palace in Badshahpur-Jharsa. This construction, which is still standing tall and proud today, remained the camp office of the National Capital Region of Gurugram district. Gurugram was a cantonment in this region in the nineteenth century, but the far-sighted Begum had realized the strategic importance of Gurugram even at that time. At that time this region was located between Jharsa and Gurgaon villages.

As the strife between Dyce and the Begum grew, the Begum understood how important the British administration's support was. After 1825, Stapleton Cotton Viscount Combermere, the leader of the cavalry wing in the battle fought against Napoleon was the only one amongst the British officers who had better acquaintance with the Begum and Dyce, who was made an important British officer. He must have been around fifty years in age at the time, although he was still physically fit and agile. The Begum knew that the British army was going through a rough patch, and desperately needed Indian friends, although they did not wish to show that they were dependent on their allied principalities.

In the first Anglo-Burmese war from 1824 to 1826, the initial failures of that pillar of British influence and power, the army, had begun to waver. This defeat gave rise to an open revolt when the Indian wing of the Bengal army refused to take part in the Battle of Burma. This is known as the 'Barrackpore Mutiny.'

To restore obedience for the presiding administration, this commander-in-chief led the Regiments of the East India Company and succeeded in capturing that part of the fort in Bharatpur that belonged to the Jat principality of Rajasthan, a fort they had always failed to take in the past two decades. Despite not having received an invitation from the British, the Begum arrived with her well-trained army to fight in the war alongside them. At that time, the British did not want to take the assistance of any local principality in that military campaign. They intended to make the people understand that the British were powerful and capable enough of ruling over them without local assistance. However, the Begum insisted on taking part in this campaign, lest people assume that old age had turned her into a coward.

This touched Combermere so deeply that he not only agreed to include her in this campaign but also maintained very friendly relations with her later. Whenever he stayed in India, the Begum would organize royal parties and feasts in his honour. Combermere was also moved by the respect the Begum extended to him. While leaving, he invited the Begum and David to London to accept his hospitality. The Begum also secured the promise from him that David would be looked after once she died. She wanted to see David as a commissioned officer in the British Royal Army. Years after Combermere had left India, the Begum continued to maintain a correspondence with him. They would periodically send each other gifts and pictures of their family members. In 1835, Combermere sent a rare statue of Christ in a prominent pose. He would frequently send invitations to David, urging him to come to England so that he could return the favour of the hospitality that had been extended to him by them.

Bharatpur principality's defeat to the British led to mounting tension and conflicts between the Begum and

Dyce. It is said that Dyce had siphoned off a significant chunk of the priceless wealth that belonged to the Bharatpur lineage of the Begum[5]. This gave the Begum the perfectly logical opportunity to begin proceedings against him. She dismissed Dyce and banished him from her *jagir.* The British government too approved this course of action. Along with him, she also dismissed those soldiers who had been supporting him or protesting in his favour. The Begum was kind to an extent, where she agreed to give Dyce three thousand rupees in cash and give his two daughters a hundred rupees as pension every month. However, this would only be done if Dyce agreed to legally give up his guardianship of David to the Begum. Despite this, Dyce's string of conspiracies and subterfuges knew no end. He not only declined to accept the Begum's terms and conditions of his dismissal and the financial help that she was extending to him after he had been exiled; he was also currying favour with the British Resident Metcalf to garner support from the British.

The Begum began behaving in a cold and unyielding manner with Dyce. She decided to not allow even his shadow to fall on the soil of Sardhana. Matters worsened to such an extent that The Begum told the British administration that she would rather give up her power than forgive Dyce. She preferred to hand her *jagir* over

5 Her husband was bestowed with a jagir by the then Bharatpur ruler, where Reindhart Sombre served.

to the British. The Begum had to admit that it wasn't a bad deal for him to spend the rest of his days on pension. Exactly thirty years previously, the Begum had given a similar offer to a British ruler when her secret marriage with a French officer, Lee Wassey had stirred a rebellion in the army. She then wanted to run away and permanently live in the French colony of Chandernagore. However, that plan had been foiled and the Begum had been taken captive after the rebellion in her army.

It was Begum's luck that Metcalf was forced to rule in her favour after being pressured by some senior British officers. Anyway, Dyce was at fault. The Begum did not reiterate or reinforce the threat she had made of surrendering her *jagir* out of rage, and Metcalf did not bring it up. He knew that sooner or later, after the Begum's demise, the British would gain complete control over the principality of Sardhana. In this situation, it was wiser to just wait for this to happen. It is, however, an entirely different thing that this wait achieved its purpose ten years later. The Begum passed away in 1836, before which she continued to handle the principality of Sardhana with full authority.

Dyce, who had been adversely affected by all this, kept roaming around Sardhana. He managed to capture the Begum's palace in Meerut through deceit. However, the Begum was miles ahead of him in the games of power and politics. She even talked about forgetting everything that had happened in the past and turning over a new leaf and even invited Dyce to Sardhana. As soon as Dyce approached

Sardhana, a battalion of Begum's army hastily took the palace in Meerut back under control. Dyce was left venting his frustration over this dramatically foiled plan.

During this time, Dyce made another desperate, but reckless attempt. When the seventeen-year-old David opened his eyes on the morning of 7 August 1827, he heard the sound of his father's footsteps. In this successful incident which had been executed in a theatrical manner which included a conspiracy against the Begum, his father had involved those old and loyal officers, who for some reason had been displeased with the Begum. They had imprisoned the Begum's loyal and sincere officers at this time. Dyce then urged the British to support him. However, in contrast, Colonel Clements Brown, a senior British officer of the Meerut Cantonment supported the Begum. He warned Dyce to restore the state of things and surrender himself to the mercy of the British administration. As soon as this information became public, the so-called rebellion turned into a fiasco.

The Begum was very grateful to Colonel Brown for this. This was the same Clements Brown that Begum not only made her confidant but also made the joint guardian of all her wealth. Four years later, David described the difficult time he was facing as a result of being caught up in the conflicts between his vengeance-hungry father and the Begum. In this period, he had neither the trust of his father nor the Begum who had been like a mother to him. Despite this, it was certain that David blamed his father more than the Begum for these complicated and strange occurrences and conflicts. Owing to this reason, he referred to Dyce as 'the old gentleman', 'the old rogue' or 'a particular person' instead of using more respectful words for him.

Even after being exiled twice, David's reckless father, Alexander George Dyce, could be found lurking in the British occupied regions near the Begum's *jagir*. Whenever he was arrested or deported, he blamed the Begum and said that she must have had something to do with it. He filed a number of court cases against the Begum, demanding his arrears of the salary and compensation. He even made his son a defendant based on the inheritance of Begum's *jagir*. He didn't stop there. Dyce secretly began filling the minds of his three children with ill-feelings and loathing towards Begum to get them to turn against her. He would separately try to overwhelm and disorient David and his daughters, Georgina and Ann Mary by talking about how much he loved them.

In this situation, the British administration had to step in to ensure that David's sisters were able to live the life they wanted. Assistant Resident Charles Trevelyan was given the task of talking to the two girls and understanding where they would prefer to live. Although both covered their faces with veils, they had to remove their veils for identity verification. Georgina was white like her father, whereas Ann had a dusky shade like her elder brother, David.

Trevelyan wrote the following about this interaction,

'After some persuasion and deliberation, both

sisters agreed to remove their veils. However, a barbed divide was still placed before them. After looking at them and interacting with them, it appears that they are very similar to their father, George Dyce and brother, David. According to the responses they made, it can be interpreted that the girls were raised under Begum Samru's care, who had played the role of their mother. Because of this reason, they would prefer to go to Sardhana instead of any other place.'

The British Resident ordered that this must be done as per Trevelyan's recommendations.

After being entrusted with the care of the two sisters, the Begum began looking for suitable grooms for them. For the twenty-three-year-old Georgina who was the elder one, Begum selected a thirty-five-year-old Italian Catholic, Peter Paul Mary Solaroli. He had joined the Begum's court sometime back.

For the nineteen-year-old Ann who was the younger of the two sisters, Begum chose a twenty-eight-year-old Scout Officer. He was a lieutenant in the East India Company at that time and was deputed in Calcutta. There was a widower named John Roz Troop. Upon receiving an invitation from the Begum, he resigned from his job and began preparing to leave for Sardhana. He performed the wedding rites in both Catholic and Protestant styles there.

Ann Mary wrote the following about the process of choosing suitable grooms for the two sisters and the wedding rituals,

> *'Before our weddings, the Begum had kept both of us in seclusion. When British guests visited, we were often around. I had gotten a fleeting glimpse of Captain Troop from a distance but there was no interaction between us before the marriage. My sister was treated similarly.'*

Both sisters got married off on the auspicious day of 3 August 1831. The situation that their husbands were in was also different. Solaroli had made his place in Begum's administrative circle. He became a rival to David's growth and status. Although the Begum had supported Troop financially, he wasn't particularly important in the court of Sardhana. Later on, also, Solaroli's children inherited a lot of wealth from Begum, whereas Troop died childless.

Although the Begum was gradually spiralling down the hole of old-age, her physical, as well as mental abilities, were still intact. She was welcoming old-age with reluctance and was maintaining a firm grip over the administration. After marrying off David's sisters in 1831, the Begum wanted to complete her will.

On 28 December 1831, David turned thirty. Two days before that, Begum had signed the will in both Persian and English languages. David was made the co-executor of the will and he was given the ownership of every bit of property that had belonged to the Begum before her death. This included the Begum's property in Sardhana, Badshahpur, Delhi, Agra and Meerut. David was also made the Colonel-Commander in the same way as his father George Alexander Dyce who had received the same honour thirty years previously. The Begum urged David to attach the surname of Sombre to his name. The other executor of this will, Colonel Clements Brown was given seventy-thousand rupees. The Begum had made Major Edward Barry and another British officer along with her priest, Bishop Julius Caesar, the witnesses of her will. The will was made public by then.

This strengthened David's position as the will was a coherent and authorized government document which made him in-charge of the affairs of Sardhana and sanctioned his status as the Begum's heir. Instead of dividing her *jagir* between David, his sisters, and other charges, the Begum decided to give her entire property to David alone. As an example, Ann May-Troop was given fifty thousand rupees and Georgina-Solaroli was given eighty thousand rupees. Nothing was kept for their husbands in the will.

CHAPTER 31

Au Revoir Begum Samru: Who Next?

THOUGH she had specifically declared David as her legitimate heir, after the Begum's demise, rumours began circulating about who would inherit the jagir. However, those close to her and the British administrators knew that the Begum had signed an agreement with the British, years ago, in 1805. According to this, the whole of Sardhana was to be annexed by the British. The majority of her assets were to go to the British. She had no objection to this, provided that the administration agree about the pensions to the handicapped and ailing people of her principality, and a part to be given to her adopted son. The Begum wanted nothing more than that.

Upon getting the news of Begum's demise, Mr Hamilton, the collector of Meerut proceeded to Sardhana immediately. The armies of the East India Company prepared themselves to get hold of Sardhana and Badshahpur. Upon arriving, they seized all the weapons from Sardhana's army and arsenals. In the presence of the Commissioner, Hamilton read out this agreement and the Begum's will to the assembled dignitaries. The Begum's assets, which were estimated to be around half a crore at that time, were distributed according to the final terms of the will. Although according to this agreement, the Begum's wealth was to go to the British government, the administration had permitted her to retain her personal wealth.

In her will, Begum had allotted twenty thousand rupees for her doctor and assistant, Dr Thomas Trevor. She had also directed that the son, daughter Johanna and the wife of her brave warrior, George Thomas' should get eighteen thousand rupees and seven thousand rupees respectively. Commander Anthony Reghellini was to get nine thousand rupees for his services, his wife Victoria was to get eleven thousand and his five children were to get five thousand rupees each. Abdul Hassan, a commander in the Begum's army, was to get two thousand rupees. A Trust was also made for David's two sisters, Georgina and Ann May. A sum of one lakh thirty thousand rupees was kept in this trust. Begum directed that the two sisters should be given the interest that the trust would yield.

The Begum's will also had a provision for those who were supposed to get pensionary benefits after her death. In all, 805 people in this list were given different pensions between five rupees to eight hundred rupees per month. This group included fifty ordinary loved ones, twenty-seven disabled Christians, sixty nine Christian widows, three hundred and eighty-five locals, two hundred local widows, and eighty four people belonging to other religions.

In this pensionary directive, George Thomas's son, John Thomas was given three hundred rupees per month. Anthony Reghellini was also given a pension apart from his salary. Dyce David Sombre's two brothers-in-law, Paul Solaroli and John Roe Troop were given a pension of eight hundred and fifty rupees every month, which was equivalent to their salaries. Minister Harakaran Das was murdered during the Begum's reign when he had gone to Bamauli near the hamlet of Baraut for revenue collection. Begum gave her approval to giving his son, Bishop Julius Caesar a pension of four hundred rupees that was equivalent to his salary.

The disabled population included Hindus, Christians and Muslims. They also included those who did not live in the Begum's *jagir*. According to the directives of the will, some residents of Delhi, Bareilly, Raebareli, Rohtak, Bassi, Kanauj, Lucknow, and Benares were also entitled to pensionary benefits.

In this, the Begum's successor, David Ochterlony Dyce Sombre was given a major portion of Begum's principality. He was the great-grandchild of David Walter Reinhardt Samru. He was the son of the daughter of Zafaryab, who had been anointed as the king of Sardhana by the rebels. He succumbed to cholera in 1799. Before his betrayal and revolt, the Begum had married him to Julia, the beautiful daughter of one of Begum's favourite army officers. They had two children together. The son died young and was buried in a graveyard in Agra. The other child was a daughter named Juliana, who was born on 19 November 1789. The Begum married her to an English colonel in 1806. Their son, who was born on 28 December 1808 was named David. He was the one who was later adopted by the Begum. He was the great-grandson of David Walter Reinhardt Samru, who Begum loved dearly.

There was perhaps something missing in these moments of mourning, for David's father, George Dyce appeared out of nowhere and began demanding his share of the Begum's inheritance. David even appealed to Hamilton to give him one lakh rupees in cash and twenty-five thousand rupees per month for the rest of his life. However, the stubborn and reckless George adamantly declined this offer. Hamilton then issued firm orders that ousted him from Sardhana and put an end to this chapter.

The time had come for the Begum's prayers and final rites. As soon as this was concluded, David had to appeal to Hamilton again. He had three main points- First, handing over the Begum's arsenal, which the British had unnecessarily seized and was part of the Begum's assets and therefore part of her inheritance. Secondly, the promise to give a pension to the eight-hundred people who were dependent on Begum and for which a a directive had been given by the British, but remained unfulfilled. The third was about the property of Badshahpur-Jharsa. According to Dyce, the agreement of 1805, had no provision for

Badshahpur to remain under British control since it was located outside the Doab region.

Lieutenant Governor Sir Charles Metcalf summarily dismissed these objections raised by David. Since Sardhana fell under the jurisdiction of Agra, Metcalf was authorized to decide concerning this issue. Concerning Badshahpur, Metcalf wrote the following report about what he believed was a failure on the Begum's part to record the event,

> *'This was a mistake that could be attributed to overlooking, a simple human fault. However, this might have been done 'deliberately' by the Begum to take advantage of our carelessness. I have reasons to believe that from our side, this couldn't have been done deliberately.'*

For this reason, it was considered legal and valid for the British to capture Badshahpur in the eyes of the law. David's appeals were drowned underneath piles of government documents. There was another thing to take note of. The soldiers of Sardhana's dismantled army had been let off without getting the salaries that were promised to them. Hamilton heaped the blame on David for getting his inheritance and not giving the soldiers their salaries. Concerning the eight hundred dependents of Begum who were supposed to be given pensions, Hamilton said that their legal claim to pensionary benefits were not authenticated by the British government's records. Therefore, the pension wasn't to be given. Later on, David decided to give those people a pensionary benefit himself.

It was clear that despite maintaining good ties with the British, they did not respect the word they had given to the Begum as was expected. After the Begum's death, the British used the terms of the contract for their benefit and tried to get their hands on her properties and deprive her adopted son, David of his legal inheritance. Neither history nor the British respected the wishes of the Begum in the matter of inheritance and legacy.

Unfortunately, Begum Samru's reign was not appreciated either by the British elite or by the ordinary Indian public. Baseless and offensive stories were circulated about her, doing her no justice. There was a lot of misogyny too. Nobody could stand the idea of a woman who had risen from the dust to occupy the pinnacle of glory in the political and administrative firmament of the pre-colonial era. She was not given the respect that she deserved.

There are still countless questions regarding the Begum's inheritance. It is less surprising that we do not have any proper evidence of Begum Samru and her husband, Reinhardt Sombre, birth and family. The East India Company also neglected to keep Begum's official writing safely. What was the fate of the written records that David's father George Dyce had?

People have tried to locate Reinhardt's descendants to discover the legal treasure that belonged to Sardhana, which was to be their rightful inheritance. However, things haven't moved forward on that front either.

CHAPTER 32

David's Journey to England and his Demise

AS soon as he turned thirty, David became the sole owner of the Begum's gigantic personal wealth. No one had legal guardianship over him now, and nor was there any responsible advisor who could advise him on the prudent management of this jagir. Despite owning this wealth, David was usually despondent and sad. David was restless and was attracted to the glamour of Western culture and the enchanting anecdotes and incidents that made him dream.

David indeed was an Indian and he was educated here. However, his father was Dutch and it was natural for him to feel an irresistible inclination towards his forefathers. Four years after the Begum's death, he went to England. He entrusted the management of the remaining part of the *jagir* to his brother in law, Paul Solaroli. This was also the last time David met his father. When his father, Colonel Dyce, who always got entangled in conflicts with the Begum, died in April 1838, David was in the middle of his sea voyage to England.

Before David embarked on his journey to England, he first toured several different principalities in India, especially Lucknow as well as British East India Company's headquarter Calcutta. He also toured China. He reached England in June 1838. From there, he fulfilled his desire to go to Rome. He wanted to honour the Begum on her third death anniversary on 27 January 1839 with great pomp and splendour in Rome. He chose the magnificent Carlo church in Corso, Italy for this. The event was conducted with great pomp and ceremony. He also built a beautiful memorial in Begum's memory and sent it to Sardhana so that it could be installed in the church there. It is the primary memorial in the church today.

The people in England were drawn to David. They came to know about this youth with clever and fearless views. On 26 December 1840, David married Mary Annie Jarvis, the daughter of Edward Jarvis. It is said that Annie was an excellent singer, dancer and composer. She was known for being the assistant of the Duke of Wellington. Although Wellington was primarily an army officer, he was also an Anglo-Irish politician. He gained popularity after defeating Napoleon Bonaparte in 1815. At that time, Napoleon had been wresting control over an entire half of the world. David Sombre was interested in local politics and soon became a public favourite. Owing to this, in 1841, he was elected to parliament from Sudbury.

It was expected that all this would have made David happier. However, his marriage resulted in mounting problems and ultimately contributed to his ruin. David's wife did not appreciate his company, and David complained about her character. Another issue that had begun to drive a wedge between them was the religion of the unborn child. They did not bear a child, and later on, Annie accused him of being deranged. To make things worse, David ran a public smear campaign against his wife's character. After revealing the marital dispute, matters worsened to such an extent that they barely talked to each other. During this time, the court case filed against David by the candidate who had lost to him in the elections turned out to be unfavourable for David. He was disqualified and ultimately lost everything.

In retrospect, this was only the beginning. One morning when David Sombre opened his eyes, he discovered that he was in captivity. Three guards were standing outside his bedroom. He had to spend four months under house arrest. On 31 July 1843, a commission came to check on him and discovered that he was mentally unstable. His health kept deteriorating. Subsequently, he was admitted to a hospital in Liverpool, where he passed away one morning of July 1, 1851.

He had tried to prove that he was healthy by getting reports from doctors in England, Paris, St. Petersburg, and Brussels. However, he could never shake off the label of a mentally ill person. The sun had dawned upon his political career also. No one was standing by his side. The owner of one of the most magnificent assets in the world was compelled to move from court to court in London and Paris as he sought justice. This prince who had been raised with love and care was living off the alms he had received from the government and a few of his friends.

Then, he published a 582-page long text which contained reports written by famous and renowned psychologists to prove that he was healthy. He also talked about his wife's bad character. Unfortunately, despite the evidence, the courts did not take him seriously.

The lonely and helpless David had passed away in the Phantom Hotel on St. James Street. After his demise, he left the Sombre lineage in anonymity. In his will, David had directed that his *jagir*, which would be worth billions in today's time, be used to build a school and not be given to his wife. Despite this, the court overlooked his last wishes because Annie had objected against his will. She claimed that David had been in a deranged condition when he had notified his will, owing to which no part of his will was to be taken into account. In this way, his widow, who he loathed from the bottom of his heart, became the legal owner of the personal *jagir* that had been lovingly given to him by the Begum. After winning the court case in 1856 to acquire the jagir, Annie was counted amongst the few wealthy women in Britain.

After his death, David was buried in Britain in an unmarked grave. In 1867, David's remains were brought to Sardhana, where he was buried in the Begum's royal graveyard. However, people continued to eye the grave with suspicion.

Annie was a clever woman. She married George Cecil Weld, who was also known as Baron Forester on 8 November 1862. Her husband was a former army officer and an active member of the Conservative Party. He travelled to India and started engaging in the upkeep and maintenance of Sardhana. He stocked items of luxury there. Annie came to be known as 'Lady Forester.' However, misfortune had latched itself onto her also. From this marriage too, Annie was unable to bear children. This final link, which was disputably linked to the Sombre lineage, was lost in the deep trough of history forever when she died on 7 October 1893.

A renowned Indian historian wrote the following about Begum Samru-

> *'In Indian history, it is not uncommon to see ordinary people rising from the dust and scaling pinnacles of power. However, it is doubtful that anyone even comes close to the Begum's personality and accomplishments. An extremely poor, orphaned girl's journey to becoming a sovereign ruler and her prowess in retaining her position amidst the political chaos of that time is in itself miraculous.'*
>
> *'This was an incident that had perpetrated the myths and accreditations of that time. She hailed from a background (as a woman) where she would have to surpass all barriers and obstacles as a brave man would be expected to do. In this sphere, the Begum not only maintained friendly*

> *and cooperative relations but also played a significant role in the political struggles of that era.'*

Even today, thousands of descendants of Reinhardt Sombre are fighting court cases to claim the property in Sardhana. However, the British insist that the property was legally under British jurisdiction and it was impossible to dismiss this. The Begum and the British had a discussion about this only three decades before the Begum's death. It is important to note that David Sombre wasn't the original legal successor of Begum Samru and Reinhardt Sombre. This meant that according to the Doctrine of Lapse, Sardhana was to come under East India Company's jurisdiction to this rule which was valid till 1858.

> *'Any property, principality, or kingdom whose ruler is either incompetent or has died without a male heir will be brought under British rule and will lose the status of an autonomous entity.'*

This was nothing but an expansionist policy using which the British usurped countless principalities and kingdoms. The principality of Sardhana was one amongst them. At least the British had allowed the Begum to keep her personal property to herself and pass it on to her heir. Despite that, the British carried out her will as per their convenience and, contrary to what they had agreed in the past, they brought her personal property under their control also. Later on, the disputes over David's condition and his wife's opinion on the matter, made it easier for the British to capture the principality. Countless principalities such as Satara, Jaitpur, Sambalpur, Nagpur and Jhansi were captured deceitfully in the same manner.

In line with its habit of deceiving others, the British administration did not give the agreement formulated in 1805 with Begum the respect it deserved. Apprehending this, the Begum had already displaced the property for David to claim. Had he been intelligent, he would not have had to face so many difficulties.

However, one cannot seek advice from the land of the dead. After all, a few moments are enough to wipe out ten years of glory and prestige.

CHAPTER 33

Sardhana Later

THE revolt of 1857 began in the Meerut cantonment, near Sardhana. In this situation, it was impossible for Sardhana to escape being dragged into the fire of this conflict, which had engulfed almost all the northern part of the country. The local people who were prey to the high handedness of the British, wholeheartedly supported the uprising and contributed all that was possible against the British. The peripheral villages also rose in revolt. Several British officers were murdered.

In this situation, a resident of Sardhana, a former Afghan commander-in-chief, Syed Mohammad Khan, also known as John Fisher Khan began supporting the British with his companions. He had a history of supporting the British in a conflict between the Afghans and the British, known as the Anglo-Afghan war fought between 1839 and 1842 and which was unsuccessful.

The British administration happily made him their

associate and rewarded Syed Mohammad Khan's betrayal by anointing him the Nawab of Sardhana. He was given the principality that had once been under Begum Samru's rule, and which had been usurped by the British following the agreement in 1836. Although most of the property was not occupied by any of his heirs, he was designated as the Nawab of Sardhana.

The story behind this Nawab of Sardhana was that after the failure of the Kabul Mission, British rebels had retreated. Then, the local ruler had punished Syed Mohammad Khan by dismissing him. After that, he, along with his family, had fled from Kabul and had settled in Sardhana. In the revolt of 1857, the head of the family, John Fisher Khan, got the opportunity and wasted no time in supporting the British. He raised an impromptu cavalry unit with the help of his relatives, companions and friends. Leading his men into battle, he marched towards Hindon with General Wilson. After that campaign, he offered his services and marched to Delhi and stayed there till Delhi had been freed from the influence of the rebels. Everyone knows that he whole-heartedly supported the British in this campaign.

In these circumstances, pleased with the services rendered by Syed Mohammad Khan, also known as John Fisher Khan, the British administration honoured him with the title of Nawab *of Sardhana* and entrusted him with the *jagir* which had once been the place of shelter of this Afghan runaway. He had many successors, out of which Syed Ali Shah and Syed Ahmad Khan remained prominent. The last Nawab of this lineage was Syed Amjad Ali Shah. Several other descendants of his such as Syed Sardar Iqbal Ali Shah, Syed Idrees Shah and Syed Tahir Shah were also heirs to the throne without being designated by the royal title Nawab.

Timeline

1751: Farzana's birth, Village Kotana (erstwhile District Meerut, Uttar Pradesh), present-day Baghpat District.

1760: In the aftermath of the father's demise, step-son throws the mother-daughter duo out of the house, they wander and eventually found themselves in the vicinity of the Jama Masjid in Delhi, little Farzana was in grief, got refuge in a brothel in Chandni Chowk.

1767: Reinhardt Sombre, also known as Samru Sahib meets Farzana in the brothel, the two came closer.

1767-1772: Sombre weds Farzana, lives in the Bharatpur and Deeg principality in the service of ruler Jawahar Singh of Bharatpur.

1773: Mughal emperor, Shah Alam II invitation to Sombre who chastises the rebel Rohilla Jabita Khan, pleases the Mughal emperor who gifts Sombre, called Samru by the locals, the principality of Sardhana.

1778: Additionally, Samru was bestowed with the post of military and civil Governor of Agra, Reinhardt Sombre's death on 4 May, army officers unanimously urge Mughal emperor to entrust Farzana with the command of the army, emperor's approval decured.

1781: Begum Samru converted to Christianity in the Roman Catholic Church in Agra.

Farzana, also known as Begum Samru and Zafaryab's name changed to Johanna Nobilis and Louie Balthazar Reinhardt, respectively.

1787: George Thomas's induction into the Begum's army, rises to become a commander in the army the Begum's attraction towards him, rumours.

French officer Lee Wassey too joined the army in those days, Lee Wassey's growing intimacy with Begum.

Rohilla Ghulam Qadir's plot to depose the Mughal emperor from the throne ruined by the Begum, to thank her for her help, the Mughal emperor honours Begum with the title 'Zeb-Un-Nissa', Rohilla leader apologizes.

1788: Mughal emperor Shah Alam's Gokulgarah campaign with Begum Samru, Begum and John Thomas protect Mughal emperor in the battlefield.

A pleased emperor gifts Begum the valuable land of Badshahpur-Jharsa region, George Thomas too honoured with a 'Khiliat'

Ghulam Qadir captures the Red Fort and takes Mughal emperor Shah Alam II hostage, reign of barbarity, cruelty and terror, Shah Alam's eyes pulled out, misbehaviour with his relatives,

Bidar Bhakt made to sit on the throne, emperor and his

sons locked up in Salimgarh jail,

Upon knowing, Begum Samru returned from Tappal, commander-in-chief, Rane Khan sent to help by Shinde.

Ghulam Qadir flees from the Red Fort, blind Mughal emperor Shah Alam II reinstated on the throne, Ghulam hunted down and brought back, sentenced to gruesome death, a number of rebels and Bidar Bhakt also executed.

1789-92: Lee Wassey's attempts to drive a wedge between Begum and George Thomas, Begum toppled him from Tappal, offended Thomas declares independence,

Begum captures Thomas and brings him back, his expulsion.

Lee Wassey's fortune shines. Rumours about Begum and Lee-Wassey's secret marriage, army officers displeased with Lee Wassey's behaviour.

1793: George Thomas earns a valuable position in Appa Khande Rao's army, his growing popularity.

1794: Mahadji Shinde dies.

1795: The Begum's campaign against Appa Khande Rao and Thomas on Lee Wassey's advice. Rebellion in her army.

The Begum's attempts to suppress the revolt, rebellion continues, Lee Wassey and Begum plan to abdicate and flee.

Begum Samru caught with her belongings, Lee Wassey's suicide, and Begum's failed attempt to do the same, taken captive and abused in the jagir.

1796: George Thomas succeeds in rescuing Begum after her pleadings, Begum is reinstated on the throne in the *jagir* of Sardhana, and her stepson Zafaryab was taken captive.

1800: The Begum heads to Agra to personally thank Mahadji Shinde for helping in freeing her from captivity.

1801: Sikhs against George Thomas, a joint campaign of the Marathas and Rajput, Deposed from the position of the king of Hansi, surrendered.

1802: Zafaryab's death in captivity, Begum brings his mother, children and wife to Sardhana.

George Thomas's demise.

The Begum's strong ties with the East India Company, and proposal to align the British with her army.

1803: On 22 July, Lord Wellesley began the proceedings to accept Begum's proposal.

1804: Begum doubts the British administration. She writes a letter to the British administrator, expressing her concerns.

Rebel Sikhs capture Saharanpur in October, British collector G. D. Gothari is taken captive, and Begum rescues him.

1805: Plot to take away Begum's *jagir* by the senior officials of the company. Revelation in the letter sent to Resident Ochterlony from her secretary on 25 February.

Half of Begum's army was at the East India Company's disposal according to the contract signed with the British administration.

Deeg surrendered completely in April.

Lord Cornwallis's second term as the Governor-General of India in July. His trust in Begum helps in maintaining the status quo of Sardhana.

1806: A happy Mughal emperor Akbar Shah II gifts Begum the *Chudi Walon Ki Haveli* in Chandni Chowk.

1807: In July, Begum insisted with the British to resolve the matter with her will, her appeal accepted on 4 August.

1808: Zafaryab's daughter gave birth to a baby boy, who was adopted by the Begum.

1822: Sardhana's grand church established.

1827: David's father, Dyce's plot to clandestinely depose the Begum, Colonel Clements Brown from the Meerut principality, supports Begum, bid foiled.

1831: Begum registered her will, day-to-day administration entrusted to David.

1834: The Begum's new palace ready in Sardhana, the establishment of a Catholic church in the principality of Meerut,

Begum registered a gift deed to her adopted son, David Dyce, Delhi's resident, urging the Governor-General for instructions regarding the course of action to be taken after Begum's demise.

1836: Begum dies on 27 January at 6:30 in the morning.

After Begum

1837: David sells Begum's *Chudi Walon Ki Haveli* to a British bank in Delhi.

1838: David's foreign journey. Reaching England in June, his father, Colonel Dyce's demise in India during the period.

1839: David celebrates Begum's third death anniversary in Rome with pomp and splendour.

1840: David's marriage with Annie Jarvis.

1841: David wins the elections to the British parliament, growing strife between husband and wife, a petition opposing David' involvement in the elections, David disqualified by the court.

1843: David declared mentally unstable, treatment under strict supervision.

1851: A lonely and helpless David dies alone in a hotel room, before that, he attempts to prove that he was healthy by publishing a 582-page book of evidence.

1856: Court case over David's property, the decision taken in favour of his wife, Annie.

1862: Annie's second marriage with Baron Forester.

1893: Jarvis Annie, also known as Lady Forester dies without an heir.

Selected References

English:

Life and Times of Begum Samru of Sardhana, by Mahendra Narain Sharma, Delhi, Vibhu Publications, The PhD dissertation submitted to the History Department of Meerut University, Meerut, published in the year 1985.

Nautch Girl of the Raj, by Pran Nevile, New Delhi, Penguin Books India, 2009.

Princesses, Begums and Concubines by BP Saha, New Delhi, Tarang Paperbacks, 1992.

Begum Samru, by Brajendra Nath Banerjee, with a foreword by Jadu Nath Sarkar, MC Sarkar and Sons, Calcutta, 1925.

Mr Dyce Sombre's Refutation of Charge of Lunacy, brought against him in the Court of Chancery, Paris, 1849.

Military Memoirs of Mr George Thomas, compiled and arranged by Wm Franklin, Calcutta, India, 1803.

Dark Legacy: The Fortunes of Begum Samru, Shreeve, Nicholas. London: Bookwright, 1996.

Samru: The Fearless Warrior, by Jaipal Singh, New Delhi, Shrishti Publishers and Distributors, Ed. 2004.

Articulating a Life, in Words and Pictures: Begum Samru and the Ornament of Histories. In After the Great Mughals: New Light on Eighteenth and Nineteenth Century Painting, edited by Barbara Schmitz. Behl, Aditya, Mumbai: Marg Publications, Mumbai, 2002.

Delhi Between Two Empires, Narayani Gupta, 1803-1931, Delhi, 1998.

Colonial Intervention and Urban Transformation: A Case Study of Shahjahanabad / Old Delhi.

Twilight of the Moghuls, Percival Spear, Cambridge, 1951.

*A Gazetteer of Delh*i (1883-4), Gurgaon, 1988 2nd Edition.

The New Landscape, Charles Correa, Bombay, 1985.

Townsmen & Bazaars: North Indian Society in the Age of British Expansion, 1770-1870 Christopher A. Bayly, Rulers, Cambridge,1983.

An Illustrated History of Modern India, Christopher A. Bayly, 1600-1947, Delhi,

1999.

The Great Mutiny: India 1857, Christopher Libbert, New York, 1978.

Swords for Hire: European Mercenaries in 18th Century India. John Murray, London1971.

The History of Zeb-un-Nissa: Begum Samru of Sardhana. By Gokul Chand, Bookwright, 1994.

A Particular Account of the European Military Adventures of Hindustan, by Compton Herbert, T Fisher Unwin, London,1892.

The Heirs of Dyce Sombre vs. The Indian Government, Dyce Sombre Westminster, 1865.

King of the World- The Life and Times of Shah Alam, by Edwardes Michael, London, K Secker and Warburg, 1970

Military Memoirs of Lt Col James Skinner, by Fraser James Baillie, London, Smith, Elder, 1851.

The Rajah from Tipperary: George Thomas, by Hennessey Maurice London, Sidgwick and Jackson, 1971.

Sardhana and its Begum, by Keegan Father William, 1879.

Hindustan Under Freelancer, 1700-1820 by Keen HG, Brown Langham, London, 1907.

*Begum Samru: Fading Portrait in a Gilded Fram*e By Lall, John, Delhi, Roli Books, 1997.

History of the Jats, by Quanaungo, K R, Calcutta, 1925.

The Last Mughal, by Dalrymple, William, Viking Penguin 2006.

Farzana: The Woman who Saved an Empire, by Keay, Julia.I.B.Tauris, 2014.

Fall of the Moghul Empire, by Jadunath Sarkar, Calcutta, M C Sarkar, 1932-50.

Hindi:

सात घूंघट वाला मुखड़ा, अमृतलाल नागर, दिल्ली, राजपाल एंड संस, संस्करण २०१८

बेगम समरू, सत्येन्द्र श्रीवास्तव, नई दिल्ली, पुस्तकायन, संस्करण १९९६.

सोना और खून, आचार्य चतुर सेन, दिल्ली, राजपाल एंड संस, संस्करण. २०१६.

सरधना : वहां की बेगम, वहां का तीर्थस्थान, वहां की बसिलिका, फादर पैट्रिक, सरधना चर्च, चतुर्थ संस्करण, २००९.

Website links:

https://en.wikipedia.org/wiki/Begum_Samru

http://sardhanachurch.org/begumsumru.aspx